Flying Solo

Flying Solo

A NOVEL

Linda Holmes

BALLANTINE BOOKS
NEW YORK

Copyright © 2022 by Linda Holmes

Published in the United States by Ballantine Books, an imprint of Random House, a division of Penguin Random House LLC, New York.

BALLANTINE is a registered trademark and the colophon is a trademark of Penguin Random House LLC.

LIBRARY OF CONGRESS CATALOGING-IN-PUBLICATION DATA
Names: Holmes, Linda (Radio talk show host), author.
Title: Flying solo : a novel / Linda Holmes.
Description: New York : Ballantine Books, [2022] |
Identifiers: LCCN 2021060306 (print) | LCCN 2021060307 (ebook) |
ISBN 9780525619277 (hardcover) | ISBN 9780525619284 (ebook)
Classification: LCC PS3608.O49435456 F59 2022 (print) | LCC PS3608.
O49435456 (ebook) | DDC 813/.6—dc23
LC record available at https://lccn.loc.gov/2021060306
LC ebook record available at https://lccn.loc.gov/2021060307

International edition ISBN 978-0-593-50093-4

Printed in the United States of America on acid-free paper

randomhousebooks.com

1 2 3 4 5 6 7 8 9

First Edition

Book design by Susan Turner

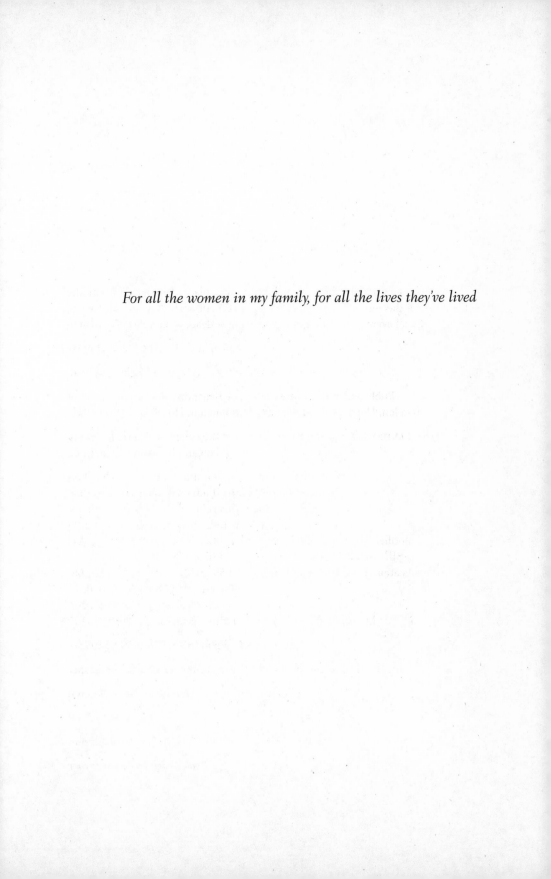

For all the women in my family, for all the lives they've lived

Flying Solo

Prologue

aurie took her fingers out of her ears only after she was out of the house, and only to pick up her bike and ride the mile and a half to Aunt Dot's. Her mom had said she could go, after Laurie wrapped her neck in a red scarf and slipped on a pair of gloves with little snowflakes on them, and after Dot said on the phone that it was okay. The boys were being loud, the four of them—fighting and wrestling and slamming doors—and Laurie had gotten tired of hiding in her room. Since she turned twelve, her mother had been letting her make her way over to Dot's by herself, even after dinner when it was dark.

When she arrived at Dot's, Laurie dropped her bike in the grass and went up to the big red door. Dot, who was actually Laurie's mother's aunt, had grown up in this house and always said her parents brought her here straight from the hospital, and she just kept coming back. Laurie rang the bell.

When Dot came to the door, she was in jeans and a purple chenille sweater, with her long gray hair pulled back in a ponytail. "Hello, honeybun," she said, and she stood aside.

Laurie loved how it smelled in Dot's house: like wood because of the fireplace, like lavender because of Dot's soap, and like the ocean because everything in Maine that's near the water smells a little bit like the ocean. There was a fire going, and Laurie pulled off her gloves and took off her scarf and carefully laid them over the back of one of the dining room chairs. "It's freezing out there," she said.

"I know. I'm so glad you're here and out of all that. You must be practically a Popsicle." Dot already had a little pot of milk on the stove, and she spooned instant hot cocoa mix into two mugs and mixed it up, then she took a can of whipped cream out of the fridge and said, "shoooop," like she always did as she built two little towers of it. Laurie wrapped her hands around her cup as they went into the living room together. "So," Dot said, "your mom said it was pretty noisy at home."

Laurie blew delicately on her hot chocolate and rolled her eyes. "Patrick and Scott are arguing about something. I don't even know what." They were teenagers, seventeen and fourteen, and a lot of the time, Laurie didn't know what they were talking about, whether they were fighting or not. She just tried to stay out of the way. "And Ryan says he's trying to figure out what the loudest thing in the house is." Ryan was the baby.

"Oh, no." Dot laughed. "Never good when an eight-year-old does research."

"And Joey is being Joey." She looked meaningfully at Dot. "And you know how *that* is." Dot nodded. Joey was ten, the drum-on-everything, break-everything, jump-on-everything, run-through-everything, eat-everything, get-stains-on-everything brother.

"Well, I talked to your mother, and we were thinking maybe you'd like to stay overnight. It's not a school night."

Laurie almost spilled her cocoa wiggling in her chair. "Yes yes yes! Should I go home and get my pajamas and stuff?"

"Oh, you can borrow something of mine."

Laurie looked down at herself. "I'm bigger than you," she said.

Dot bark-laughed. "You are absolutely not bigger than me," she said. "And even if you were, there are plenty of things you can sleep in. For all I care, you can wrap yourself up in my bathrobe. And I have some extra toothbrushes, and that's pretty much all you really need, right?"

When they finished their cocoa, Laurie followed Dot upstairs, and Dot dug around in the dresser in her bedroom and eventually came out with a long-sleeved pink shirt that said NIAGARA FALLS. When Laurie held it up to herself, it hung to the middle of her thighs. "Thank you for letting me come over," she said, and she put her arms around Dot, who squeezed her tight and kissed the top of her head.

"You know you always have a place here when you need one," she said.

Laurie laid the shirt on the bed and sat down next to it, listening to the furnace flip on. "It's amazing here—it's so quiet," she said finally. "I can't read over there, I can't even think."

"Well, you have a big, beautiful family that loves you very much," Dot said, "and I know that you love them." She came and sat down next to Laurie. "But they're loud, I agree."

Laurie smiled. "Really loud."

Dot raised her eyebrows. "Well, there's nobody here but you and me. You can sleep in as long as you want," she said, "and nobody will make a peep unless it's me making coffee. You might sleep until noon. You might sleep until dinner!"

"I'm so jealous," Laurie moaned. "You get to be by yourself all the time."

"I'm not by myself all the time." Dot laughed.

"Mom says you have a boyfriend," Laurie said.

"Oh, your mother is a gossip." Dot grinned. "I have lots of friends, and that's all you're getting, Nosy-Nose." She got up, went to stand in the doorway, and ran her finger over the painted wall, which was peeling a little. "I have to paint this room," she said. "Absolutely have to."

"What color are you going to paint it?" Laurie asked.

Dot was quiet, then she turned back to Laurie. "What's your favorite color?"

"Right now it's goldfish."

"Goldfish? Like orange?"

Laurie nodded. "I really love it. My mother says it makes her think of macaroni and cheese."

Dot nodded. "Well, let's paint it goldfish, then."

Laurie's eyes opened wider. "Really?"

"Sure. Why not?"

"Just like that?"

"Why are you scandalized, love? It's just paint."

"I don't know. You just . . . paint your walls however, whenever you want? You don't . . . talk to anybody?"

"I'm talking to you," she said. "Who else would I talk to? It's my house. They're my walls. I can cover the entire place in zebra-stripe wallpaper if I want to. I can fill it up with sand and make a beach. Compared to that, a few goldfish walls are pretty tame."

Laurie looked all around. Her parents owned their house too, but somehow she felt certain they didn't think of it this way. She imagined zebra-stripe wallpaper. She imagined herself lying on this bed, in a zebra-stripe room, with sand on the floor, with no one around, no one yelling, no one deciding when breakfast was or when was too late for hot cocoa.

A week later, Laurie went over to Dot's and they repainted the bedroom she had slept in. They did the whole thing in a bright orange with a few red swirls Dot painted with a fat brush to make it more "goldfishy." At the end of the day, Laurie had orange specks in her hair and on her jeans, and she told Dot it was the greatest room she'd ever seen. And while Dot lived almost thirty more years, and she repainted rooms and refinished floors and put in new counter-tops and renovated the bathroom two more times, that room stayed the goldfish room, always.

Chapter One

She could have missed the duck entirely. It was at the very bottom of the cedar chest, and in the manner of the princess and the pea and the stack of mattresses, Laurie might have ignored it if she hadn't pulled all the blankets out to see whether any of them seemed special.

The duck was about a foot long, made of wood, and lighter than she expected when she picked it up. She couldn't even guess how old it was, since it looked pristine, like it had barely been touched. It was without a single visible scratch, and it was worked to a finish so smooth she could make out the thinnest brushstrokes in the paint with the tips of her fingers. The colors were bright: a green head and a reddish-brown chest, a gold flush along the sides with blues and greens along the wings. Laurie stepped into the hall. "Now, why," she said, standing with one hand on her hip and the duck in the other, "would a ninety-three-year-old woman have had a wooden duck in a chest under three afghans and a quilt?"

"To get to the other side?" June called back from the living room.

"It's not that kind of riddle."

Laurie walked with it out into the living room, where June was working through the books. Or some of the books. Aunt Dot had them in practically every corner, stuffed into floor-to-ceiling built-in shelves or sitting in stacks on the floor, in danger of tipping over. "I guess she had it for the same reason she has four feather boas and a signed picture of Steve McQueen."

"Which is what?"

"She was ninety-three. Why *wouldn't* there be a duck?"

Laurie took out her phone and snapped a couple of pictures of the duck from different angles to show her mother. "It's pretty, actually. I don't know why it wouldn't be out somewhere you could look at it. Everything else is."

Dot's whole house was an extravagant display case for the fruits of her adventures. There were postcards in patterned fabric boxes, home-movie reels in bins with labels marked in ballpoint pen, and travel souvenirs that suggested impulsive shifts in Dot's collecting philosophy. There were egg cups, spoons, and little dessert plates with scenes painted on them. She'd been to Rome, to Bangkok, to Buenos Aires and Mexico City. She'd camped in a trailer with two girlfriends in Yellowstone in the summer of 1952, and she'd wandered around China on her own in 1994, when she was in her sixties. In a photo from that trip that she must have convinced a stranger to take for her, she was next to the Great Wall, her gray hair gathered in a loose ponytail at the back of her neck. She wore a light denim jacket with a patch of Elton John's face on the arm.

Dot had tried just about everything they taught at the community college—and kept every course catalog—and her work and supplies were stacked and stored in one of the bedrooms. Ceramics, cross-stitch, knitting, scrapbooks with stenciled titles like

"Christmas 2003: Cold as Hell." Painting, sketching, calligraphy, beaded bracelets strung on fishing line. There was a big blue plastic bin at the bottom, under all the boxes of crafts, that said IN PROGRESS/UNFINISHED. Those were destined to remain so now.

There was a small stash of love letters from some of Dot's known boyfriends: Paul, the teacher; John, the chemist; Andrew, the journalist. There was also one without an envelope that was signed "M," which Laurie suspected might have been from a woman, based on the handwriting. (Again: She was ninety-three. Why *wouldn't* there be a woman?) Laurie set aside but did not read these, for the simple reason that she wouldn't want anyone to read *her* letters after she was dead. It seemed wrong, though, to throw them away, so she'd just left them in their shoebox labeled CORRESPONDENCE, SPECIAL and set it on the bed.

Laurie dropped onto the couch. "Take a break with me," she said. "I finished with the jewelry box, and I cannot start a box labeled CAMERAS AND 8-TRACK TAPES without sustenance."

"Just keep petting that duck," June said, getting off her knees and passing Laurie on her way to the kitchen. "You want an iced tea?"

"You are the best friend in the history of best friends."

"Laur, it's only iced tea."

"You know what I'm talking about," Laurie said. "I've been doing this for a week and a half, and I already have scratches all over my hands from tearing boxes open and a sore shoulder for no reason I can particularly pinpoint. And I have to be here. You're just here because you're a good person."

"I've got news for you," June said, over the sound of ice clinking into glasses. "When you're the one relative who shows up instead of just letting Goodwill take everything in the house, you are also a good person."

Laurie puffed out a breath. "It made the most sense. I didn't want everything she owned to vanish just because she didn't get married or have kids. Nobody else had the time."

June appeared with the drinks in two of Dot's tall glasses, criss-crossed with a chunky diamond pattern. "I don't know. Four brothers, and you wind up holding the bag?" she said as she sat down. "Regardless, I'm very happy to be talking to you somewhere other than FaceTime. I like seeing your beautiful face in person."

"You're very sweet, given how sweaty and disgusting I am, and I feel the same way. I thought I was going to see you in person at the wedding I didn't end up having, so I'm glad I had an excuse. Honestly, it's a particularly good time to see old friends, since everyone I know in Seattle also knows Chris, and I have no idea whether any of them likes me anymore. And even if they do, I definitely don't want them to throw me a fortieth birthday pity party based on the assumption that I have given up my last chance at happiness and will now shrivel up like a prune."

"Nobody thinks that," June said, rolling her eyes.

"Tell it to *When Harry Met Sally.*"

"What does that mean?"

"Well, do you remember the part of that movie where Harry goes over to see Sally, and she's crying in her bathrobe because her ex-boyfriend, that guy who's Gerald Ford's son, is getting married?"

"That guy is Gerald Ford's son?"

"Yes. And she starts crying, and she's very depressed, and she says through these really pitiful tears, 'And I'm gonna be forty.' And he says, 'When?,' and she says, 'Someday.' That's the first punchline. The second punchline is that he says she's going to be forty in eight years."

At Laurie's expectant look, June shook her head. "I don't get it yet. Keep going."

"Well, the joke is that it's hilarious that she thinks she's washed up when she won't be forty for eight entire years. Believe me, when you watch that movie and you're going to be forty in a month, it's really different. Why can't he just say, 'Who cares? You'll be forty either way, and if you're single that's fine, and if you're married that's fine, and by the way, Gerald Ford's son and his fiancée are also going to be forty someday'? I've always wondered why he can't just say it that way."

June raised one eyebrow. "You always wondered that, or you maybe just recently wondered that?"

"Nobody likes a smart-ass," Laurie said, narrowing her eyes. "I'm just saying it seems like they didn't have to make such a big deal out of whether she did or did not have a grand romantic destiny."

"I mean, it's a romantic comedy."

"I know. I know. I just had this moment where I envisioned myself telling Billy Crystal that I called off my wedding, and saying, 'And I'm gonna be forty.' And then I see him say, 'When?,' and I say, 'In a month,' and he just says, 'Yikes.'" June's chuckle was so good, so small and melodic. It really had been too long. "Don't laugh when I'm railing against ageism."

"I'm sorry. I just think . . . it has nothing to do with you. You wouldn't be crying in a bathrobe. You would be pouring drinks and watching a movie, you know? Meg Ryan was single and despondent. You're just single."

"Well, that's true. I mean, I feel bummed that we lost some of our deposits, and I feel regretful about the hours of my life I spent sending back gifts, but I cannot claim to be despondent."

"Well, then, be at peace. Nobody asked Billy Crystal for his opinion anyway."

Laurie said, around an ice cube in her mouth, "Did you worry about getting married before you did it?"

June looked up at the ceiling, then back at Laurie. "Not really, I don't think. I worried about the wedding DJ, and I worried about logistics, like whose family we were going to spend Christmas with and whether any of our relatives were going to flip out if I didn't change my name. But I'd been living with Charlie for a couple of years by then, so I didn't think it would be that different."

"Was it different?"

"Not really. A lot of the time, I sort of forgot that we had gone from not married to married."

"You two are amazing. It's like after you met in college, you just floated from there to here."

"Oh, hardly. I got completely freaked out when we were having Bethie. That was a whole other person puking and pooping and yelling at us all the time. *That* was different. Even though she was a good baby. And Tommy was also a good baby, very mellow and quiet, although for some reason he smelled worse more of the time. I don't know. I guess I'm saying everything's an adjustment."

"I haven't seen your kids in so long, when I walked in the other day, I was sure for a second you had traded them for other, much older kids."

"I think that sometimes, too," June said.

"Do you miss when they were babies? They were so cute."

"I liked it when they were babies," June said. "But now they're old enough that they have backpacks and frenemies and real opinions about things besides hating everything when they're tired. And that's fun, too. I'm glad they got to see you. I think after all this time, they thought you lived in Skype."

Laurie had learned to knit so she could make a blanket for Bethie, and then she never did it again. "I'm sorry I wasn't around more. I feel like I wanted to be Aunt Laurie, and I ended up being somebody they barely remember."

"That's not true. Even if it was, what are you going to do? It's a long flight here from Seattle. And you travel so much for work already."

"Yeah." Laurie picked up the duck, which had been sitting next to her on the couch. "I am so in love with this thing." She ran her thumb along its back, looked at the painted feather patterns, felt the bright green head with her fingertips. "I think it's a wood duck."

June put down her drink on a crocheted coaster on the side table. "It looks like wood."

"No, not a wooden duck, a wood duck. A kind of duck that can nest in the woods." Laurie looked at the bottom, which was a plain light wood with a faint mark that looked like a circle with the initials CKM inside. "CKM," she said quietly. "It says 'CKM' on the bottom."

"Calvin Klein . . . Mallards?" June offered.

"Outstanding guess, but probably not. I honestly have no idea where this would have come from or why Dot would have it."

"It's a decoy, right?"

"Yeah. And even though I'm embarrassed by how little I knew about big parts of her life, I'm pretty sure she didn't have anything to do with hunting." She kept running her finger over the mark on the bottom. "Baby wood ducks can jump fifty feet out of trees."

Laurie had been a wildlife journalist, writing about critters and bugs and birds and fish—just about everything that swam, walked, wriggled, or flew—long enough that June expected a certain amount of animal trivia. "Are wood ducks endangered? Did you spend six months chasing them across Michigan or something and then write a heartbreaking article about how they're getting slammed by climate change?"

"Some ducks are endangered," Laurie said, "but not these ducks, at least not right now. They were before, partly because of hunting, but then the Migratory Bird Treaty Act"—she looked over and saw that June's eyes had gone wide—"they were protected long enough to recover." Laurie smiled and ran her fingers down the wings. "But I did write a story for *The Outdoors* about a kind of botulism that knocked out a lot of waterfowl up in Oregon and Washington, and some of them were ordinary ducks, like this guy. So I'm not totally without relevant waterfowl experience."

"That reminds me, you said you had an assignment in a few weeks, but you haven't told me what it is."

Laurie put the duck down next to her. "Turtle trafficking."

"People traffic turtles?"

"Absolutely. They catch them in traps, gather them up, ship them off to places where they're in demand as exotic pets. Box turtles especially. So I'm going to South Carolina to meet a reformed turtle trafficker named Puppy Tavishaw who's helping the fish and wildlife guys bust them."

June stopped what she was doing. "Puppy? His name is Puppy?"

"Just one of the many things I'm looking forward to investigating while I'm embedded with *Law & Order: Turtle Unit*."

"*Spe-shell Victims Unit*," June offered.

"Turtles are chased by two separate yet equally pokey groups. These are their *slow*-ries," Laurie said. "Please, let's stop before I start googling turtle species that rhyme with 'criminal minds.'"

June went back to her work. "Hopefully, Puppy isn't dangerous."

"I think the most dangerous part is probably the threat of getting about six million mosquito bites. That, and the fact that I have to take pictures myself, at least for online. I'm still not completely used to it. Which reminds me, wait here, I'm ready to move on to the next box."

By the time Laurie returned to the living room with the CAMERAS AND 8-TRACK TAPES box, June had put her feet up on the ottoman. "Okay, it's time to see what's in here. I found one camera on the kitchen table, so I don't know what this is." The ancient masking tape gave way easily, and the dusty flaps of the box puffed motes into the sunlight.

At the very bottom of the box, there were two short rows of 8-track tapes lined up. "So for music, our selections include Dolly Parton, Kenny Rogers, The Beach Boys, Fleetwood Mac, Smokey Robinson, Santana, David Bowie, and Van Halen."

"Dot listened to Van Halen?"

"Well, let's see. This is *Van Halen II*. From this label it looks like it came out in 1979. Dot would have been, what, about fifty? That tracks. I hope to still be listening to cool new music in ten years."

She picked up the tape, and found something stuffed into the cardboard sleeve. When Laurie slid it out and unfolded it, she grinned and looked at June. "It's a ticket stub. Dot saw Van Halen in Boston, at the Paradise Theater, on March 27, 1978. Opening for Journey." She handed it to June.

"Wow. My mind is completely blown. The idea of my grandmother or even my mother rocking out is so baffling to me."

"I'm clearly going to have to pick through all her music, in case she has anything else stashed in here. The rest of this bin is supposed to be cameras, but everything's in these fabric boxes." She took the lid off one, and inside were two Polaroid cameras. One looked older than any of the Polaroid cameras Laurie had ever seen, and one was the same kind of OneStep her parents had when she was a toddler. She unloaded all the fabric boxes, and she kept finding instant cameras. A total of five Polaroids, two Kodaks, and a Fujifilm. Some looked like they were of an 8-track vintage; others looked like they were probably made right before digital cameras upended instant photography. One or two looked practically current.

The last box she opened was labeled on top 2007. Laurie pulled the lid off, and inside were Polaroid photos. Long rows of Polaroids, or Fujifilms or whatever, filed with unlabeled dividers that separated them into bunches. She pulled one stack out. This was a trip to New York. The Empire State Building, the Statue of Liberty, the marquee at Radio City Music Hall. There was a picture of Dot, then almost eighty years old and silver-haired, her beaming face pressed next to that of a man who looked about the same age, under the marquee for *Avenue Q*. There was a single word written in Sharpie in the white border under the photo: "Leo." She turned the picture around and showed it to June. "I knew she liked Broadway."

June leaned forward. "Who's Leo?"

Laurie shook her head. "I don't have any idea. She was well into her retirement by then, and I know she traveled all over with all kinds of people. I have no idea who Leo might have been, but clearly, they were having a lot of fun together seeing the dirty puppet musical."

The rest of the box held a combination of travel pictures, pictures from birthday parties and a couple of weddings and what seemed to be a football game at the high school, and pictures of people Laurie only occasionally recognized. There was one of her mother and father, and a few that had been taken at her brother Patrick's wedding. She only vaguely remembered Dot walking around with an instant camera, stopping at every table to grab a couple of shots.

"Why do you think she packed her cameras with a box of pictures from 2007?" June asked as she went back to sorting books into boxes by type and condition.

"Maybe these are the most recent ones she had," Laurie said as she put them back into the box and picked up one of the older cameras. "I know they stopped making instant film for a while, so maybe she stopped when she got a digital camera."

"Maybe all the newer ones were naughty."

"I wouldn't be surprised if they were, but I would be surprised if she left those around for people to find. I do think there are probably more pictures somewhere." She turned the camera over in her hands. "Like, a lot more pictures."

Chapter Two

Not long after they found the cameras, there was a knock. "That will be the Grim Reaper," Laurie said, heading for the door. She opened it to find a guy in a Decemberists concert shirt and jeans looking down at an iPad. He looked up and smiled. "Hi, I'm Matt, I'm from Save the Best, I think we talked on the phone?"

Save the Best was a service that would come and inspect the house of a person who was either dead or downsizing to determine whether any of their stuff was worth selling and haul away the rest. They called this particular service "bereavement decluttering." Which, Laurie supposed, was better than calling it Almost Literally a Flock of Vultures Circling Your Dead Relatives.

He didn't look like a vulture, though. He looked like a philosophy professor as you might encounter him buying granola at a Whole Foods. She suspected he actually went to that concert to buy that shirt. He'd bought the ticket, he'd put on the orange wrist-band, he'd had the overpriced beer, he'd stood near the back out of consideration for shorter people. (Probably.) His eyes were gray but also blue, and he had a little bit of a tattoo poking out from under his sleeve. Maybe something vaguely Celtic. Maybe something pre-tentious like a platitude in Latin.

She gathered herself. "Hi, I'm Laurie Sassalyn, thanks for com-ing." He followed her in and sat on the couch while June and Lau-rie settled in the wing chairs. "So where do we start?" Laurie said.

"Tell me about you, and tell me about your aunt." He left his iPad sitting at his hip for now.

"Well, I'm Laurie—I said that—and this is my friend June Devon. Dot was actually my great-aunt. My mother's father's sister. She was ninety-three."

"Wow, ninety-three, what a run." He looked like maybe he used to be an athlete. Soccer or rugby, but now his knee was blown out and his doctor didn't want him to play, but he still showed up for beer league because all his friends were there, and he wasn't the player he had been, but he was always the one who paid for the first round after—

"Laurie." June was looking at her with her eyebrows raised. "Are you with us?"

"Yes, sorry. It's just a lot." Laurie resettled herself. "Anyway. This whole house was hers."

"Was she widowed? Any kids?"

"No, she was a one-woman show. She worked for the school system, in the business office, until she retired. Then she was . . . well, I guess you can see how she was. The place is packed to the gills with her things. We've been going through as much as we can, saving some personal stuff, but I don't have any other family up here anymore, and most of this, we just . . . we don't have a place for it. I mean, she has college textbooks and a vinyl record collection and enough books to open a library. If I use my rental car to move everything out, I'll still be working on it a year from now."

"So you're not from around here?"

"I grew up here, we both did. Junie lives here, but I live in Seattle. I haven't been back in ages, that's why I didn't know how full the house was."

"And this wound up being your job, ironing it all out." He had a good voice, kind of velvety. Reassuring. Understanding. *Parts of me are extremely neglected,* she thought before sitting up straighter and nodding.

"Like I said, Dot didn't have kids. My parents live in Florida, my mom just had her hip replaced, and my dad just had back surgery."

"You don't have siblings?"

"My brothers?" She and June looked at each other and eye-rolled almost simultaneously. "I have four, but if they came up here, they'd just rent a backhoe and push it all into a hole in the back-yard. Officially, they're all busy."

"The good daughter." He smiled. "You won't be surprised that I see this a lot. Probably three daughters for every son. And the fur-ther out you get in the family, the truer it is."

"The patriarchy will get you every time," Laurie said. "But it's fine. I'm not a hero, I'm just the person who opens every single box hoping not to find any spiders or sex toys. For different reasons, obviously, but with about the same amount of anxiety."

She was talking too much. As always. But he laughed. Next, he flicked through screens on his tablet, explaining the contract she'd be signing. "Like we talked about on the phone, feel free to pack up everything that you want to keep. Take as much or as little as you want, and take all the time you need. Today, I can give you my best guess about what might sell—can't make guarantees, just a good-faith guess that will be based on my experience and the experience of my business, which I've been running for about fifteen years. I carry this guy"—he held up the iPad—"so I can do research on the fly, consult with colleagues, things like that. I'll bring you an estimate of what I expect the saleable items will bring. You can take those things with you, you can get an independent appraisal, or you can give them to me. If I take them, I'll ask you to make one more choice. You can consign those, so you'll get paid a full share if they sell, or I'll pay you a flat amount that's usually around fifty percent of the consignment amount and you'll be done with those items right away whether they ever sell or not. We would make that a credit against your bill. Making sense so far?"

It was hard not to think about her own belongings. Her concert shirts, her fountain pens, her own not-instant camera, her pressure cooker. Whose job would those things be if she walked out the door and was eaten by a bear? Should she be making lists? Someone should have her mother's bracelet, and it should not be any of the boys. "Sure, yes."

He went on. "Then we arrange to pick up any donations. That's often your furniture in good condition, kitchen items, some linens, books we can give to the library, things like that. The vinyl will be TBD, we'll see what she's got. So we take all that and donate it, you don't need to do a thing. Then we come back one last time and we take the things you don't want that are probably at the end of their useful lives. That's the clothes that are worn or they're not likely to get more use, plus all your trash, plus the things we refer to as the grind. The grind is your bent paper clips, your half-empty shampoo bottles, used cosmetics, some kinds of costume jewelry and knickknacks—just things we're not likely to find good homes for. And those things will get a dignified send-off."

"I'm glad to know Dot's eye shadows will get a proper burial."

"Right." He smiled. "So it should be pretty painless."

June, who had already helped go through three boxes of hand lotions, let her eyes go wide at the word "painless," and Laurie swallowed a laugh before she answered him. "I'm not sure she owns very much that's worth money. She owns a lot of things with sentimental value, I guess you'd say. I know they were special to her, but I don't know if, you know, a lot of people are going to buy the egg cup she got in Rio. I don't think she bought this stuff as collectibles, per se, do you know what I mean? She just collected it." Laurie leaned back in the chair and put her hands over her face. "This is just a gruesome job. I feel so bad, like a grave robber."

Matt nodded. "You are far from a grave robber. Remember, she had these things for as long as she needed them, and they probably brought her a lot of happiness. But they most likely won't bring you any, so there's not a lot to gain from your coming down hard on yourself because you want to let stuff go. Keep a few things you really like, things that remind you of her, and let me take care of the rest, okay? I'm here to make everything easier."

"Yeah. Yeah, that would be great, actually." Laurie was pretty convinced she only ever smiled awkwardly, but she tried to smile not-awkwardly in this case, because she really was grateful. It didn't escape her that because someone had recommended this service to her parents, who were paying for it, she wasn't going to have to carry out twenty garbage bags of souvenirs herself. She didn't want to ask June to come over too often, so there was nothing to do but just get through it. Matt stood up with his iPad.

"I'm going to start in the bedroom if that's okay. You guys stay out here, keep setting aside anything that you want, and I'll have a list for you of the saleables in a little while." Laurie directed him down the hall to where the big bedroom was. Just as he went in there, he said, "By the way, I don't wear a jacket and I sew my pockets shut"—he tugged on the pockets of his jeans to demonstrate—"so people know I'm not giving myself any five-finger discounts."

"That's a good idea. But I trust you," Laurie said as he set off down the hall.

When he was gone, June looked up from the boxes of books she'd just been stacking. "That's the Grim Reaper?" she said quietly.

"I'll admit I envisioned him with a sharper scythe." Laurie leaned back against the couch. "Honestly, if he had one, I'd probably have let him in anyway, because all I want is to get this done. My back is going to hurt, because I'm going to be forty *in a month,* so I think tomorrow, I'm just going to head over to the library and see if I can grab a couple of fresh paperbacks that I can read on the couch when I can't do this anymore."

"Sounds divine. Just so you're warned, you know Nick runs it now?"

"I do."

"His parents retired."

"I heard."

"Also, he's divorced. For a couple years."

"Yes, I know. June, I promise, I really just want my books."

June held up both hands. "Just wanted you to know. You still read cozy mysteries?"

"Right now, it's anything with a person in a dark doorway casting a very long shadow and holding a knife. They're called . . . I don't know. *Brutal Silences, Captive Secrets, How to Strangle Your Gardener,* whatever keeps my mind occupied."

June put her icy glass against her cheek. "You should ask out the Grim Reaper. Maybe he wants to talk about heirloom jewelry and what happens to old encyclopedias."

"He seems nice," Laurie said. "Do you think he seems nice?"

"I do think he seems nice. It's not a joke. I am actually, unironically suggesting you should ask him out. Take a break from trying to figure out your future. Have some dinner, maybe have some very low-stakes sex—besides, you'll be way ahead of the game with a guy who's seen your great-aunt's underwear drawer before you even spend time together socially."

Laurie surveyed the room, the boxes and bins, the things she was setting aside, and the big trash bags they were filling. "I honestly thought returning a room full of wedding gifts would be the most overwhelming thing I would take on before my fortieth birth-day." It had been almost a year since she and Chris had called it off—well, since she did—and a little less since she finished send-ing back the presents. "Junie, I think I'm falling way behind you, friend-wise."

June rolled her eyes and started ticking items off on her fingers: "Apartment hunting in Philadelphia when I was working at the bookstore, editing my college applications, going with me when they froze off my back mole, wearing an uncomfortable dress at my wedding. You are fine. And believe me, selfishly, I would rather be making good this way than by holding your hand through a divorce. Yikes." She punctuated this last word with a shudder.

"I don't know if I would have even gotten a divorce," Laurie said. "I might have just stayed married to him, making soup and slowly turning into dust."

June frowned. "Soup?"

"I started making a lot of soup in those last couple months. Soup when I was depressed, soup when I was trying to think, soup when he was around, soup when he was away. It was like I was planning for a post-apocalyptic future. The wedding was the apocalypse."

"Maybe the breakup was the apocalypse."

"I didn't know that was coming, though."

June raised one eyebrow, a talent Laurie had always envied. "Maybe you did."

"Ah, you're very clever."

They kept putting books into boxes, just books and books and books, and Laurie kept filling a small shoebox with little mementos. She kept a refrigerator magnet that said KISS MY GRITS, and a set of coasters with art deco patterns on them, and a ceramic owl the size of her thumb that sat on the kitchen windowsill.

After a while, Matt emerged from the bedroom. "Okay. So, are we ready for a first pass on the valuables from the bedroom?"

They all sat down together. He explained that while Dot didn't have a big collection of expensive jewelry, her opal ring might sell, plus a watch with a couple of small diamonds on it. He also thought he could get some money for her quilt, which was of good quality and in good condition. But that was about it. He gave them a quote, and Laurie told him to put it all on consignment, hoping that in the end, the money she made might cover her plane ticket. Then she held up her great treasure. "Did you see my duck?" she asked.

"The decoy?" His grin sloped to the side a little and made an asterisk wrinkle appear by the corner of his eye. "I did. Do you know where she got it? Any hunters in the family?"

Laurie shook her head. "Not even a little. I thought maybe you'd know. I also don't know why it was in the blanket chest instead of out on the shelves with the rest of her stuff."

"Do you mind if I take a closer look?" he said, and Laurie handed it to him. "It's in really solid condition. How about I give you $50 and see what I can get for it? I make more than that, we'll split it."

Laurie smiled. "I'm pretty attached to it. I think I'm going to keep it."

"Laurie knows a lot about ducks," June offered. "She writes magazine articles about frogs and swamps and things." She didn't add that Laurie also wrote for alumni magazines and trade magazines and other not-glamorous outlets that paid her dependably and hired her regularly.

"Really? That's amazing. I'm kind of a nature dork; what have you written recently?"

"Well," Laurie said, "I wrote a thing for *The Atlantic* about the Texas blue lizard, a species that probably doesn't exist but is legendary anyway."

"That was you? I read that. I loved it," he said with a smile. "I can't blame you for hanging on to the duck. I would, too. Do you mind if I take a couple of pictures of it? I have a buddy who knows all about these things, and I'm sure he'd love to see it. Maybe he'll even know something about it."

"Of course," Laurie said. "The more eyes on it the better."

"That's very nice of you," June said pointedly. "Laurie will have to figure out how to thank you."

"No need," he said. "I'm happy to help." He took a few pictures with his phone while Laurie tried to look at June so hard that her forehead would catch fire. "Make sure you take good care of it," he added.

"Oh, I will."

It took him a couple of hours to work his way through the rest of the house while Laurie and June unpacked dresses and purses and took care of almost all the clothes in the closet. When they all gathered in the living room again, he didn't offer to buy much. There was a hand-carved tray he thought might bring about a hundred dollars, and Dot's mother had left her a silver teapot; that was good for a little more. A few other things, small things. But nobody was going to buy her Polaroids or her old cameras. As he finished the paperwork for the contract, Laurie sat on the couch and fidgeted. "So," she began, "do you live here in Calcasset?"

"Camden," he answered. Pretty close. "You said you grew up here?"

"Yeah, until I left for college. My parents moved to Florida around then for my dad's job. And now that they're older, it's nice to be there since it's a lot warmer, obviously." She paused. "Do you have kids?" For some reason, when she wanted to know whether a guy was single, she always heard herself ask if he had kids, which was not the right question, since it was both overbroad and not broad enough, but it was easier to pass off as idle curiosity. Just regular questions: Where are you from? What do you do? Do you have durable domestic attachments?

"I don't," he said. "I have a dog. But he's very demanding."

Behind him, June made a face, a little "aw" face, like she'd just seen a kitten pick a flower.

"By the way, I sent the pictures of the duck to my buddy. He recognized it, says he thinks it's mass-produced, so it doesn't really have resale value. My guess is that your aunt forgot all about it. You'd be surprised how often people pick things up, they keep them, and before they know it, it's twenty years later, or fifty, and the thing is still in the basement or the cedar chest or it's inside an old suitcase. I wish I had a more exciting answer for you." He folded his arms. "People are mysterious, is what I guess I'm saying." Was that a twinkle? It might have been a twinkle. It was at least twinkle-adjacent. Twinkle-ish. "I think if I put it in my store, it'll sell as a nice piece of decor, so I'm still willing to offer you those fifty bucks if you want to take a flyer on it." He paused. "So to speak."

She shook her head. "I think I'm attached to it now, but that's very nice of you." Just as Laurie was starting to consider taking the breath that might have been exhaled in the form of the words "do you" and "want to have lunch sometime," Matt the Grim Reaper got up and shook her hand.

"Okay," he said. "I think we're about all set for now. You just let me know when you're done here, and I'll take the rest of your sale pieces and schedule the donation and disposal pickups. Will that work?"

She said that it would, of course it would; what else was she going to say? "I'm not ready for you to leave yet because I enjoy the crinkles around your eyes, so please reschedule the truck that's retrieving my great-aunt's furniture"? So yes, the answer was yes, that would work. "Sure." They shook hands again, and she signed some more paperwork, and he set off in his truck. When he was gone, Laurie turned to June. "I may be out of practice."

"Not at all," June said. "It was wildly hot, that polite handshake. I felt like I shouldn't be watching."

• • •

They puttered around for a bit, and then Laurie and June went out to dinner. They had fried fish and shrimp and they tore pieces of bread off a big loaf, and there was a responsible amount of white wine and more talk about the Grim Reaper. It wasn't like Laurie didn't have his number; she had his business card. She could still call. Laurie dropped June off on the way back to Dot's, and they hugged goodbye.

Upstairs in Dot's second bedroom, the one with the painting of the tall ships, Laurie sat with the box that said CORRESPONDENCE, SPECIAL. She wasn't going to read the love letters. She wasn't going to pry. But the work of the last few days had put a rock in the middle of her chest, made of obligations and frustrations, and it was reluctant to budge. She would skim one letter, just one, one from John—how scandalous could a letter from a chemist be, anyway?

She took the top off the box and flicked through envelopes until she saw one with a return address that said "J. Harlan." The sender was in Bangor. When she slid the letter out of the envelope, the first thing she saw was the date: 7.14.73, with dots between the numbers. She immediately felt wrong even scanning it—she saw "miss you" and "can't imagine" and "hard times" and "your smile." She wasn't just in Dot's house; she was in a room from Dot's life, she felt, where she shouldn't be. Looking under the bed and behind the curtains and in the closets. It seemed wrong. She could tell, though, that this letter was written to a woman who was not happy. That year, 1973, would have been right around when Dot's school had been consolidated with the one in the next town and she'd had to get another job. That part of the history Laurie did know, because that was when Dot moved from the business office at the elementary school over to the high school.

Laurie got to the last page, the second side of the third sheet of ivory paper, and looked for his signature. She wondered how it was signed. "Fondly"? "Yours"? "With burning desire"? "Chemically"?

As it turned out, it was simply "With love." It said, "With love, John."

But what stopped Laurie was just above that. One sentence. A closing, offered with evident tenderness. It said, "And anyway, if you're ever desperate, there are always ducks, darling."

"Ducks," Laurie muttered.

Chapter Three

In Dot's jewelry box, there was a crowded charm bracelet with eighteen hearts dangling from it. Each one had a name on one side and a birth date on the other. Four were for her two nephews and two nieces, including Laurie's mother, Barbara. Fourteen more, in a slightly newer style, were for their kids, including Laurie and her brothers.

Out of all those hearts, it was Laurie's family that had stayed in Calcasset. They were the ones who saw the charms in person whenever Dot put on the bracelet at Christmas or Thanksgiving. Laurie carefully took off her charm with a tiny pair of pliers and slipped it into her box of keepsakes. After consulting with her mother, she removed the rest of the charms, too, and packed each into a tiny plastic sleeve, setting them aside to later be sent to the people whose birthdays they marked.

When Dot was still working, she had kept her travels to the

summers. It was after she retired, when Laurie was twelve or thir-teen, that she'd accelerated her adventures. She sailed on cruises, took trips with friends, took trips with "friends," and went back-packing with tour groups and church groups. But there had also been plenty of journeys on her own, like the ones to Paris and Seville and Key West and Tokyo, filling her house with everything she could stuff into her suitcases. She lovingly lined it all up on shelves, in cabinets, on tables, and on windowsills, until her house sagged under the weight of everything she had managed to see.

Dot had died in November, and the air was sharply cold outside when she was buried next to her parents. After the funeral, Dot's friend Martha from church had hosted a gathering at her house, and there were snacks and there was coffee, and people Laurie knew as well as people she didn't know at all walked through and kissed her on the cheek. Then Laurie and her parents and her brothers had packed into the SUV her father, Dennis, had rented—with Laurie, as always, climbing all the way into the very back so she wouldn't have to be compacted between her brothers. She hated to be compacted. They went back to Dot's house and sat down around her dining room table. Barbara poured decaf, and Barbara and Dennis sat at the ends of the table. Laurie suspected they took some pleasure in the fact that all their children were in one place, which hardly ever happened anymore.

"We have some things we need to figure out," Barbara had said. She explained as economically as she could that in Dot's will, she—Barbara—was named as the executor. But they were estimating it would take at least six months for the estate to be probated so that they could clean out and sell the house, and Barbara, who was already skip-ping a lot of her regular activities because of hip pain, was rather incon-veniently scheduled to have surgery right at the beginning of the summer. Dennis wasn't doing much better, and not long after that, he had some long-delayed back surgery. It was just bad luck, that was all, but they had to figure out what they were going to do about the house.

Dot's estate was to be divided up equally among her four nieces and nephews. The only real value, they figured, would lie in the house itself, which Dot had grown up in and inherited from her parents when they died. No one in the family was clamoring to live in it, and in order to sell it, they would have to empty it of ninety-plus years of Dot's belongings, going back to her childhood. This job would probably land on the family around May or June. "It's going to be a big job," Barbara had said. "None of you has to do it, but nobody else in the family is going to do it. Most likely, our choices are to figure it out among the seven of us or to turn a lot of the work over to somebody we would pay. But we can pay somebody if we need to, so don't worry about that."

Patrick had spoken up first, in the confident tones of doctor privilege as well as with the authority of the eldest—Number One, Laurie always called him. "I could get maybe a couple of days off," he said, "but with the kids and the hospital and Marianne starting her business, I can't take it on. I'm sorry." Patrick's kids were ten and twelve, and his wife Marianne had just started doing some kind of IT consulting that Laurie didn't understand.

"Unfortunately, I can't either," Joey said. For him to speak up next made sense, since, despite being Number Four, he was the most competitive with Patrick. The two of them had had closely aligned interests in sports and science when they were growing up, and Joey had once burned a hole in the couch trying to prove that Patrick's science fair project was flawed. "I'm not organized enough, I hate paperwork, and there's no way I could get that kind of time off." Joey did not have a wife and didn't have kids (*yet,* as Laurie's mother would have rapidly added), but he did have a very demanding boss he called Brutus and a job he had been in for only a couple of months. He was a business consultant who worked with medical device companies, which was why every time they got together, Laurie asked him if he was working on any new sex robots.

Scott, who was Number Two, shook his head and held up both

hands. "Sorry to play the new baby card, but: new baby." Scott had been in trouble for about the first twenty-five years of his life, until he started looking after his mental health, but right now, he was the most assertively domestic, the one with a new baby. Her name was Lilac. (Dot's exact words on this development had been, "How fragrant.")

Ryan looked over at Laurie, then at his mother. Then he took a deep breath. "If we're lucky, Lisa's going to be pregnant then. If we're *lucky*. It's just the worst timing." Ah, Number Five. The baby who wanted his own baby. "Plus," he added, "I hope I'll be working." Ryan was a New York actor, and he was regularly out of work.

They looked at Laurie, and Laurie looked around the room. Every closed cabinet door was holding back piles of vinyl records, piles of papers, piles of magazines. On one shelf alone, she could see and count twelve egg cups. There was upstairs, too. There was a basement. There was an attic. There were four bedrooms. There was a garden shed outside.

"Laurie, don't feel like you have to do this," her mother had said. "We can perfectly well spend a day together picking out some things we'd like to remember her by and then hire someone to do the bulk of the work. We're not the first people to ever have this problem."

Laurie nodded slowly. "What would they do with her things?"

Her mother shrugged. "They would donate what they could. They would sell what they could."

"And they'd throw away the rest of it," Laurie finished. "It's her whole life," she added. "It seems sad."

"It's sad that she's gone," her mother said. "But she wouldn't expect you to sit here and fuss with all this. You know she wasn't like that. It would take you weeks."

"Honey, you have your own place to look after," her father said. "You have work to do, you'll have jobs, and it will be summer. We'll get someone to do it."

"I agree," Barbara said.

But Laurie just kept looking around the room, from shelf to cabinet to drawer. "I don't think so." She shook her head. "No. You know, she used to let me come over here whenever I wanted. When the house was too noisy and there was too much yelling, or when everything was crazy, she would let me come over and sleep in the guest room upstairs, in the orange room. You know she gave me a taste of bourbon when I was in high school? She even stayed home with us the first time Scotty went to the hospital." She broke the spell and smiled. "I can do it. I'll come back in the spring and do it. I can make the time."

That night, when Dennis and Barbara were asleep in the green guest room upstairs, Laurie and her brothers poured drinks and pulled blankets over their legs and stretched out all over the living room furniture. "Are you sure you want to do this, Laur?" Ryan asked. "She's got so much stuff. She has what a hoarder would have if they were organized and only had nice things."

"I'm fine," Laurie said. "Go home and get your beautiful wife pregnant."

Ryan looked at his watch. "She's sleeping right now, but I can try to get her pregnant tomorrow."

"Get sleep while you can," Scott said. "Lilac sleeps for maybe three hours at a time right now." He turned to Patrick. "When did yours start sleeping through the night?"

Patrick rubbed his eyes at the thought. "I think they were both about eight months? Ten months? It's not an all-at-once thing; they start sleeping more and then they go back and sleep less, and I guarantee you that at some point you're going to feel like they're doing it on purpose, like it's a psychological experiment." He took a sip of his drink. "It's not, though. They don't start experimenting on you intentionally for another few years."

"That's great, that's great," Scott said. "Just when I think my brain is fixed."

"Your brain is fine," Patrick said. "You've been doing well, right?"

"I have," Scott said. "By the way, Laur, speaking of mental states, it looks like you're going to be up here to celebrate the big four-oh. Are you ready for that?"

She frowned. "I'm trying not to think about it. I have enough to worry about. I have to tell you, I'm sure it's much worse with babies, but I never knew how much work it was just owning a house. My furnace went out a couple weeks ago, and it took some time for me to come to terms with the fact that I couldn't just call the landlord and tell them to come fix it. That I *was* the landlord. It was like a horror movie. I might have screamed."

"Wait until something breaks that pours water all over your floor," Patrick said.

Laurie put her fingers in her ears. "La la la la I'm not listening." She relaxed deeper into the couch. "I did get somebody to come in and clean once a month, but I don't know if I'm going to keep up with that."

"Why's that?" Ryan was chewing on a handful of leftover Chex mix from the memorial service. When Laurie squinted at him, he shrugged. "I took some in a baggie. They said I could."

Laurie shook her head. "Anyway. A couple of weeks ago after she cleaned, I get back to the house, and there's this neat pile on the armchair in the corner, and it's three of my bras. It was kind of alarming, but then I realized she found them in the couch. And I'm just not ready for a stranger to know I take my bra off in the living room at the end of the day without standing up. I think it's too intimate."

"She probably doesn't think that. She probably just thinks you have sex on your couch a lot."

"That's not better," Laurie said. "Then she's just thinking I have a sex couch, while the whole time it's actually just me being lazy and not wanting to stand up."

"So," Joey said, "it's about a stranger seeing your underwear."

"Oh, this isn't about the bras," Ryan interjected, swallowing another mouthful of Chex mix. "This is just like when we weren't allowed in your room. Do you remember when you used to put Scotch tape over the edge of your door so you could tell if anybody went in there while you were gone?"

"Oh, I remember that," Scott said. "You had that sign, KEEP OUT I MEAN IT. And Mom made you take it down and replace it with one that said KEEP OUT PLEASE."

Laurie had made the sign when she was thirteen. She had come back home before dinner after spending a day watching MTV with June, and she'd seen that her desk drawer was open. She had stomped into the room that Ryan and Joey shared, because they were responsible for 90 percent of the snooping, given that Patrick and Scott were older and wouldn't ever admit they were the slightest bit curious about her or her stuff. She flung the door open hard enough that the knob crashed into the wall, and found them on the floor building a complicated Lego set. "Who was in my room?" she snarled, her cheeks still pink from riding her bike home. After several minutes of interrogation, Ryan had admitted that he went in hunting for a pair of scissors for some project or other.

It wasn't a particularly bad example of an intrusion into her personal space; he hadn't read her diary. That had happened later, when she was fourteen; Joey was grounded for a month. Laurie had established years ago that he no longer remembered doing this, even though *she* still thought about it every time she started a new journal. But at the time, she had felt her face go hot, and she'd yelled at the boys with such fury that her mother had come flying up the stairs to intervene. Laurie had felt the pressure building in her head, the heat on the back of her neck. *They will not stay out,* she had said. *I ask and they ignore me and they think they can come in and open anything they want.* She had ended up at Dot's for dinner.

The next day, her mother had agreed that it wouldn't hurt

anything for her to put a sign up on the door of her room to "remind" them. And after Laurie drew it with markers, her mom insisted on only the one edit.

"Man, it's a good thing you didn't get married," Scott said. Everybody was very quiet. Ryan looked at Laurie. Joey looked at Patrick. "What?" Scott added. "It's true. I mean, I don't think you could have kept Chris out of your laundry forever."

"You know what you are?" Patrick said, looking at her over his glasses. "You're exacting. You always were, and you probably always will be. You want a thing how you want it, you want it left where you put it, and you don't want everybody's hands all over it."

Laurie shrugged. "Maybe I'm a hummingbird."

"What does that mean?" Ryan asked. "Is this a nature thing? Do I have to watch PBS to understand?"

"Most birds fly in big flocks," Laurie said. "They're social. But some hang out by themselves. Like hummingbirds. They mostly just do their own thing unless they're eating or making baby birds, and maybe I'm that. Living a hummingbird life."

For a minute, all her brothers seemed to be digesting this idea, but soon, Patrick scoffed noisily. "Eh, I still say you should have married Angus. What happened to Angus?"

Angus was the boyfriend before Chris. He was a hiking guide, and he worked at an outdoorsy store that earned him discounts on backpacks and boots. He shared Laurie's love of turning over rocks to look at critters. He had a big bushy beard, and a couple of times a year, he played guitar in a Fleetwood Mac cover band. He'd been part of the boys' group chat for two NFL seasons and then vanished from her life and, she assumed, theirs.

"Yeah, how is Angus?" Joey said. "Is he still single? Can we get him back?"

Ryan held up one hand. "All right, this is as much as I can take about Laurie's love life." He had decided to bail her out. Ryan, because he had happened to visit her just after the breakup, was the only one of her brothers who knew what, in fact, had happened to Angus. He was not still single. He was married now, and he had a six-month-old daughter. What had happened to Angus was simple: He had wanted kids. "If she's a hummingbird," Ryan continued, "she's a hummingbird, whatever that means."

"Do you want that, though?" Patrick asked. "You were about to get married. Are you sure you want to commit to being by yourself forever? It seems kind of lonely."

Laurie looked around the room. "Dot was a hummingbird," she said. "I don't think she was particularly lonely. And look at all the stuff she got to do."

"Yeah," Scott said, looking around the room. "She probably had sex on this couch."

Chapter Four

Most mornings, Laurie made breakfast while she FaceTimed with her mother, which was much more convenient now that they were in the same time zone. The morning after she met the Grim Reaper, her mom answered with "Good morning, I hurt my ankle." She aimed the phone straight down, so Laurie could see the big brace strapped around her leg.

"Oh no! What happened?"

Her mom hesitated, and her face went a little pink. She said, "I was trying to catch the ice-cream truck." There was indeed a truck that tootled around their Florida neighborhood for much of the year, playing "My Heart Will Go On" and serving Drumsticks and Chipwiches out the side window. Laurie's parents had been known to indulge in the occasional Dove bar. "He stopped for the kids across the street, the twins, and I was trying to find cash—you know I never have cash anymore—and when I got out there, he was starting to pull away. So I ran down the sidewalk, and I tripped over a box full of shirts your father ordered from Tommy Bahama."

Laurie had to admit it was never boring to ask her mother what happened, in almost any situation. "Okay, but what happened to your ankle? Did you break it? Did you go to the emergency room?"

"Dad drove me to the hospital. We had to sit around for three hours so they could tell me I sprained it and give me some crutches. By the way, if anybody ever tells you your armpits are made to support your entire weight," she said as she swung the camera over to show her crutches leaning against the wall, "don't believe it."

"I'm so sorry. You didn't mess up your hip, right?"

Barbara waved her hand. "No, it's no big deal. How are you doing at Dot's? I was going to check in with you last night, but I took to my bed to watch *Bridgerton* and it was lights out before I knew it."

"We did fine. The guy came, the guy who's going to pick up everything. I'm trying to pack up what you asked for and whatever I think we should try to keep. I got the framed pictures from the mantel, her big Dutch oven . . . I'm trying to make sure I get everything on the list. I did want to ask you about one thing."

"If you don't mind talking to me while I'm eating breakfast." Her mother bit into an orange section. "Fire away."

"Do you know anything about the duck decoy that was in the cedar chest? It was under these blankets, like she was hiding it or something. It was weird, because of the way everything else is just all over the place, on her shelves and in cabinets and things. It doesn't really go with her other stuff, either. It's sort of rustic, you know? For Dot? It's pretty, but it's not sparkly. Most of her stuff is sparkly, or it's a souvenir, or something like that."

Barbara frowned. "I don't know anything about a duck decoy, no. I assume it's from a yard sale or the rummage sale at church, maybe. She certainly wasn't a hunter. She probably forgot about it. You know how she was about saving everything, and she went everywhere."

"Yeah, I guess so." To bring up the letter or not to bring up the letter? Better not to. "It just seemed odd. That it was buried like that, when her place is so organized and everything is lined up and displayed, I don't really get it. I took some pictures of it." Because they were chatting by iPad, she could pull the pictures up on her phone and hold them up to the screen for her mother to see.

Barbara leaned forward and squinted at them. "I can barely tell what I'm looking at, but it doesn't seem familiar. Maybe it was a gift and she hated it, so she tucked it away and never thought about it again. Did you keep it?"

"I did for now," Laurie said. "The antiques guy, Matt, he said it was a cheap little doodad, didn't seem important. He offered me fifty bucks for it."

"Well, that's up to you. I think the lady who takes on the huge job gets to make the decisions. Do whatever you think is right. Aunt Dot probably had a lot of mysteries in that house. Ninety-plus years of independence leaves a lot of room for questions."

"Am I going to find mysteries if I have to clean out your house someday?"

Her mom smiled and picked up her coffee cup. "Not like with Dot. No ducks here."

"You know, the more I looked at her pictures and things, the more I wish I'd talked to her about the wedding. About deciding not to have it, I mean. The last couple of times I called her, I was going to get into it more, and I thought maybe she would ask, but we just didn't talk about it."

"I'm sure she would have said something like 'better this than a divorce.'"

"That's what June says, too."

"She's very wise, as she always has been." Barbara looked at her watch. "So, I have a follow-up appointment at eleven-thirty this morning."

"Well, that's good. I guess they can give you lessons on how to walk on your big braced leg, in case you have to stomp on any mice in the next few weeks."

"Once," Barbara said. "I stepped on a mouse once, and my children have never let me hear the end of it."

Laurie laughed and glanced at Dot's clock on the wall. "The library's going to open in about fifteen minutes, and I think I'm going to go over and grab some books to read."

"Dot doesn't have enough in the house? I seem to remember she had enough books to choke the Library of Congress."

"I just want some fresh ones," Laurie said. "I was over there the other day right after I got here, and I kind of liked it." What she did not say was that the library had three big sofas in a horseshoe formation in the middle of the fiction section upstairs and an endless supply of magazines. "I won't be long."

"Did you know Nick Cooper is running that library now? He took over from his mom and dad?" She did know. It was the sofas and the magazines . . . and that.

"Yes, Mom. June told me. And no, I haven't seen him, and yes, I know he's divorced, and yes, if I do see him, I will say hello for you."

"You're way ahead of me, sunshine."

"I know. Please take care of your ankle, get your ice cream from the store like a normal person, and I'll check on you tomorrow. Love you tons."

"Love you, too."

The Calcasset branch of the Whipwell County Public Library sat on a hill on the corner of Kirk and Cabot Streets, a block down from Grocery Stop and two blocks down from a little coffee shop that was just called The Cozy Cup, which hadn't been there when Laurie moved away. A small parking lot, a bike rack, and a book drop bin sat in front of the big stone building, more like a church than the kind of brutalist block big cities had, or the office-park splat of a structure that too many suburbs got stuck with in the 1970s. This building had been here since 1898 and was on the National Register of Historic Places. This was a proper library.

Laurie parked out front and slung her tote bag over her shoulder, filled with the mass-market paperbacks she'd checked out when she first got to town a week earlier, all of which she'd already raced through. Inside the front doors, she found the slot near the circulation desk and slid them in, one by one, letting them thunk into the mostly empty bin. She raised one hand and offered a little smile to the woman behind the desk, who nodded back. *Who,* she wondered, *are all these people who live in the place where I once felt like I knew everyone?* And then there was the one person she did know, who hadn't made an appearance yet.

The paperbacks were on a set of short shelves near the middle of the library's main floor. Laurie ran her hand along their spines, some of which were so broken that the titles were almost obliterated, looking for things that sounded like they would have lots of murders and detectives and maybe some beautiful people having sex in European cities. She pulled *Fatal Memories* and *Guns on the Riviera,* and just as she was getting to the end of a row of books, she heard a voice next to her.

"Ma'am, I'm here to arrest you. Your books are about twenty years overdue."

It took a minute. He was older, obviously, just like she was. She often saw men with the same hair they'd had in high school, but his had evolved. Shorter, neater, maybe a little lighter. Still, the face was the same, and the smile, especially, was the same. She'd always had to catch her breath when she saw him, and she figured now it was probably just because it had been so long. Probably. He put his palm to his chest. "Nick? Library enforcer? Old pal? Don't pretend you forgot."

"Oh, *Nick,*" she said, drawing it out. "I *guess* I remember you."

"You better."

Before she could spend too much time wondering whether she should hug him, it was already happening, and he was so familiar that she almost slid her hands down into his back pockets. How long had they lasted before they made contact, nine seconds? "I'm glad to see you. I was here the other day, but I guess you weren't around." He ran the library now, circ desk to stacks, and when she'd come before, she'd casually glanced down every corridor and row of materials, and she'd happened to wander past every section on both floors. She hadn't, purely fortuitously, run into him. Now she held up the books in her hand. "I'm grabbing some pulp. I get bored."

He had a smile like a camera flash or a clap of thunder: distracting. But then his expression changed. "I heard you were coming up here to see about Dot. I'm sorry I missed the service. I was stuck here, actually. I hope she would understand—she came around a lot. I think she was here about three weeks before she died, just dropping off spy novels and picking up more."

"I wouldn't be surprised if some of your books are still at her place. I might need a truck to return them, though."

"So you're taking care of the house?"

"Yeah, she has a whole lot of stuff. My mom and dad couldn't really do it, and the boys are all over the place. So I'm taking some time up here to deal with the house in between jobs."

"While you wait for the next animal whose story needs telling."

She nodded slowly. His eyes were so green.

Now they had reached that point. The point where she could say, *Well, great to see you, everything here looks amazing,* and he would probably say something like *Give my best to your family.* But she racked her brain for other options. And just as she started to get desperate, he said, "I was about to walk over to get some coffee; do you want to check out your books and walk with me?"

She felt her whole body loosen with relief. "I would love that. But when I was here last time, Viola over there vouched for me. I think before we go, I should get a real library card so she doesn't have to keep breaking whatever rule that is," she said, noticing his shoulders, his sparse freckles, the way he still stuffed his hands into his pockets and pulled his shoulders up. She had always loved that.

"You have come to the right place," he said softly.

He took her over to the circ desk. "So. Your name is Laurie Ellen Sassalyn," he muttered, tapping away on the keys.

"Sharp memory."

"Your local address is at Dot's."

"Yes—2623 Butterfly Street."

"That's right," he said. "You know, a few years ago, one of the houses over there had a break-in, and people were walking around asking if I'd heard about Butterfly Street, and I kept thinking how much it sounded like the title of a Strawberry Shortcake mystery or something." He tapped a little more. "You were born . . . July 16 of . . . 1982?"

"Yeesh. You keeping a dossier on me, Cooper?"

"I remember things." He looked up. "Hey, you've got a birthday around the corner."

"Don't remind me."

"It's a big one. I know because I just had mine."

"Yes, I'm going to celebrate by consuming the essence of several virgins to restore my youth."

"Gross."

Just then, a young woman with a name tag that said JOLIE came around and tapped Nick on the shoulder. "I'm sorry, Nick. Frank Ashton says you were saving some Nova Scotia travel guides for him?"

"Ah, I was," Nick said. He looked under the counter and pulled out a short stack of books. He handed them to her. "Tell him to call me if none of these are right."

"You do requests," Laurie said.

"Yes, I am a personal research concierge to a wide variety of people who hate the internet," he said, pushing a few more buttons on his machine.

When he had printed out and laminated her card and put the bar code sticker on the back, she scanned the books and dropped them into her bag, and he held open the door as they stepped out onto the sidewalk. They walked in silence past the drop bin and the bike rack, and then finally, he bumped her with his shoulder. "Other than for thirty seconds at June's wedding, I don't think I've seen you in . . . twenty years?"

She nodded. "Something like that." She had been single at June's wedding; he had not. "So how's Ginger?" she asked. "Still motoring?" Nick's grandmother lived in a converted lighthouse out on the water with her dogs. You couldn't drive all the way out to the house on the jetty, so she used a golf cart, and sometimes it would show up in town, too, even though it wasn't street-legal. It had a license plate on the back that said SPEEDY.

"Yeah, she's going strong. Same as always. The team is really good this year, so that makes her happy." Ginger owned the local minor-league baseball team, the Calcasset Claws. She'd moved to town twenty-five years ago, after her husband died, to join Nick's mom and dad, and much of the rest of the family had followed. "My folks downsized after they retired. They have a townhouse in Rockland. They're playing a lot of tennis."

"Ah," she said. "My mother has discovered swimming." They took a few steps in silence. "How about you? Are you happy?" He had gone to Boston and New York for school—undergrad, master's—but he'd been back here ever since, according to the social media posts from him that trickled through her line of sight from time to time, most of which were about travel, and about a wife and then no wife.

"Pretty happy, yeah," he said. "I like what I do. It's not easy, but it's got some purpose to it."

Laurie looked up to see a car driving alongside them with its window down. A girl in the passenger seat, maybe fourteen, looked up from her phone. "Hi, Mr. Cooper!" she called out with a wave. "Thank you!"

"You're welcome, Angela. Hey, Anna Beth." He waved.

"Hey, Nick, thanks again!" The woman in the driver's seat called across, and the car drove off.

"Boy, did you pay them to come along right then?" Laurie asked.

He laughed. "That's Angela and her mom. Angela had an assignment for a summer class; she had to find out something she didn't know about one of her heroes. I spent a little time this morning walking her through the fine points of some of our better databases. And believe me, it's not easy to give a tenth-grader who idolizes Beyoncé any information she doesn't already have."

"Did she find anything?"

"I don't know. She said she'd come back when she was done and fill me in. I'm on tenterhooks."

Laurie shook her head. "It freaks me out that there are so many people here now that I don't know. I'm sure I lost out on a ton of hot gossip."

"Well, let's see. I told you how the team is doing. The community theater did *The Music Man* this year, it was a hit. They even rounded up a passable barbershop quartet."

"Did you play Marian the librarian?"

"Cute. What else . . . we have a new T.J. Maxx on the edge of town that has Calcasset's third escalator." He held up three fingers, and she laughed.

"Amazing, I'll have to go ride it up and down sometime."

"We have a baseball coach at the high school who used to pitch for the Yankees."

Laurie turned to him. "How did *that* happen?"

"His fiancée lives here. Do you remember Evvie Ashton? She was younger than we were, lived with her dad?"

"I don't. I've clearly forgotten everything I ever knew."

"You should have come back more."

Laurie sighed. "I know. At some point, I started talking to Dot and June on the phone all the time and I just stopped visiting. Everybody else kind of faded." She smiled. "You are the exception, of course. I'm very happy to see you."

He put a hand on his belly. "Well, I am honored. I'm happy to see you too." He rubbed his chin. "Should I ask you about the wedding? I did hear about the wedding."

"Everyone knows everything," she sighed.

"Unintended consequences of an overly connected society," he said.

"Unintended consequences of my mother having Facebook. Does that service do anything other than trick you into disclosing things you could have just kept secret?"

"In my experience, it will also remind you that eight years ago, you took a really great picture with someone you were married to but aren't anymore. Of course, you don't have to say anything about the wedding if it's particularly sensitive."

"It's not particularly sensitive, but that is a conversation that we should definitely have somewhere other than walking past this sign that says PLEASE CURB YOUR DOG."

He put his hand on her elbow as a car pulled out of a driveway in front of them, and then they continued. "Fair enough. So you're working hard over at Dot's?"

"Yeah, with Junie. We hired this guy to come over, and he's picking through all her stuff, and after we decide what to keep and what might sell, his people will clean out the rest."

"Did she have any buried treasure in the closet?"

"No, not really. She had a lot of trinkets, and some letters, and enough travel souvenirs to sink *The Love Boat*. You've never seen so many nearly identical postcards of blue water."

"Nothing scandalous, though."

"Well, I'm trying to resist reading her love letters. It's not easy."

"She seemed like she had quite a life."

"To say the least," Laurie agreed. "I think she was a hellraiser. I'm not sure what a hellraiser even looked like in the 1950s, but I'm pretty sure whatever it was, she qualified." She paused. "I did find this duck."

"A duck?"

"Not like quack quack, not a live duck. This wooden duck, like a decoy. It was in her cedar chest, way down at the bottom. Forgotten, I guess." She kicked a pebble off the sidewalk. "It's weird, though. Because I did read this one letter, one of her love letters."

"Of course you did."

She rolled her eyes. "Oh, you would have, too, don't judge me. Anyway. There was this line in there about how if she ever was desperate, there were always ducks. I don't have a clue what it means. For all I know it could have been a policy with a duck-themed insurance company or something. But it's weird, right? This letter about ducks, and there's a duck in the bottom of her trunk under all these blankets?"

"Did you ask the downsizing guy?"

"I did. He took a look at it, and he said it wouldn't sell for much. I hung on to it, but I think I'm going to let him buy it off me for fifty dollars. I can't take everything with me that's interesting, or I'd . . . you know, I'd take everything with me."

They got to the coffee shop, and he opened the door for her again, and she slid inside where it was nice and cool. "Okay," she said, "this is much better." They both got big cups of coffee wrapped in Cozy Cup sleeves, and he gestured toward a couple of leather chairs. "You want to sit?"

"Sure."

Once they were settled, he looked at her expectantly. "So. The wedding."

She smiled. "How much do you know?"

"Just that it got called off."

"Right. So you want the whole thing?"

"Absolutely."

"Okay. Well, we hadn't been dating for that long before we got engaged, only about a year. I don't know, maybe it wasn't long enough. It's a long time when you're over thirty-five, I feel like. But we got engaged, which seemed like we were making appropriate progress or whatever."

"Did he give you the ring and get down on one knee and say 'Laurie Sassalyn, will you do me the honor of agreeing to be my wife so we can make appropriate progress or whatever?'"

"No, but I'm not sure he wasn't thinking it."

"How romantic."

"Anyway, a few months before the wedding, we were registering for gifts. The wedding was supposed to be in August, and this was February, because apparently people need months to buy you a present even when you tell them exactly what you want. I found the whole thing sort of mortifying, like I was making a list of demands, but I know it's what's done."

"Well, when Becca and I got married, we got a giant green dish that I never stopped calling 'the golf trophy,' so don't knock the registry."

"You don't even play golf. Or do you now?"

"Of course not, come on. I'm divorced, by the way."

"I heard."

"Right, because your mother has Facebook."

"Exactly."

"Okay. Continue."

"We were at one of those big stores, I forget what it was called, Homes-N-Things or whatever. And we were walking around with those little guns. These scanners you aim at stuff, and it goes *beep*, and it's added to your registry. We beeped a Vitamix, some really nice linens, some regular stuff like a salad bowl or whatever. And then he wanted this waffle maker." She looked over at Nick, and he was looking at her with raised eyebrows. "What?"

"Nothing. Are you kidding? I love this story so far. I'm riveted. Five stars. I wouldn't change a thing."

She laughed. "Okay. Anyway, he wanted this waffle maker. But not just any waffle maker. It was called the WaffleSmart, I think. It came with these metal plates that swapped out, so you could make waffles with different designs on them. I think it had a flower and maybe a rabbit and a map of the United States. You could buy add-ons, you know, Darth Vader waffles, Ohio State waffles, Red Sox waffles."

"If this turns into a story where you called off your wedding over Red Sox waffles, you are going to be a New England legend."

"I wish it were that exciting," she said. "Anyway. Removable plates, all these different settings. You could make your waffle crispy on the outside and fluffy on the inside. You could make it lightly toasted, or extra crusty, and I think there were settings for whole grain and gluten free, as if the waffle knows the difference."

"That's what makes it smart."

"Oh, no. What made it smart was that there was an app. There was an app that you installed on your phone that would set the timer for the correct cycle. Then it would alert you when your waffles were done. So this whole thing is built on the assumption that making waffles is an operation you need to be able to monitor remotely. Who is ever that busy when they're making waffles? Other than somebody working the brunch shift at a hotel buffet?"

"It seems excessive."

"Can you guess what the app was called?"

He tilted his head. "I'm going to go with . . . GoWaff."

"That's impressively terrible and, in that sense, pretty close. It was called Waffle Me."

He shook his head firmly. "I don't like that at all."

"No."

Nick considered all this, then rested his coffee cup on the arm of his chair. "I'm not going to lie, I tend to burn waffles, so this might have won me over, too."

"I'm not done, though. When your waffle is done, it sings 'Oh, What a Beautiful Morning.' If you don't like that, you can change it to 'Also Sprach Zarathustra' or—this is the truth—the world's squarest version of 'La Cucaracha.' And the icing on the cake is that this thing costs 350 dollars. I am not making that up, it is a waffle maker that costs 350 dollars. He wants to put it on our registry and tell people that we want them to buy it for us. He wants us to say to our friends, 'We are the kind of people who would like you to spend 350 dollars on a waffle maker that plays "La Cucaracha." '"

Nick sipped his coffee thoughtfully. "That is a man who really respects the most important meal of the day."

"Oh, no. That's the genius part. Chris doesn't eat breakfast. If I made coffee, he'd drink coffee and maybe eat a PowerBar. If I didn't make coffee, he'd just eat the PowerBar. But he doesn't eat breakfast."

"Did you bring that up? I bet you did."

"Oh, I did. Right there in Homes-N-Stuff."

"I think it was Homes-N-Things."

"Whichever. I also asked him where he was going to put it, since he had moved into my house and we were pretty much out of cabinet space between the actual dishes and the food dehydrator he had bought himself and then used to make jerky a total of two—as in 'one, two'—times."

"How was the jerky?"

"Wretched. It tasted like wet cigarettes. We could have used it to repel raccoons. And now he wanted us to find space for a 350-dollar waffle maker that sings show tunes and sounds like a Cinco de Mayo office party at a law firm. Do you hear my voice? I'm getting loud all over again."

"I'm enjoying it."

"Anyway, even though I didn't call it off for another few months, I'm pretty sure that was when I knew it wasn't going to work out. He kept saying that he wanted to use it to make brunch, which we never ate, or to entertain, which we never did. It was like he was describing *some* life, but not *our* life." Laurie tried to take the tension out of her voice. "I know this sounds ridiculous as an explanation for breaking my engagement."

Now Nick was quiet for a minute. The door opened and closed; a woman and a little boy came in and went up to the counter to order; a girl with a backpack slung over her shoulder walked out. "Nah. Believe me, you don't want to get married if the marriage you're going to have is not the same marriage as the one you'd like to have."

"Boy, that's it exactly." She picked at the edge of her shirt. "Anyway, I called it off."

"When?"

"Three weeks before it was supposed to happen."

He whistled. "Whoa. I'm sure that was wrenching and everything, but undoing a wedding also sounds like the biggest pain in the ass ever."

"Yeah. Once he took a couple of days to get drunk and hate me, Chris was very helpful, probably about half because he's a genuinely lovely person and half because he wanted to see if we could get any money back. Spoiler alert, by the way: not much. I canceled the hall and the band and the flowers. He canceled the food and the bartenders and the minister. My mother made the cancellation calls to the guests. We divided up sending back the gifts. I had to deal with the dress, obviously."

"Did you get your money back for that?"

"It's a funny thing," she told him, holding up one finger. "It turns out that when you have a wedding dress made, there's no backsies. So you either keep it, or you let them keep it and try to resell it, and you lose most of your money. Which, in my case, was a bunch of thousands of dollars."

"Laurie," he said as he fidgeted with his coffee cup, "that is a racket."

"It is a racket. My friend Erin back home is planning her wedding right now, and there was a printer that she had used for these fancy party invitations once and they wanted to charge her six times as much for her wedding invitations, which were basically the same. And she asked why, and the guy said it was 'the market.'"

"So you have to hope somebody buys your dress?"

"No," she said. "I didn't want them to get the best of me with this ridiculous system, so I just paid for it and kept it."

"So you have this dress now?"

She nodded. "I have the dress. I am not at all sure I'm ever going to get any use out of the dress, but I have the dress. Maybe I'll wear it on Halloween sometime. Otherwise, it will decay in my closet at home, and one day, they can bury me in it."

He tilted his head. "So you would be a very old lady who was buried in a forty-year-old wedding dress?"

"Exactly."

He considered this. "Huh."

"What?"

"Nothing. That'll show 'em?"

"Hey, whose side are you on?"

"I'm on your side. And the dress is not going to decay in your closet. I'm sure you're going to use it when the time comes, and you're going to look great." He drank his coffee, and they just looked at each other for a minute, a dark curl of his hair falling onto his forehead.

She put her cup down. "Wait. How are you hot now?"

He laughed—he cackled, really—and he slid his jacket off and put it over the arm of the chair. "I'm not, believe me."

"I'm not sure you're the expert."

"Don't take my word for it. I had a woman on a dating app a few weeks ago message me to say I was a six, but if I cut my hair and went to the gym I might be as high as an eight."

"Why would she tell you this?"

"I don't have a clue. I think getting information you didn't ask for is one of the basic features of dating apps. Whatever you actually want to know about people, it's not what you're going to find out. I asked a woman what her favorite book was once, and she said, 'Yoga.'"

She rolled her eyes. "Oh, don't ask people what their favorite book is, though."

"Why not?"

"Because even though you, in particular, ask that question in your capacity as a non-jerk, it's a question a lot of jerks ask, because they want to use it to develop a cultural profile of you that they can work to adjust later."

"Is that true?"

"Absolutely. I once told a guy I loved *The Firm* and he told me that if I loved legal thrillers, I should read the best legal thriller of all: the Bible."

"I don't know what that means."

"Neither do I. But I do know you are not a six. You are hot now, and I resent the fact that you became that way while I was gone."

"Maybe we're thinking about it wrong. Maybe I was always hot."

"You were not," she said. "You were cute and nice. That's different from hot."

"Well, you thought I was hot then."

"How do you know?"

"You dated me."

"I dated you because you were cute and nice. I was sixteen, and you were cute and nice. 'Cute and nice' is what you aspire to date when you're sixteen and you're a complete dork, everybody knows that."

"You were not a complete dork."

"Oh, I was."

"You really were not."

"How do you know?"

"I dated you."

"Like I just said, dorks date people who are cute and nice."

"Wait, who do hot people date, then?"

"Other hot people." Laurie looked down at the cup in her hands, and then she looked at him. "Oh my God, Nick."

"What now?"

"You're a sexy librarian. I hope it makes you happy."

"Very."

"Yeah?"

"I mean, not the sexy part, that's obviously a huge hassle with the crowds of admirers and everything. But the librarian part is good. I'll admit it's not the easiest job in the world, taking care of something people are constantly trying to starve. Every few weeks, some genius somewhere says something about how there should be a Netflix for books, and I have to buy a new night guard so I don't grind my teeth down to little stumps."

"Yeah, I read the other day about a start-up that said they wanted to create, you know, 'green spaces with fitness equipment,' and 'staff who could preserve the natural resources' in return for modest monthly fees, and I honestly wouldn't have been surprised if they'd said they wanted to have a bear as part of their green branding who would send out push alerts to say that only premium subscribers can prevent forest fires."

He laughed. "Exactly. On the other hand, I was Calcasset Citizen of the Year last year."

"Get out of here!" she said. "That's awesome."

"I mean, they get around to a lot of people eventually, but it made my mom very happy."

"I assume she has also been Citizen of the Year."

"Four times. My dad three times."

"Wow, a dynasty. Your parents are going to be the Goldie Hawn and Kurt Russell of Calcasset Citizen of the Year. What did you get?"

"There was a dinner at the Pearl. Very nice, very tasteful, my grandmother wore her silver jacket."

"Of course." She took a sip of coffee. "So you never think about getting into a different line of work?"

"Oh, once every six or seven minutes. But then I get to stop some guy who's working on his résumé from dropping Girl Scout cookie crumbs into the keyboard, and I tell myself it's all worth it."

"That's what makes it worth it?"

He shrugged. "He has to work on his résumé somewhere."

Just then, the doors opened, and a couple came in laughing. The woman spotted Nick and waved. "We finally got finished," she called out. "You're my hero." Nick threw her a thumbs-up.

"Who's that?" Laurie asked.

"That's Bruce and Shelly Foster-Forester. They're building a tea shop in that place over by the fire station that used to be a stationery store, and then it was jewelry? Anyway, they checked out a Shop-Vac from the library the other day."

"You can check out a Shop-Vac?"

"You can," he said. "We have a tool library. Started it a few years ago, right after my mom retired." Nick's mother and father had run the library together since Laurie was a kid, and he'd started working there in high school. "That way, everybody doesn't wind up with bolt cutters taking up space in their garage because they had to cut a lock one time."

"I've been with you for like five minutes and two people have literally yelled out to thank you. In public."

"Oh, yes, I'm very important," he said, putting his hand over his heart. "I am the man to speak to if you need Beyoncé information or a floor buffer."

"I think it's great," she said. The espresso machines hissed, and Laurie thought about how Nick used to sit behind her and give her backrubs when they were waiting for a movie to start, then scoot around the end of the row to come sit next to her when the lights went down. "It's good to see you," she said.

"It's good to see you, too. I'm sorry you're not back under better circumstances. I know how much you loved Dot."

"I appreciate that," Laurie said. "I wish I had seen her more. Not that she was sitting around waiting to be visited. She had a lot of adventures, I think."

"And a duck," he added.

Laurie repeated it: "And a duck." She felt herself start to bounce her knee the way she did when she worked on crossword puzzles.

"That duck is really bugging you," he said.

"It really is."

"Sass," Nick said, looking at her hard, "I think you have to keep that duck."

"Nick," she said, nodding slowly, "I think you're right."

Chapter Five

Back at Dot's, she googled "antiques dealers near me" and found a place that mentioned hunting and fishing memorabilia on its website and was just a couple of towns over in Wybeck, about a half hour away. She hopped into the car, with the duck on the seat beside her in a small box, wrapped in a blanket.

The air was cool and dry, and she put on one of her podcasts and opened the window partway. The sun was welcoming but not sweltering, and while she loved the luscious green of the Pacific Northwest, and while it didn't rain *all* the time the way her mom often asked her if it did, this kind of sunshine was not one of her chosen hometown's strengths. The houses were far apart on the state routes between these Maine towns, and she glided up and down hills, trying to concentrate on driving while also identifying the birds that periodically sailed past in the blue sky or flittered by a fence post.

She'd been in Seattle for fifteen years, and she did think of it as home. But Maine was where she was *from,* where she was *made.* She was made as a ten-year-old asking her brother to come over and help lift up a rock so she could see the starfish and hermit crabs and sea urchins. She was made watching live lobsters wherever she could, which was practically everywhere. Not because she liked to eat them, but because the segments of their bodies and their deep brown armor were like nothing she'd ever seen outside of the world of bugs. And she was made by the birds she learned to spot while sitting on lawn chairs in the backyard with her father, accumulating advice and mosquito bites at a rapid clip while they shared a bag of M&M's.

When she got to Wybeck, she found Ransom & Sons Antiques along a quiet street, between a post office and a yarn shop. The front windows were crowded with clocks, lamps, paintings, little side tables, and a tall white vase speckled with black.

She opened the door and the bell rang, but at first, she couldn't see anyone. The aisles were Brooklyn-bodega narrow, and the inventory was spilling out past the end of every row. Just as Laurie was about to say something, she saw a man poke his head out from behind a stack of boxes. He was tall and thin with white hair, and she liked him instantly. "Afternoon," he said.

"Afternoon," she said back. "I'm wondering if you can help me. I have a question about whether something is worth anything."

He wiped his hands on a white rag and came toward the front of the store. "Well, whether something is worth anything is right up my alley, so I'll give it a shot. I'm Joe Ransom." He held out his hand, and she shook it.

"Hi, I'm Laurie Sassalyn, and I have a question about this." She set the box under her arm on the glass counter, above a display of fishing lures. She unwrapped the duck and set it down in front of him. "I'm cleaning out my great-aunt's house, she passed away recently, and I found this in her cedar chest. I don't know anything about it, but it seemed like she had kind of set it aside, and I was wondering whether you might be able to tell me anything about it. I'm happy to pay you for your time, obviously."

He waved one hand. "If I didn't like a mystery, I'd have a hardware store." She could tell this was not his first time using that line. He put on a pair of glasses that had been hanging around his neck. "So you've got a decoy here, obviously of a wood duck. Lovely crest, beautifully made."

"I did get that far."

"Well, you're on the right track, then. How old was your great-aunt?"

"She was ninety-three. I don't have a clue how old this is, though."

He picked it up and looked closely at it. "Huh. It's in very good condition. In fact," he said, tipping it back and forth to let the light hit it, "it's in such good condition that I don't think it was ever used."

"Is that unusual?"

"It is. These are collected now, of course, like folk art. People like 'em, and they sell for good money sometimes. But decoys were mostly made for real hunters, not just for decoration. When I see one that's been around a while, it's generally either been repainted at least once—usually a lot more than once—or it's been subjected to a lot of time outside, sometimes in salt water. Sometimes it's even been shot at."

"Wow, that's a lot for a floating duck to have to put up with."

"It sure is. In fact, one reason people pay a lot of money for the really old ones is that most of them haven't made it this long without their heads or their tails breaking off. This guy looks . . . old, but also like it just came out of the shop, which might make us think it's not a real antique."

"Oh, okay. I did have somebody tell me they thought that might be true."

"Hang on, don't give up on him yet. I'm just getting started." He turned it over. "Huh. Look at that mark." He took out a magnifier and ran it over the paint on the wings. "Huh. Well, isn't that interesting." And then he said it again: "Huh. Interesting. Did you say where your aunt lived?"

"I didn't. Just over in Calcasset."

"Huh." That was four. Four *huh* noises. How many made up a true exclamation? What was the exchange rate? "So what I'm noticing about this is that it's in the style of a guy named Carl Kittery. He made decoys from, oh, I want to say about 1940 to 1980. I think his last piece might be 1982. Do you see how the wing is painted? This pattern?" The wings had painted white Vs, made of very thin lines and neatly lined up, alternating bigger and smaller rows. "This is his very specific way of painting feathers, like a signature. Although I've never seen a wood duck from him, so that would be unusual. And the other thing is, he has a mark that you generally find on his decoys, and it's similar to this, but it's not quite this."

"Oh."

"See this 'CKM'? That's for 'Carl Kittery, Maine' in his mark. But it should have a year after it. It would say 'CKM65' or 'CKM78' or what have you. And on top of that, his mark would have had three little dots underneath the circle that signify his wife and two daughters. There's some variation in the first ones, the very early ones, that don't always have the full mark. He hadn't even developed it yet, his daughters weren't born and he was a young man making pieces for hunters. But for one of those early ones to turn up now would be a real surprise, and this doesn't look that old. I've sold Kitterys myself, and I've never heard of partial marks like this. So this looks a little more like it was somebody trying to imitate the mark without quite forging the mark."

Laurie nodded. "So it's . . . it would be a stretch, believing this is the real thing."

"It would, but on the other hand, there are makers who change their marks, or who, for reasons of their own, don't mark pieces at all. Nobody can tell you it's impossible. Since I've never seen a wood duck from Kittery, it could be that this was something he tried out as an experiment and didn't ever sell, and maybe he didn't complete the mark for that reason. It's very similar to a Kittery to not be a Kittery, and it's been made with a lot of care."

"So it's just hard to be sure."

"I'm afraid that's right. Probably the only way to know for sure would be to find some kind of a record of how your aunt got it. With this mark and no history of how it came to her, it's going to be hard to authenticate, so it'll be hard to sell."

"If it was real, would it sell for a lot? I have a plane ticket I'm trying to cover."

He smiled. "You'd want to know if it was a real Kittery, that's for sure. A 1962 Kittery sold for a little under eighty thousand dollars last year, and as I said, this is the only wood duck I've ever seen from him, if it is from him, and that would make it worth more. So I'd say, yeah, it could cover your plane ticket." He made a couple of scribbles in a spiral notebook. "Give me an email address, and what I'll do is I'll send you a picture of what the full stamp looks like from one that I sold a few years ago, and you can see if any other information about it turns up. If it does, let me know, because he's interesting, this fella. It's a beautiful piece of work, whether it's really a Kittery or not."

"I like it." Laurie laid her hand on the duck's back. "I'm just curious about it. I'm not necessarily trying to sell it."

"I'll tell you," he said, "I'm a pretty casual decoy guy; if you want the best shot at a good appraisal and some expert advice, go through Wesson & Truitt, they're in Hartford. Single best auction house for decoys, best resource you can find. If anybody can give you a reliable ruling, those are the guys. Talk to Jim Baines." He scribbled on another sheet from his spiral pad, tore off the page and handed it to her. In his somewhat shaky handwriting, it said, *Wesson & Truitt,*

Hartford, Jim Baines. "And write down your email address for me, I can get you the information on that mark."

"I appreciate it, Joe."

"If you find anything else you want to sell, bring it right over. Look around and you'll see, I carry a little bit of just about everything."

It took a couple more days for Laurie to get well and truly sick of going through souvenirs and table linens and holiday decorations, as well as stir crazy from being by herself listening to podcasts during the day and reading books at night while her back ached. She broke it up by taking what her father used to call her critter walks, peering at tree stumps and stopping for every rustle of leaves. And then on that Thursday around suppertime, she was listening to Dot's Doris Day records and drinking red wine when she opened a closet in the third bedroom that she hadn't explored yet and saw thirty-three identical blue fabric boxes in five tall stacks.

They looked just like the box of 2007 Polaroids, and they were in order, each labeled with a year from 1974 to 2006. She pulled 1983 off the top of a stack and sat down on the daybed. More photos. More and more photos. Here was a party in someone's living room, everyone turned toward the camera and smiling—nobody Laurie recognized. A woman sat on a man's lap, both of them laughing. Someone had paused in the middle of pouring a drink, a martini glass in one hand and a shaker in the other. Where was this house? Who were all these people?

Laurie had been a toddler then. This would have predated even her memories of Dot bringing chocolates at Christmas and ruffling her hair, Dot sleeping on the living room couch at Grandma Natty's because the rest of the family consisted of couples and kids sharing various rooms upstairs and downstairs.

Beautiful travel pictures, yes—some were taken in postcard

places like what seemed to be Hawaii, but also a man standing under a tree pointing to a sign that said BAXTER STATE PARK. In one, two women posed with baskets of wild blueberries. She was fairly certain one of those women had also been in the party picture, sitting on the man's lap.

There was a picture of what Laurie recognized as much younger versions than she could remember of her mother and father, faded but familiar, seated on Grandma Natty's rosebud-print sofa, Mom's head dropped onto Dad's shoulder. Laurie and her two older brothers must have been running around somewhere, evading the camera and probably eating the Chips Ahoy! that Natty always had in her koala cookie jar.

She looked back at the closet. Thirty-two more boxes. She picked up the phone and texted June. Any chance you want to come over tonight and go through some pictures with me?

Laurie and June usually didn't say yes or no to each other. They moved along to planning. Gotta get the kids fed and down, but Charlie's here. How about 7:45?

Laurie texted back a thumbs-up. She sang along with the music for a minute, took a sip of wine, and then picked up her phone again. Then she put it down. Picked it up. Put it facedown. Drank the rest of the glass of wine. Picked it up.

She'd saved his number under "Library Consultant." Hello! I'm going to make you regret sharing your number with me by asking whether you would like to use your hard-earned organizational skills by coming over tonight and helping me sort through 32 years of Dot's assorted Polaroids that I just found in a closet. (They are not explicit that I know of.) I can promise snacks and wine. June is also coming. Please check this box if this sounds like the most fun you've ever had. Send.

She lay back on the bed, feeling her heart *donk-donk-donk* in her chest, staring at the round brass light fixture in the ceiling. This was the orange room they had painted together, where Laurie would stay when she came over. When her parents were going out, sometimes they'd leave her brothers at home and let her come and curl up with Dot and eat popcorn and then stay overnight. It would be just the two of them; Dot sometimes called it "girls' night."

Her phone pinged, and when she picked it up, she had a text from Nick. Sure, it said. Happy to help. 8:00?

She sent back yet another thumbs-up. And then she texted June. P.S. Nick is coming over also.

June pinged her again almost immediately, in all caps: PLOT TWIST.

They sat on the floor of Dot's living room, three members of the Calcasset High School Class of 2000, drinking wine out of juice glasses so they wouldn't tip over on the carpet. They decided to divide up the work roughly by decade: Laurie took the first ten boxes, June took the middle third, and Nick took the last third. The rules they agreed on were that general travel photos could go, pictures with family (most of whom Nick and June could recognize) should stay to be picked over further, and it was perfectly acceptable to keep, as Laurie put it, "anything awesome." And of course, there was the rule that ruled the other rules: Absolutely anything that had any connection to any kind of duck, wooden or real, had to be saved and pointed out immediately.

They dove in.

"So," Laurie said as she started flicking through her stack, "do you guys see much of each other anymore besides when I make you do chores?"

June frowned. "Here and there. But when did I last actually talk to you, Nick? The Spring Dance?" He nodded. The Spring Dance was, incongruously, an annual charity baseball game played by the minor-league team Nick's grandma owned. "We see each other at the store and stuff. But I mostly spend my time around other people who are also chasing their kids all over the place. Nick and I would see each other more if he shared my keen interest in Little League."

"I only socialize with books," Nick added, throwing two pictures into the KEEP box in the middle of the circle. "Other than that, I'm basically a seaside hermit."

"Well, that's no good," Laurie said.

"This town and I are stuck with each other," he said, tossing in a couple more pictures. "I've made peace with it."

Junie paused and had just a little more wine. "Is it okay if I ask how Becca is?"

He didn't look up. "You can ask. She's good. If you believe in amicable divorces at all, we had one. She's in Michigan. As you may have seen on Facebook, she is In a Relationship."

"Do people still change that status?" June asked. "That seems so creepy. I mean, I say that as someone who has been with the same person since 2001. By the time Facebook came around, I was off the market." She passed a picture to Laurie. "Look at this. That's got to be your brother running the cereal box race." The cereal box race around the bases was the between-innings entertainment at Claws games, and Laurie's brother Ryan had won, wearing the Chex box, when he was nine. "Anyway, fortunately, yes, I was married before my relationship had to really deal with the internet."

"Well, that is lucky," Nick said.

"Have you done the online dating thing at all?" June asked. "Either of you?"

"I tried," Laurie said. "I can't say I tried for very long. I just could not handle signing on every day to be greeted by a bunch of guys saying 'hey.'"

"What's wrong with 'hey'?" Nick asked. "Maybe they're trying to start a conversation."

"How am I supposed to answer 'hey'?"

He shrugged. "Say 'hey' back?"

Laurie switched to a new box. "I feel like it's a very indiscriminate 'hey.' I feel like these guys go through and 'hey' at eight hundred women, and they see who will 'hey' back, like they're blowing a horn at the top of a mountain and waiting for goats to come running."

June shook her head. "I'm not sure that's how those horns work. And I'm almost positive it's not how goats work. And you would know."

"Fine. I'll get back on Winkr or Nudgr or Smasho or whatever and write 'hey' back to twenty guys, and we'll see if any of them is my future husband."

"I think Smasho is the most promising of those possibilities, although maybe not for getting married," June said, shifting to rearrange her bent legs. "How about you, Nick? You out there?"

Nick shook his head. "I told Laurie, I'm apparently only a six. Plus, the first app I got on, I wound up on a date with my dentist."

"You didn't recognize her from her picture? You didn't recognize her name?" June started on a new stack of Polaroids.

"Hey, I see her once every six months at most, and she wears goggles and a mask, and her name is 'Dr. Smith.' In her picture, she was wearing sunglasses and hugging a Chihuahua and her name was Leslie. I had already ordered a drink when I figured out where I knew her from."

"And she didn't recognize you?" June said.

"She said I was out of context. We both realized at kind of the same time."

Laurie shrugged. "So? Just find somebody else to clean your teeth."

"She takes my insurance and I had to get two root canals last year," Nick said, straightening a stack of sorted shots. "I'd rather look for another date than another dentist. She was very understanding. I think she was flattered. It's too bad there's not a graceful way for me to leave it in a Yelp review. 'Very attractive woman, even better dentist.'"

"But you feel ready to meet somebody?" Laurie asked.

"I don't know," he said. "I kind of hate being single. It was a lot easier being married. I liked having the house, the other person who was there for everything. I get up in the morning now, and I look around, and I have that feeling of freedom that only comes with realizing nobody else cares what you do at all. I hate it."

"Are you setting dish towels on fire and stuff? Slipping on broken eggs trying to make your own breakfast?" Laurie asked.

"Hey, I'm entirely self-sufficient, that's not the issue. I just didn't want to have to figure out what to do on Sundays by myself. I'm totally out of practice."

"That's the part I love," Laurie said. "I know single people are supposed to be fearful about choking to death in their apartments or whatever, but it makes me feel absolutely blissful having no plans with anybody. Not all the time, you understand. But sometimes, if I want."

Nick nodded slowly. "That's dark, Sass."

"I like being the boss," Laurie said. "I like being capable of taking care of myself. I feel good about not being reliant on somebody else."

"Oh, thanks," June said, with an edge of sarcasm.

"What?"

June put down the photos in her hands. "I think it's great that you like your life. But you make it sound like I'm not independent because I'm married and I have kids."

"I didn't mean it that way," Laurie protested. "I just meant you have another person who can share the weight of things."

June's eyes widened. "I mean, I have that sometimes. Remember when Charlie was working out of Philadelphia for like six weeks? And I wound up driving Bethie to the ER because of her asthma, with Tommy screaming his head off? I was trying to finish everything I was supposed to be doing and getting them fed and getting the garbage

out and suddenly driving an improvised ambulance. I have to tell you,
I think I'm capable of being pretty self-sufficient."

Nick was very quiet.

"I'm sorry, Junie," Laurie said. "I take your point."

June narrowed her eyes at Laurie, then smiled and picked up a
picture that she held out in front of her. "This is me and you. It's my
house on Cragen Ave. I think this is the year your parents' anniversary party was over there. Maybe '90?"

"Oh, sure, during the kitchen renovation." In the picture, Laurie's ponytail was falling out and both of June's knees were ban-
daged, and both girls had prominent front teeth missing: Laurie's
on top and June's on the bottom. "I loved this shirt because it said I
BRAKE FOR LIZARDS. You can't really tell, though, because the picture is a million years old."

"Speaking of a million years old," June said, "remember the buried treasure we found in that yard?"

Laurie laughed. "Oh my God, I tried so hard to forget." Nick
looked up, puzzled. "You tell," Laurie said with a nod.

June pointed to the picture. "I moved to this house in 1989, and
Laurie and I absolutely loved this huge yard it had. We made up all
kinds of games, we raked paths in the leaves and raced each other
around, it was our personal paradise, pretty much. Then we saw something about buried treasure on TV, and we decided we wanted to check
the yard to find out if we had any. There was this big tree, and at the
bottom, we found a little circle of rocks. Somebody clearly put it there,
and we figured it was probably somebody who was hiding their gold or
burying their emeralds, or whatever seemed most logical to us when
we were seven. So we decided to do a little archeological dig."

Laurie put her hands over her eyes. "I brought the shovel."

June started to laugh. "We start digging, and my parents don't
see us. So they don't stop us, and we're digging, and then we find . . .
a bone." She held her hands about three inches apart. "But a little
bone. Like this."

"What did you do?" Nick asked warily.

"Naturally, we assumed it was a baby dinosaur," June said. "We figured we were going to become famous, and we thought we should probably take it to a museum. So we kept digging, and there were some more bones, and we set them in this little pile. And then my dad comes out to see what we're doing, and at first, he's just mad that we dug a hole in the yard. Then he sees the bones."

"I'm guessing he didn't think they were a baby dinosaur."

Finally Laurie jumped in. "He realized pretty quickly that we had located the remains of a rare domestic catasaurus."

"Oh," Nick said, scrunching up his face, "you guys dug up a cat?"

"Cat bones," June clarified. "Laurie thought it was fascinating."

"It's true, I was goth as hell." Laurie shrugged. "It's too bad we didn't ask Dot to come over and photograph the cat bones, because I guarantee you that picture would still be in the 1987 box with her dinner parties and her cruise to the Bahamas."

"You know what gets me about that?" June said. "Instant film used to be really, really expensive. My mom used to set up shots for ages because she didn't want to waste any. Dot was taking a couple hundred pictures a year. She was really committed."

Nick held up the box he was working on. "And this is 2005. There were plenty of digital cameras by then. Half these boxes could probably be on a hard drive."

Laurie smiled. "They probably could." She ran her finger around the white border of a picture of her parents at Christmas. It was faded and discolored, aged in the way it wouldn't be if it had, in fact, been on a hard drive. "Maybe she liked watching things change when they got old."

June paused over the work she was doing. "Can I ask you a question, Laur? Do you want to be going through all of these pictures, or do you feel like you have to go through all of them? Because I don't mind at all, I love seeing you, and I would hang out with you and sort boxes of socks if you needed me to. But you know you don't have to do it just because you can."

Nick looked up and flicked his eyes back and forth between the two of them, then he kept working on 2005.

Laurie put everything down and lay on the floor, pulling her knees into her chest to stretch out her back. She thought about Dot holding a camera at her parents' anniversary party and at a state park. Someone had taken the picture outside *Avenue Q*, someone Dot had tapped on the shoulder and asked politely. She sat back up. "Junie, when your parents die, who's going to go through their stuff?"

June blinked. "Mary Jo and I, probably."

"Are you going to look at their pictures?"

She nodded. "Sure."

"Every picture, right? At least for a second? Or at least one in every album, one in every box, to see what all there is?"

"Most likely."

"How about you, Cooper? Are you going to look at all your parents' pictures someday? Are you going to look at your dad's baseball cards and all the fishing tackle and flip through their college yearbooks?"

He looked at her and he smiled, just a little, and she remembered for some reason the jacket he used to wear, with the shearling collar, which she would grab on to when he kissed her. "I'm sure I'll do that. But it's kind of my thing, professionally speaking."

"I might run out of steam at some point," Laurie said, looking idly at an unlabeled and faded shot of fall foliage. "I just think Dot should have that, too. Even though she doesn't have daughters. Or a librarian." She sighed. "You know what I mean?"

It got quiet, and then Nick raised his half-full glass. "To Dot. And every picture."

"To Dot," June said.

"Dot," Laurie echoed. They all awkwardly leaned forward on their knees for a dull juice-glass clink, and they went back to work.

They debriefed Nick on his path to running the library, which ran through grad school, his return to Calcasset, his dad's retirement, and then his mom's. Laurie told them about being out on a story about frogs in Borneo and getting caught in a rainstorm so sudden she climbed a tree and stayed in it for an hour and a half just to make sure she wouldn't get washed away. June recounted how Tommy had learned to love instant mashed potatoes when he got his tonsils out, and now he wanted to eat them all the time.

They'd been on the floor together for two hours or so when Laurie leaned forward with a picture from the 1970 box. In it, a man with his back to the camera was at a workbench. "I don't know where this is," she said, shaking her head. "But tell me what that looks like to you, the thing on the bench all the way over on the right." She handed the picture to June.

"It looks like the front end of a bird." June handed it to Nick.

He nodded. "Looks like half a duck."

The head was tawny brown and didn't have a crest; this was certainly not *her* duck. But it looked very much like the front of a duck, nonetheless. "Do you guys have any idea who that is?"

"I haven't," June said, "but I mean, it's his back. Other than that he has hair that's turning gray, it could be just about anybody."

"Yeah, it's pretty hard to tell," Nick said. He looked at the front and the back of the picture. "People don't label anything, it drives me crazy." He handed it back to Laurie. "Do me a favor, both of you. Think of the librarians, think of the historians, and label your stuff."

"You mean it's not enough to just write 'Leo' on the bottom of a picture?" Laurie asked.

"It's not ideal."

"Well," Laurie said, "I guess it's my fault for not paying more attention."

Chapter Six

Laurie had talked to Dot on the phone a week after she canceled the wedding. She was sitting alone in her house in the middle of a huge pile of boxes, one of which was the WaffleSmart. The big boss at one of the magazines she wrote for, whom she didn't really know, had sent it on behalf of the company. It had been a very nice gift. Now it was another one to try to return gracefully.

Since she hadn't ever opened the box, with its picture of a heart-shaped waffle, she pasted a big label right on the outside, wrote the office address on it, and moved it to the pile she was planning to take to the post office. It joined several checks she would be mailing to people who had sent money, a few other boxes (including a "popcorn concierge" she had looked up online and discovered cost sixty dollars for five "varietals"), and all of the apology cards she would send to the people on Chris's list, whose gifts he was returning.

Surrounded by boxes and envelopes, with labels and scraps of tape sticking to her socks, surveying the evidence of her mistakes, Laurie pulled her phone out of her pocket and texted June. Damn, there is so much stuff here, Junie. Why did we invite so many people? I should have just married him.

Next time just ask for money, came the response.

Next time LOL, she typed back.

Do you need to hop on the phone?

June was in grad school, and she always had a lot of work to do whenever she wasn't up to her neck in her kids. No, keep studying, she answered. Just tell me that it's impossible that there are an infinite number of gifts in this dining room, even though it seems like there are.

Definitely mathematically impossible. I should know, because grad school!

Grad school for history!

Still counts. I'm officially smart.

Laurie sent back three hearts and returned her attention to the rest of the boxes. She picked up a squared-off package with a Florida address on it that she was fairly confident was from a former colleague of her father's. She thought it might be a candy dish, or maybe a ceramic animal or something. She ripped off the brown paper and found a plain white cardboard box. Inside, a heavy piece of crystal about the size of a grapefruit sat on a dark wooden stand. On the ball, it said, CHRIS & LAURIE, 8-28-21, HERE'S TO THE FUTURE.

"Oh," she muttered. "It's a crystal ball." This was custom. It couldn't be returned to the store. Someone had told her that she didn't have to return items that were personalized, since they'd have no value, but someone else had told her that everything had to go back, no matter what. She would have immediately sent it back, except that in this moment, the idea that someone she didn't know had sent her a large and heavy glass object for which they simply expected her to find room in her house, despite the fact that she didn't even know who they were, rankled. Intellectually, she knew it was kind, but it *felt* entitled, as if a near-stranger were claiming a piece of her mantel, her cupboard, her coffee table. Did they really think she would *want* this, or did they somehow relish playing a role in this little ritual in which people ceremonially force unwanted bric-a-brac on one another as a way of getting revenge for having to sit through an unsatisfying meal in company they did not choose? Did it matter that now they would not have to sit through the meal after all?

She set the crystal ball on the floor. Her hand crept over to the hammer she'd used earlier to rehang her picture of Mount Katahdin where Chris had put his Foo Fighters poster during the months he'd lived there. She held the hammer, moved it back and forth from one hand to the other, tapped the carpeted floor very gently with the head of it. The mental picture of the ball shattering, the glass flying, the explosive crash sounding—it was interrupted only by the thought that she should probably put on safety goggles. Did she have any safety goggles? Were there any with the tools downstairs? Did she still have her swim goggles?

Just then, the phone rang. She put the hammer down to pick it up. "Hi, Dot."

Dot still had a landline in her kitchen, and Laurie could hear her puttering around, turning the faucet on and off, probably pouring some water into the little flowering plants on the windowsill. "Hello, honeybun. I'm just calling to yoo-hoo at you, I hope I'm not interrupting."

"Of course not. I'm just sending back wedding presents."

"Mm, how's that going?"

"Boring and painful, so, a typical Friday night."

Dot laughed. "You know, it's just awful that after everything else, now you've got to go to the post office. I can't stand the post office. They're always out of parking and there's always someone in front of me with an armload of packages that have to be insured. One of them told me she sells buttons on eBay. She insures the buttons. Can you imagine?"

"They must be pretty good buttons." Laurie leaned back against the wall. "How are you?"

"Not bad for ninety-three," she said—her usual answer. "I saw the DiCaprio movie. Where he's that cat burglar."

"Oh, how was that?"

"It was very boring," Dot said. "I know he's an artist now, but I really liked him better when he was going down with the ship." Laurie could hear her pouring wine. "How are the boys?" Laurie was the official communicator for all her siblings. The boys weren't big on the phone.

"Patrick got promoted at the hospital. He's the head of something now, but I forget what. I think Scott's paternity leave is just about up—did he send you the pictures of Lilac in the Batman pajamas?"

"I don't think so."

"Well, you should definitely have those, so I'll send them after we hang up. Joey won some kind of a softball tournament with his team at work. And Ryan is starting a run in a play. Off-Broadway, something about the Cuban Missile Crisis. He and Lisa just got a bigger apartment; she's making the costumes for that *Our Town* revival."

"How's your mother? We haven't talked in a while. Your aunt Colleen told me she's been swimming."

"Well, she's been swimming ever since they moved down there, it's practically the state sport. But yes, she started doing senior synchronized swimming at the Sarasota Y recently. She's going to be in a recital. The theme is Hooray for Hollywood."

The sound Dot made was closer to a hoot than a laugh. "Good for her. Whatever it takes to get your legs over your head. She'll be a regular Esther Williams." She paused for a sip. "I know you don't know who that is."

"I know who she is. She was the underwater movie star."

"That's right, she was. And she lived to be ninety-one." Dot was a student of famous nonagenarians: which diseases they had, how much money they died with and which relatives tried to extract it through various sketchy methods, and especially whether they stayed in their own homes to the very end. She insisted she was living at her last address, and she was right, of course.

These calls went the same way every time. First came what Laurie was doing, then what Dot was doing, then Laurie's brothers, then her parents, then the other relatives in descending order of importance until Dot lost the ability to fake interest or Laurie ran out of gossip. Then they would cover any recent discoveries on Netflix—on this occasion, Dot was excited about something she claimed was called *Handsome British Army Doctors* "or something dashing like that"—and then the news, which included a U.S. senator who had recently been indicted for fraud, whom Dot called "that liar, that disgraceful liar." This was their routine.

"All right, love," Dot finally said, "I'm off to the tub with my wine. I'll call you soon. I love you so."

"I love you too. Have a good bath. Behave yourself in there." She put the phone down beside her on the floor. Dot had recently installed a special tub she had seen advertised during *The Price Is Right* that had a door in the side she could step through to get in and out easily. She was not willing to leave her daily soaks, she said, to the vagaries of her "incorrigible New England joints."

Talking to Dot always made Laurie think about the way Dot's house had saved her life, or at least her sanity. What would she have done without the quiet retreat she didn't even know she needed yet when she was a kid? It wasn't that Dot spoiled her or gave her things her parents wouldn't. She was just there, and she'd open a door, and inside was peace. No negotiating like there always was in a house of seven people; no bargaining. They'd just take the two ends of the couch and watch *Dr. Quinn, Medicine Woman* or Dot's VHS copy of *South Pacific* until Laurie's mom showed up to take her home.

. . .

Laurie, June, and Nick were about halfway through the Polaroid boxes when June's phone rang. She looked down at it and said she had to take it, but she'd be right back. "It's my husband," she said. "He apparently needs me desperately." She disappeared into the bedroom.

"I'm going to pick up some of this stuff and get it into the dishwasher before I break something," Laurie said, getting to her feet and carrying a few small plates and glasses to the kitchen. Nick followed, and he stood a barely platonic distance from her as she ran hot water in the sink. "Is this fascinating, Cooper?" she asked. "Me doing the dishes?"

He smiled. "Don't knock it. I'm just soaking everything up before you leave again."

She felt his eyes on her, and she knew she was blushing, and as much as she tried to swallow the smile, there it was. "Here we are again," she said. "Flirting in the kitchen. This is how we got in trouble at Dana Koppke's sixteenth birthday."

He frowned. "I'm pretty sure you started it at Dana Koppke's sixteenth birthday. I was just doing the dishes, up to my elbows in soapy water. And you"—he stepped closer—"kissed me right on my clueless mug." He pointed to his cheek. "I've never washed it, you know."

"Oh, *brother,*" Laurie muttered down toward the glass she was cleaning, and she heard him chuckle. "My greatest hits. For the record, I was at least smart enough that I was mortified." She glanced at him for the shortest moment she could manage. "I can only imagine what you told everybody."

"I didn't tell anybody. I was trying to figure out my big move."

She swirled water in a glass. "You waited a week to call me, you know."

"Of course I did. I thought I might have imagined it, since you immediately ran out and never said anything about it again."

She opened the dishwasher, and he had to step back. "Exactly. It was step one in my big romantic plan in which I had absolutely no step two." She lined up the plates and the glasses and shut the door, wiping her hands on a towel that was folded on the counter.

"Well, it worked on me," he said, taking hold of a salt shaker on the counter and spinning it in his fingers. "So there's that."

"Yeah," she said, "there is that." She looked at his hand moving. "I forgot how fidgety you are."

"Ah, that. Becca called it 'twitching.' It drove her nuts."

"Ah," Laurie said. "Is *that* why she so foolishly let you go?"

He nodded slowly. "Yes. That and a very appealing job offer that took her very far away."

"You couldn't go?"

"I really couldn't."

"No libraries in Michigan?"

"I couldn't," he repeated. "I was in the process of taking over from my parents, and it was just the worst possible time for me to go."

"So it was bad timing." Laurie had come to the library a lot during their senior year in high school, when Nick was working there part-time. They would talk, make out in the stacks, shelve books, make out a little more.

He nodded again. "The county wanted to close the branch. Combine us with Wybeck and Brayer, lay off the staff, take back the budget, send all the patrons forty-five minutes away. We would have been screwed, but they did say they were going to put a vending machine that made lattes in the new building."

"And you stopped it." Of course he did. Of course. *Hi, Mr. Cooper; thanks, Mr. Cooper; thanks again, Nick; you're my hero.* She couldn't stop staring at him, at the corners of his eyes, the shape of his shoulders, the way his fingers were nimble and still spinning the glass shaker. "How did you manage that?"

"I went to probably a hundred meetings," he said. "Boards and councils and advisory groups. I ate a hundred stale doughnuts, drank gallons of the most vile coffee on the planet. We needed money for repairs that the county didn't have, so we had car washes and book sales and a very memorable bachelor auction with a bunch of our local baseball players."

"I honestly thought people only did bachelor auctions on television."

"On television and in the world of my grandmother."

"Well, it sounds exciting. Who went for the most?"

"Shortstop. Nice guy. Raised a hundred bucks. We would have needed like five thousand of him to save the place, but he did his part." He put the salt shaker down. "It took about three years to get through it."

"And it's safe now?"

"If there's one thing I've learned," he said, "it's that you're only safe till the next city council vote."

"Is that your parents' advice?"

"I think it was the theme of my fifth birthday party." He took a deep breath. "So, anyway. Right then, I couldn't leave. And because it was the job she'd always wanted, she couldn't stay."

"I guess being married long-distance is not ideal."

"Honestly," he said, "maybe we'd have tried it for as long as we could if everything had been perfect otherwise. But it wasn't. So we didn't."

"I'm sorry that happened," she said.

He leaned toward her a little. "And?"

"And what?"

"And, why did you really not get married? And don't say it was a waffle iron."

Laurie had fallen for him so fast when she was sixteen. It was one of those things—a guy you've known since you were little suddenly shows up one day in the right pair of jeans and the right shirt and he smiles and you break out in a sweat. That was how she had described it to June: *Junie, he walked into that party and I felt like I had the absolute and utter flu.* June didn't get it; she was only interested in new boys. To her, Nick was still just one of the kids they grew up with who fished off the dock and rode his bike across the narrow bridge to Kettle Bay Island and played soccer on the town fields.

"It was a lot of things," she said. "He just wasn't the right person." He kept looking at her expectantly, but she just shrugged.

Finally, he spoke. "Well," he said, "lots of fish in the sea, so to speak."

"Who knows?" she said. "I might not be meant for company. I haven't successfully had a real date since I broke up with him. Now it's this *thing* that's hanging over me. It's such a pain in the ass to even throw yourself into it, you know? Well, you *do* know. It's like you and the dentist. You get to a point where other things seem more pressing and suddenly it's been a million years since you had a first date that didn't turn out to be a horror story and you're very, very out of practice."

"I'll take you out," he said, shrugging.

She felt those words everywhere, and also that shrug, with its resolute casualness. "That would not be a first date," she said.

"Practically. I mean, you don't know. I'm reliably told that I'm hot now, so who knows how many other things have changed? I could be a completely different guy. And you're leaving anyway, so if you don't like me, you can just slink back to the other coast like it never happened."

She was already nervous that it was not going to be possible to make it like it never happened, and not because she didn't like him. "I guess we could do that," she said.

"Good. There's a new place I haven't been to, out toward Rockland, that supposedly has great steaks. It used to be a German place and a Thai place. I think when you lived here it was Italian. Marino's, Marini's, red wine and white . . . tablecloths." His voice faltered a little. "We don't have to if you don't want to."

He had bought her a necklace for her eighteenth birthday with a panda charm that dangled from it. She was pretty sure that back in her jewelry box at home, she still had it. He'd known she wanted to study biology and work in a zoo. It hadn't quite gone that way. "No, let's go. Let's go this weekend. Let's go Saturday."

He smiled—was that relief? "Great, good."

Just then, June appeared in the kitchen doorway and cleared her throat. "Hello, mischievous teenagers."

Laurie turned toward her. "Did you get Charlie all squared away?"

"Oh, yes," she said. "He just missed me."

"Any particular reason?" Laurie asked.

June smiled. "Because I'm not there."

aurie's friends in Seattle had been worried about her going all the way out to Maine and taking on Dot's whole house by herself. A couple of them had offered to come with her for at least part of the time, including Erin, who was only a couple of months away from her own wedding. "I don't even care, Laur," she had said. "I can talk to caterers remotely. If a box falls on you and you don't come back and I can't see you in the first good bridesmaid dress ever in history, I'm going to be *irate*." Erin and Laurie both wore an 18 and traded clothes now and then, and this wedding was honestly the first time a bride had ever offered Laurie a dress that she thought suited her.

But on the phone on Friday afternoon, it was becoming clear that this was not one of Erin's happy-bride days. "You had it right," she declared on the phone as Laurie paced around the kitchen making lunch. "People should not get married."

"Okay, please imagine me giving you the biggest eye roll you've ever seen," Laurie said. "I'm not against other people getting married. I'm just against myself getting married. Do not tell Justin I told you not to get married. Do not tell your mother I told you not to get married. I absolutely think you should get married. Don't cancel your wedding because you hate the caterer."

"I don't even hate the caterer!" Erin said. "I just don't understand the caterer. Why do they keep asking me questions? I don't want to think about napkins. I would pay extra not to think about napkins. I don't want this much control."

"You understand you may be an unusual bride in that way," Laurie said.

"I'm going to give the caterer a pair of dice and tell them to roll a number every time they consider calling me about something."

"I can't recommend that," Laurie said. "That's how you end up with shrimp." Erin hated shrimp.

Erin offered a frustrated groan. "Talk to me about something else. How are you? How's the house?"

"It's fine." Laurie ran through the events of the last few days, ending, of course, with "So now I have a date."

"Oh my God, your old boyfriend," Erin said. "That is a nostalgia tour if there ever was one. I can't think of anyone I have ever broken up with who I would want to go on a date with now, especially someone I dated in high school."

"College, too," Laurie said. "We were one of those high-school couples who were definitely, totally going to stay together in college even though they're going to opposite coasts. You know: 'we're not like everybody else,' 'we're going to stay together,' 'we're really in love,' all that jazz."

"How long did you make it?"

"Two years. We were about to start junior year, and he was talking about going to grad school after we graduated. And I realized that he wanted to come back and live here and have a job here, and I was not thinking about that at all, you know? I had a lot of things I wanted, and going back where I started wasn't on the list, even if it had been the best place in the world. I just wanted something new, something bigger and different. I was thinking about whether I wanted to live in the mountains or in New York, and he was thinking about which of three streets he wanted to live on that were all within five miles of where we went to elementary school. So all we were going to do was put several more years into this in-between situation where we rarely saw each other, and then we were going to break up anyway. So I pulled the plug."

"I hope you did it in person."

"Of course I did. I tried to do it fast, tried to do it nicely. Cried the whole time, but whatever."

"Oh, no," Erin said. "You're going to break his heart again."

"We're going out as friends," Laurie said.

Erin's "Ha!" was not exactly amused, not exactly scornful; it was kind of sympathetic. "Oh, 'as friends.' He was your first love!"

"Yeah, but now I'm old and he's divorced and we've both had sex with other people, and it's really not the same." She waited, but Erin was quiet. "It's just dinner."

When she was finished talking to Erin, Laurie loaded a box of board games into her car. She'd promised them to June for the kids and offered to drop them off, since any excuse to get out of the house was a good excuse.

June was taking classes online for her master's degree in history, and Charlie worked for the county. They had a house with a yard big enough for the kids to have a whole setup with swings and ropes and ladders, for June to have a garden, and for Charlie to keep a few hens. When Laurie got there, they'd had dinner already and the whole family was out back: June doing some weeding while Tommy crouched nearby, Bethie climbing up the ladder and sliding down the slide over and over, and Charlie cleaning out his coop.

"Hello, Devons," Laurie called out as she let herself in through the gate. "I am here with some very dusty games."

Tommy looked up briefly, then went back to whatever he was examining in the dirt. But Bethie hopped off the ladder and ran over to examine the box. "How do you play them?" she asked as she peeked into it.

June wiped her hands on a green towel and walked over. "I think what Bethie means is 'thank you,'" she said, and she put her hand on her daughter's shoulder.

"Thank you," Bethie said, appropriately chagrined.

"You're very welcome," Laurie said. "Honestly, I only know how to play some of them. And I only like some of them. My personal opinion? Don't play Careers," she said.

"How come?" Bethie asked.

"Because thinking about whether you'll earn enough money as an astronaut is not much of a game." Laurie put the box down on the table on the small flagstone patio. Also on the table was a rectangle of red Legos that outlined an area maybe the size of a shoebox, with walls about three inches high. "What's this?" she asked.

Bethie immediately turned her attention to the question. "I'm making a barn," she said, trailing her finger over the shape. "For horses."

"It looks great," Laurie said.

"It was going to be a school," she said. "But I changed to a barn."

"Well, it's good to be flexible." She turned to look out at the yard. "Garden looks wonderful too, Junie."

"Thank you, thank you," she said as Bethie went back to taking the games out of the box and examining them one by one. "I'm determined to get good tomatoes this year if it kills me. How's the progress at the house?"

"It's good. I'm very tired."

"I'm sorry I can't help this weekend. We've just got kid stuff out the wazoo. Softball, birthday parties—my kids are too popular, I think."

"That's okay," Laurie said. "I have some plans, actually."

June raised her eyebrows. "What's going on?"

"Nick and I are going to have dinner tomorrow."

Laurie was ready for June to be scandalized, or intrigued, or excited, but she wasn't prepared for the way June sort of tilted her head, almost sympathetically. "Oh, Laur," she said.

"What's wrong?"

"You don't think it's going to be messy? Starting this up again when you're leaving?"

"I'm not starting anything up. We're having dinner."

June laughed. "Who do you think I am? I'm not new here. I was there the other night. This is not dinner. This is dinner and maybe a sleepover," June said, lowering her voice to a whisper for the last three words, as her daughter shook a pair of dice that had come out of some box or another.

"You wanted me to date the Grim Reaper, and I can't have dinner with Nick?"

"Oh, come on," June said. "I said low stakes. I said *fling*. Nick is not a fling."

Laurie blinked. "It's just dinner," she repeated.

"And he knows that?"

"Yeah. I mean, I'm sure he does."

June nodded and reached up one hand and put it on Laurie's shoulder, then dropped it back to her side. "Oh boy," she said. "Well, have fun."

Chapter Eight

On Saturday afternoon, Laurie was just back from a trip to the grocery store for Diet Coke and frozen pizzas when someone knocked on Dot's door. When she peered through the small square window, she saw the Grim Reaper himself. She swung open the door. "Hi there."

"I hope you don't mind that I stopped by. I had a meeting down the street"—he pointed vaguely eastward before stuffing his hands back into his pockets—"and I wanted to catch up with you for a second if I could. I have good news, actually."

"In that case, you should definitely come in." She stepped aside. Today, it was a faded Ruth Bader Ginsburg T-shirt. He sure did know how to play the hits. "I don't get enough good news."

He sat on the edge of one of the wing chairs and pulled a folded envelope out of his back pocket. He handed it to Laurie, and when she straightened and opened it, she found three hundred-dollar bills and a record that showed he'd sold the quilt and the jewelry. "I didn't have any trouble selling your stuff," he said. "Or Dot's stuff, I should say. I hope it greases the wheels a little. I wanted to ask if there was anything else I could do to help."

He was very tall. Even while he was sitting, it showed in the way his legs folded up, sort of grasshoppery and angular. "I think I'm going to be okay. I'm gradually working my way through the closets and the trunks and the boxes. It takes forever. Or it takes me forever, at least. I'm looking at every book, because she had a way of using funny little things as bookmarks, you know? I found a birthday card from my great-grandmother that Dot was using to hold her place in *The Warmth of Other Suns*. Sometimes there's a method to her madness, like her ticket to *Company* that's in her Sondheim book. But sometimes, it's just, you know. She was reading and she stopped."

He smiled. "Do you have enough help? Make sure you have enough help."

"My friends are helping," she said. "We did a marathon session sorting her Polaroids the other night. I don't suppose you sell old instant cameras."

"Put them aside. I can take a look later." He glanced over at the mantel, to the duck's temporary perch. "Any news about that guy?"

"Maybe," she said. "I went by a store up in Wybeck, and the guy there told me it could have been made by somebody named Carl Kittery, who I guess was a famous duck guy? But it doesn't have quite the right marking, so it's apparently very hard to tell. I'm supposed to take it to this place in Hartford, Wesson & Truitt, so that somebody can tell me what's going on with it."

Matt leaned forward. "You're kidding. I know that place. I'm taking a tennis racket down there that some lady thinks might have been used by Bobby Riggs."

"The time he got his ass kicked?"

"No," he said. "Not the time he got his ass kicked. A different time. Anyway, they're basically sports generalists. I could take it for you." He pointed at a legal pad on the coffee table. "I'll write you a receipt, I'll take it when I go, and they'll do an initial consult and tell you whether they'd advise spending the money on a full appraisal. I'm going Tuesday and it'll probably only take them a couple hours, so I can bring it back to you this week. Plus, because I do work with them a lot, I can get you a discount on the consultation. People in this business will really take you to the cleaners if you're not careful."

Laurie went to the mantel and took the duck down, running her hand over its smooth, brown back. She knew the feel of it by now, the crest that came to a rounded nub behind its neck, and the curve of the chest. She handed it to the Grim Reaper. "This is nice of you," she said. "I can definitely use the help." She gave him the legal pad and a blue ballpoint pen.

He smiled down at the paper as he wrote out the receipt that indicated he was taking a duck decoy for the purposes of an appraisal. "Well, I like selling old stuff, but what I really like is when somebody who's going through a hard thing can go through a little bit less of a hard thing." He dated and signed the paper and handed it to her. "We're going to solve this mystery."

When he was gone, she looked at her phone. It was 4:30, and Nick had said he'd swing by to get her at 6:30. Laurie could have spent the next two hours trying to figure out how she should try to look, but instead, she decided to watch three consecutive episodes of *Veep* on her phone, hop into the shower, and then slip on a close-fitting pair of black pants and a slouchy gray top with a deep V-neck and black booties. A little rosy lipstick, a little tinted moisturizer to even out the splotchy places on her cheeks that she blamed on her imperfect history with sunscreen, a little mascara, and she was ready to go. She was about to answer the knock at the door when she reached out and grabbed a pendant from Dot's dresser—an enamel charm of a round blue Earth.

When she opened the door, Nick was there, holding three small yellow flowers. "I thought about roses," he said. "But that didn't seem like you. And I thought about lilies or something, but that didn't seem like me. Fortunately, my neighbor saw me leaving the house, and she wanted to know where I was going. She gave these to me, right from her own garden." He handed them to Laurie. "Lanceleaf . . . something. Corinthian? Lanceleaf Corinthian? That sounds wrong."

Laurie smiled. "Thank you. That's very sweet of your neighbor." She turned and grabbed a tall glass off the counter. As she ran water in it for the flowers, she turned back to him. "You look great."

"Thank you. So do you. It's nice picking you up somewhere other than your parents' house."

"Yeah, now you can pick me up at my *aunt's* house." She dried her hands and, just as she started to follow him out, she grabbed one of the flowers and slid the stem into the top of her bag so the yellow petals peeked out. "I have to stay fancy," she said.

The drive to the restaurant in the soft gold light took them through the middle of Calcasset, past the high school and the ball-park and the Compass Café, where two of Laurie's brothers had worked in the kitchen when they were young. He pointed to the new Episcopal church and the new Best Buy, and three times, he gestured to a place where something had once been and wasn't anymore. The saddest was the salon where Laurie had gone to get her hair done for the prom. They remembered together how she'd had it pinned up in back and how it had fallen down over the course of the evening because she danced too hard—with him, but with June, too.

The restaurant was called Tyler—not Tyler's, and not The Tyler, and not Tyler's Something-or-Other, but Tyler. As if it were less a restaurant than a toddler eager to get off the wait list at an exclusive preschool. Out front, a water feature burbled beside a sign that was made to look as if it had been hastily stenciled onto a wooden pallet but had probably cost more than the water feature plus all the water it would ever need.

Inside, a hostess called Nick "sir" (okay) and Laurie "madam" (weird) while bringing them to a table by the window that looked out at a funny little garden that looked like the inspiration was part Zen, part mini golf. They both asked for fizzy water, and the hostess described the steaks as the result of cow lives that sounded nothing short of idyllic, then she left them to go over the aggressively laid-back paper menus. "I bet the food is really good here," she told Nick. "And I bet they are sweating about making this place work."

He widened his eyes and nodded. "I appreciate the effort, which is effortful." Someone brought the fizzy water, and someone else took their orders—steaks for both, because why not?—and brought a little bowl of bread and a steel cup of butter. The music was gentle coffeehouse anesthetic, not quite fancy but also not cool. "So," Nick said as he tore a piece off a miniature loaf of French bread, "what's the duck news? You were going to send it to some-place in Hartford, right?"

"I was," she said. She explained how Matt had materialized and taken the task off her hands, exactly the way she needed. "This way, I'll know it's in good hands, it's taken down there in person and everything."

"What do you think your odds are?" he asked.

"That it's real? That it's worth money? No idea. I'm not sure I care that much about that. I mean, obviously, it would be great, but that would go to my folks and Dot's other family, just like it will when they sell her house. It's not like I'd pocket it."

"So you're still planning to sell the house?" He wasn't looking at her. He was busily buttering some bread.

"Of course," she said. "What else would I do?"

He shrugged. "Keep it?"

"I already have a house."

"I know."

She raised her eyebrows. "Nick, you know I'm not moving here, right?"

He nodded. "Sure. Yes. Of course."

"I'm not moving into Dot's house."

Now he looked up. "If you say so. You just look pretty comfortable kicking around that kitchen, that's all."

"I'm also pretty comfortable kicking around the kitchen I already have."

"Okay. So you're not in it for the money, you just want to solve the duck."

She smiled. "Yeah. I know it's weird. It's probably nothing. It's just the way she had it in there, under the blankets, and then that letter, and now the picture that we found. I just want to know. I'm just curious. I know you probably think it's strange."

Nick had always kept his hair fairly short, because when he let it grow longer, its close waves would grow into total chaos. But there was this one curl he had—she used to call it his Superman wave—and it would drop down over his left eye. And when Laurie used to gaze at him a lot, which was most of high school even before they started dating, it was one of the things she gazed at. She could never decide whether it was the result of calculation or good luck, whether he spent ten minutes making sure it would fall the right way, as she would have, or whether he just ran his hands over his head every morning and was blessed, as she figured boys mostly were. She was thinking about this at the moment when he said, "I don't think it's strange. I think it's great."

She blushed. *Oh boy. New subject.* "So now that you've single-handedly saved your place of work, what's next?"

He immediately took out his phone. He scrolled through some screens and then showed her a picture of a blue van with colorful type on the side. "This is the Rockland Bookmobile," he said. "I want one just like it."

"It looks expensive."

"It is," he said, "but we need it. We also need the county to get a better mobile app, and we're still in the middle of all these repairs. We're trying to figure out how to do it without closing down, since every time you close, somebody starts arguing over whether you should ever open again." He put his phone away and sighed. "I basically never stop thinking about that building. I see construction paperwork and grant proposals when I close my eyes."

"Do you like that?" she asked.

"I think it and I are one now," he said with a smile. "I think I've fused so completely with that place that I don't think about liking it or not, you know? I just do it." He shrugged. "How about you? Do you like your work?"

"I do," she said. "It's not a particularly stable way to live since I've been freelance. You know I had a staff job when I was first in Seattle?"

"I heard, yeah."

"Had that until five or six years ago. Then that all collapsed. I'm lucky to work as much as I do now. I get to schedule myself, which you can tell from the fact that I hopped on a plane out here to do all this." She waved her hands around.

"Well, it sounds like you're doing amazing," he said. "Even if you did end your engagement over a waffle iron."

"Not *over* the waffle iron. Maybe after being *enlightened* by the waffle iron. Like you said, he just thought things were going to turn out one way, and I thought they were going to turn out another way. And I couldn't get used to living with him." She ran her finger around the edge of her plate.

"Why's that?"

"I really like living by myself, honestly," she repeated. "I can have breakfast for dinner, I can have dinner for breakfast, I can take a bath at two-fifteen in the afternoon on a Wednesday. And I sleep so well there. I don't talk about it very much, but I've slept like garbage for most of my life."

"Really."

"Really. The whole thing, waking up with my clothes twisted and my sheets in knots. I had terrible dreams. I would wake up in the morning and feel like I hadn't slept at all. I'd pass out in my breakfast or while I was trying to write. But then I moved into the house, and I bought this new queen bed after I had bounced on about a hundred mattresses. And I had these sheets, these linen sheets. They are so cool in the summer and cozy in the winter. It is the first bed where, when I sleep in it, I am just out. I am *out,* for hours and hours. When I wake up, I feel like I have a full battery."

"And when you lived with him, you didn't?"

"It was like having a hot water bottle in bed with me. It threw off everything. I was afraid to move because I didn't want to wake him. I was afraid to sneeze because I didn't want to wake him. I couldn't splay my arm out, because it would land on his chest. I woke up at two in the morning, day after day after day, and I'd lie there listening to this ticking clock he brought over that was like listening to the audible expiration of my youth."

"Did this happen with other boyfriends you had before him, or just him?"

"My boyfriend before Chris, we didn't live together. Mostly, I went to his place instead of him coming over to mine. I liked it better that way. And it didn't seem weird that I didn't sleep well, since I wasn't at home."

"Should I ask what happened to that guy?"

Laurie took a sip of her drink. "Well," she said, "Angus was great, honestly. I was very happy with him. We had all kinds of things in common, he was funny, he was comfortable, he was really smart."

"Sounds good so far."

"Yeah." It had, in fact, been good so far—but only so far. "Unfortunately, he wanted kids, and I didn't. When we met, he thought he *probably* wanted them and I thought I *probably* didn't."

"Any particular reason?"

"I like kids. I love my brothers' kids, I love June's kids. I just wanted other things more," she said. "I never had that thing, the thing where people say they always wanted to be a parent, always dreamed about kids. I just never felt it. And we were together for a couple of years, you know, right at that age where if you want kids, you're not really in a *hurry*, but you're starting to think about when you *will* be in a hurry, you know what I mean?"

"I do."

"We went to his cousin's wedding, and I saw him with this adorable little girl who was there, maybe three or four? He was just great with her, totally at home, and he was *so* happy. He was just over the moon in love with this kid, you could tell." She sighed. "We came home, we talked, and we broke up. That was a few years ago, and he has a wife and a daughter now."

"Sounds like it ended the only way it could."

"It did," she said. "The only thing I should have done was figure out sooner that it wasn't going to resolve itself. Anyway, a year later, I met Chris. And I liked him, and he did not want kids, and he did not mind that I was, as Angus used to say, 'sturdy.' And by then I was thirty-eight, and he was age-appropriate, and he was looking for someone who was age-appropriate. And I just thought . . . he was a stroke of luck."

Nick nodded. "However," he offered.

She smiled. "However. When we moved in together, I hated it. It ruined things I liked about him. It made me resent him. And I just thought . . . this is not sustainable. And for whatever reason, that crystallized when he wanted to put a big dumb waffle maker in my modest kitchen cabinets, which I could not even get myself to call *our* kitchen cabinets."

Nick thought about this, took a bite of bread, finished it, drank a slug of wine. "Maybe you needed a bigger bed."

She laughed. "I love my bed. And we went on vacation once and slept in a king, and guess when my dumb ass ended up staring at a generic clock radio in the middle of the night?"

"Two in the morning?"

"You know it." She sighed. "It wasn't the bed. It just wasn't right. Some part of me was screaming, 'don't do it, don't do it, don't bind your life to this guy just because he's fine and he didn't rule you out.' And that's when I started to think, you know . . . if it's not this guy, maybe it's not anybody. Maybe I'm not a June, maybe I'm a Dot. Maybe I'm supposed to die with boxes of love letters and pictures, and one of my brothers' grandkids will find something of mine and figure out something about me, something special that nobody knew. Maybe even something nobody asked me about."

"I don't think you're a June or a Dot," he said. "I think you're just yourself. And that should satisfy anybody, including you."

Laurie felt a melt of warmth that started somewhere in the core of her and prickled out to her arms and her legs, and she knew she was gazing at him again, but she was *not* moving into Dot's house, she really *was* going back to Seattle. "I missed you, Cooper," she finally said.

He took a drink of his water, but when he put it down, he didn't look quite as date-drunk as she felt. "You know what? I made a mistake."

She blinked. "What do you mean? What mistake?"

He picked up his napkin and set it on the table. Out of his wallet came enough money to cover his dinner and hers and the tip. He set it next to his bread plate. "You trust me, Sass? Can I change the plan?"

"Of course."

"Okay. We have to go. I brought you on the wrong date."

Laurie picked up her bag even as she watched him scribble a note on his napkin. "What is wrong, Nick? This is a perfectly good date."

"What I brought you on," he said as he took her elbow, "is a first date for people who don't know each other. I completely missed the opportunity to take you on the correct date for you, as a duck enthusiast and person who is as curious about weird things as I am."

"Which is what?"

"I really can't believe you haven't figured it out. Come on. No lagging."

Just before she walked away from the table, she turned back and looked at the napkin. *Date emergency,* he had written. *Apologies.*

Chapter Nine

The library closed at 7:00 on Saturdays, so by the time they got there, it was locked up and the lights were out. Nick pulled his ID out of his wallet and held it up to the pad by the front door, which beeped and welcomed him with a little green light. He opened the door wide. "Welcome."

It looked very different when it was closed. It sounded different; there was a different kind of quiet. Nick flipped a switch that turned on just the lights over the main desk. "Step into my office," he told her, and he swung a section of the counter up and out of the way so they could pass through.

"I've never been behind the desk before," she said. "Is this where I get to break in and obliterate all my fines? You're right, this is a very exciting date, even if it seems kind of corrupt."

Nick pulled two chairs over in front of a monitor with a huge screen. "Have a seat, patron," he said.

"Is that a real library word?"

"You bet your ass."

"You can't just say 'customer'? Or 'user'?"

"As my father likes to say, we are not FedEx or Facebook." He dropped into the seat next to her and signed in to the terminal. "And don't try to look at my password. I don't want you recklessly overusing Interlibrary Loan."

"Well, sheesh, Coop, can't I have any fun at all?"

"Okay," he said. "Tell me again the name of the duck-maker. Carl something?"

She smiled at him without turning her head. "Carl Kittery. I did google him. I didn't find out very much."

He turned the monitor slightly so she couldn't see it. "Okay. Pop quiz. Tell me what you learned."

"Oh, *brother*. Okay. He was born in, I think, 1915?"

"Wikipedia agrees."

"You're a librarian, and you use Wikipedia? What am I paying you for?"

"You're not paying me anything, because you're not a taxpaying resident of Whipwell County. Besides, Wikipedia is a perfectly good starting point as long as you look at the citations. Stop stalling."

"Grew up in New York somewhere." She impressed him with her recollection that Kittery got into duck hunting as a kid, near the Niagara River, and that he started carving ducks with his father, but didn't start to sell his work much until about 1940. "Now help me look him up, Cooper, don't be a tease."

He turned the monitor back around. "All right. Let's look at some things. This is one of my favorite databases for magazines and stuff." As he logged himself in and started typing, Laurie saw a handful of saved searches drop down, and one of them said, "Laurie Sassalyn conservation." She reached over and put her hand on his arm.

"Excuse me, what is that? Have you been googling me?"

He stopped and looked at her. "I read your stuff. I read about the alligators, and I read about the bees, and I even read that one about the Amazonian spider colony, although I have to say, I really regretted it."

Without breaking eye contact, she scooted her chair a little bit closer. "Okay. Continue."

"All right." He could type much faster than she could, even though she spent so much of her life transcribing interviews. She watched his hands, how they had the same sun splotches as her cheeks, and it was the first time she could honestly say she'd been turned on by typing. "Now, don't distract me while I'm working my magic. Not that I wouldn't love to sit here while you slither over to me to breathe hotly on my neck."

"I don't slither," she said. "I scooch."

"Whatever. Just remember, librarians can sense fear." He pointed at the screen. "They wrote about him in *Niagara Nature Monthly* in 1968."

"Oh God."

"What?"

She collapsed onto the desk with her forehead on her wrists. "I'm just realizing they can barely keep *Rolling Stone* in print and there used to be a magazine called *Niagara Nature Monthly*. Can you imagine how much work I would have gotten for *Niagara Nature Monthly*? I would have been out there stomping around in the river . . . now. That might not have meant spiders, but I bet I would have ended up partying with like thousands of crazy-ass fish." She sat up. "Okay. I'm recovered."

"So let's keep reading before you get too depressed." Almost right away, he whistled. "Wow, this auction site? It says they sold one of this guy's ducks for 78,000 dollars last year."

"I know. The Wybeck guy told me." Just then, Laurie's phone buzzed, and when she picked it up, she saw that it was June texting.

How's the date?

She smiled and shook her head. *You wouldn't believe it. I'll call you tomorrow.* June texted back the eyes emoji, for obvious reasons.

When Laurie looked up, Nick had found *Niagara Nature Monthly* and a scan of the piece. As he scrolled, he came to a photo, and Laurie put her hand on his arm. "Look at this. There's a picture," she said. Dated 1964, the photo showed Kittery in a woodworking studio, surrounded by partially finished decoys, bending over a block that was just beginning to take on the character of a bird. His face was in profile, tense with concentration, a man who, at nearly fifty, wore his gray hair down to where it gently curled against his collar. "It says here that his work was just starting to be in demand at this point. And still by real hunters, mostly. There's only one line in here about people collecting decoys as art. He says himself he thinks it's silly."

Nick nodded. "Must have seemed like it to him."

The photo, scanned in black-and-white from the magazine archive, was ghostly and overexposed, but as Laurie stared at it, something about it seemed familiar. She'd seen this man, maybe. And maybe even this place where he was, with the window behind him and the wood-slat walls. "Nick, do you think this could be the room in that Polaroid? With the half a duck?" She nodded toward the screen.

Nick cocked his head to one side, then the other. "It could be. It's not the best photo, obviously. But I agree, given everything else, it does make you wonder."

She scooched again, so close she could almost feel the heat from his cheek. "The caption says it was taken in his studio in Bar Harbor. I'm telling you, I think this is the room in that picture. Maybe the guy with his back to the camera was this guy. Maybe they knew each other." She leaned back in the seat. "You really did find the right date."

He smiled out of the side of his mouth. "Well, good."

He was still so close. He smelled like shampoo, maybe. Or detergent. When he was sixteen, he'd worn some kind of spicy cologne that she could sometimes detect on the shoulder of her shirt when she got home. More than once, she'd curled up on her side and twisted around in bed until she could breathe it in while she fell asleep. He left a hoodie in her car after the junior year bonfire, and she wore it to breakfast every morning for two weeks, telling her parents she'd stolen it from Nick, but not telling them how the best part of some of those mornings was the moment when she pulled it over her head.

"Okay, I'm going to print off some auction updates for your file, because I don't think they have that much heft to them." They sat at the monitor in the pool of light, taking notes from little pieces here and there, filling in gaps about Kittery—his wife, his kids and grandkids, the growth in the value of his work throughout the '80s and '90s.

"What else have we got?" Laurie asked.

"Well, there are a couple of what look like little pieces from the Niagara County Historical Society. Which, by the way, also had a magazine, in case you want to get depressed again because you can't write about the long history of people going over the falls in barrels."

"Did people actually do that, do you think?"

"Let's see," he said. She wanted to ask him questions all night. Push on his curiosity, exploit his absolute allergy to saying *Who cares?* Chris had been big on that reaction when she was diving down deep rabbit holes. "Yes, it looks like they did. Annie Edson Taylor in 1901. She was sixty-three. She hoped to make money. Apparently, she did not make the big bucks, although she did survive."

"Wait, she went over the falls in a barrel when she was sixty-three? Because she wanted to make money?"

"A one-woman argument for Social Security," he said.

"Apparently, the last person who went over and survived did it in 2019. Wait, what were we talking about again?"

"The Niagara County Historical Society, Carl Kittery, my duck."

"Right." He leaned over toward her until she could feel him brushing against her hair. "I have one more trick that is harder to use than it should be in a lot of cases, and that's public records." He went back to typing.

"Oh hey, look," Laurie said, tapping her finger on a listing that said *Property record, Hancock County*. "Isn't that where Bar Harbor is?"

"It is," he said. "Hey, get your smudgy finger off my screen."

She removed her hand but scooted over even more, until their shoulders were fully touching. "I want to look at that one." When he pulled it up, she sucked in her breath. Carl Kittery, born June 1915, had owned a house in Hancock County from 1960 until 1982. "So he could have been selling down here in Calcasset," she said. "Right? I mean, he could have been at a fair or a boutique or something. It's, what, two hours away?"

Nick nodded slowly. "It's interesting, that's for sure. Is all this enough for you to start with if I print it up and you take it with you?"

"Absolutely," she said. "And I couldn't have asked for a better date."

"Well," he said, "it's not over yet. You haven't seen the view at night from the reading room. It used to be kind of musty and full of books nobody checked out, but now it's a very nice place to relax."

"I saw it the first time I came in, when I was walking all around looking for you."

He turned to look at her. "You were?"

She nodded. "I was. But you weren't here."

"Mm, my loss. Let's go up." He took the papers from the printer and led the way up the wide carpeted steps, and at the top, he flipped on a single light way over in the corner. The reading room had six round wooden tables with chairs arranged around them, and newspaper racks lined up against one wall. All four sides had huge, nearly floor-to-ceiling windows, with rolling shades that mostly served to keep the room from getting too hot in the summer.

"This is so great," she said. "Just gorgeous."

"Spiffing it up was my dad's project," he said. "It was his pride and joy."

When Laurie was a kid, she could remember her own father coming all the way here just to read the paper while the sun streamed in, and while she understood later that there were times when it wasn't easy to be at their house, it never occurred to her to wonder why someone would want to sit and read the paper in the library. On the contrary, why wouldn't everyone want to?

They sat at one of the tables, and Laurie ran her hand over the smooth top. "Very nice, very classy." She touched a metal plate near the edge of the table that was engraved with block letters: POLLY SHAHEEN. "People sponsored tables?"

"My dad is a creative fundraiser," he said. Nick handed over what he'd printed downstairs and a yellow highlighter. "In case anything looks interesting," he said.

"It matches my flowers," she said. And now, maybe, just a little bit, *he* was blushing?

As this new quiet, this promising and loaded quiet, fell on them, she looked over, out the east windows. From up here, the upper floor of the highest corner in Calcasset, you could see all the way to the water a few blocks away. Boats that would be anchored until very early in the morning bobbed in the harbor and bells rang, and the little orange blots were knots of buoys tied up so they wouldn't get away. "You have a nice view here."

The swell in her chest looking out that window was matched by how hopeless it felt to try to talk about it. Talking about this view was like talking about the weather—just a nod to a slice of reality that instantly flattened it. There wasn't much for him to say, so she wasn't surprised to feel his hand pick up hers and just hold it, and when she looked over, he was looking back. Their chairs pushed together, they both slumped down, sat back, let their necks rest on the backs of the chairs. "You take good care of this place," Laurie said.

"It's come back from the dead a lot, you know?"

"You must be really proud of it. Everybody loves you."

"It's not me," he said. "It's the library. This is one of the few places in this entire town people are allowed to just come and be. Even when they don't need anything, they turn up and rattle around. I have a lady who comes once a month and reads upstairs while her house gets cleaned. I have a guy who I was pretty sure was living in his car who used to come in when it was cold, and to tell you the truth, I don't know where he went this last winter. But we haven't closed yet. It's my job for the place not to go under, and we haven't."

She looked over at him. "You're a damn good person, Cooper."

Their heads were turned toward each other, just looking, and then she was the one—at least she was pretty sure she was the one—who started it, who sat up and leaned over to kiss him, putting her palm against his cheek. His hand was on the back of her neck and she felt it everywhere, just everywhere. And more than twenty years after the last time it had happened, it felt exactly like kissing him when he was sixteen and also nothing like it at all. It was familiar *and* totally foreign, like it felt when she hadn't driven stick for seventeen years and then borrowed June's old Civic. She still had the moves, even if she was very much out of practice.

Nick kissed, as he always had, with a certain amount of what she could only call conviction. It was notable particularly after she'd spent more than a year with Chris, who kissed with something more like resignation. Chris kissed only to get to sex more quickly, and while it wasn't *bad* kissing, and it wasn't *bad* sex by any means, kissing was not its own reason for them to wind their bodies around each other on a couch or in bed, first thing in the morning or at the end of a movie. Nick had kissed thoroughly, even as a guy who was as young and dumb as she had been back then, because he liked to. He apparently still liked to.

He didn't have that jacket anymore, of course, that jacket with the shearling collar. So she took two fistfuls of his shirt and pulled him tighter, hearing herself gasp for breath, hearing one of them—both of them?—make little sounds from their throats. And then she stopped, pulled back, looked into his eyes. Literally panting, literally trying to get air, literally breathless. It popped into her head completely unbidden: *And I'm gonna be forty! . . . Someday!*

Finally, she let her hands trail down the front of his shirt.

He smiled and slid his hand up from her hip, over her waist, up to the side of her breast, and he said, "Want to go someplace and fool around?"

She dabbed the corner of her mouth with her thumb and smiled. "I'm a short-timer, Cooper."

He shrugged. "Want to fool around for a short time?"

Yes, I do please, yes, I very much do please, let's flop on top of the table please, I don't even mind if I fall off. But when she looked at him again, she felt herself falling through twenty years, hearing him ask her why they had to break up when they only had two more years to be apart and they'd already done two years. Why couldn't it work? What was the problem? *Oh, dammit, dammit.* She took his hand from her side, moved it. "Nick, I don't know. I really want to. I really, very much want to, you know that. But I . . . don't know."

"Did I say something wrong?"

She could not say *you are too good.* She could not say *this will only get worse.* So she just put her hand over his. "I'm really leaving. I'm not moving back."

He nodded. "Okay."

"I know I started . . . that. I did. And I'm not trying to be weird about it, I just don't want to start something pretending it's going to be anything other than what it can actually be. And as much as I'd like to just sink into this for a few more weeks, I think it's going to get really complicated."

He nodded and hooked his finger through hers. "Fair enough. Probably just as well. The Missing Laurie Sassalyn routine knocked the wind out of me when I was twenty. I don't know if I'd be able to do it again a month from now. I kind of thought maybe a little nostalgia thing, you know? But you're right, I'm not sure I know how to wade into this with only one foot, now that I'm here."

When Laurie had broken up with him between sophomore and junior year, she'd given back that hoodie, given back the paperbacks he'd left on the table by her bed. She'd told him the truth: She knew he was permanently in love with Calcasset, and she wasn't. He saw it as his future, and she saw it as the place she'd always love, but like you love an old movie. He would go back after he graduated from college; she would not. And, maybe in order to feel less guilty, she'd somehow told herself he'd take his basic Nick-ness, his tendency to make friends everywhere, and just keep going.

Knocked the wind out of me. She nodded. She took back her hand and rubbed his shoulder. "I'm sure I'm going to regret this in about ten minutes."

They gathered up the papers, and he locked up the library and drove her home to Dot's. He didn't walk her to the door. Probably better for both of them.

Chapter Ten

The next time Laurie saw the Grim Reaper was that Thursday, and this time, when he sat himself down in her living room and put the duck on the couch next to him, his expression looked significantly cloudier. "So I do have some news. I'm going to let you read it. Here's the report they gave me."

It was printed on Wesson & Truitt stationery, under their bright blue logo.

Wood duck decoy, approximately 2008. Produced in bulk in the style of Carl Kittery and distributed to museum and souvenir shops as part of a promotion commemorating the history of American folk art. Also sold at traveler locations including Logan Airport. Original sale price approximately $25.99. Current value similar. Many examples available through online auction sites and estate sales, selling for approximately $30.00. Further appraisal not necessary or recommended.

She just stared at it. "Oh," she said. "Oh, okay."

"I know this isn't the news you were hoping for."

She put down the paper on the couch next to her. "No, I mean, everybody said from the beginning it was a long shot." To her, it was still a beautiful wooden bird that had secrets under its wings, even with the knowledge it had been picked up at a museum store or a craft store or maybe just a dollar store. "I guess she didn't have it out because it was junk, you know? She did have really good taste."

Matt shook his head. "That's not the way to think about it. Junk, not junk, who knows, right? You see a painting and it's real or it's a forgery, but either way, it looks the same on your wall. You like the duck? Then you like the duck. Keep it, put it somewhere, tell people the story."

"It's funny," Laurie said. "It turns out Kittery had a house up in Bar Harbor. Maybe a studio, too. I think I just got a little carried away. Kind of cast a spell on myself. And I think if I kept it, I'd just keep feeling really dumb about it."

"Look, you don't need to feel dumb. It happens to me practically every day," he said. "I'll see a sketch or a letter or a vase or something, and I get totally obsessed with it. Totally preoccupied with finding out what it is and where it came from." He took a breath. "Listen. I still like your duck. I think it's a nice piece. I think somebody is going to want it for an office or a dining room or something. I'll tell you what: I'll still give you fifty bucks for it. Just like before."

"It's not worth anything," Laurie said.

"Doesn't have to be expensive to be worth something," he told her. He was wearing a Fiona Apple shirt that said THIS WORLD IS BULLSHIT. She liked him. But not *quite* as much as the first time he'd come over. He was attractive, but he wasn't reading-room-in-the-dark attractive.

"Fair enough," she said. She handed him the duck. He took the receipt he'd given her the other day off the coffee tables, and he added a note on the bottom that said she'd sold it to him for fifty dollars. He tucked it into his pocket and handed her the money. "Please don't feel bad about it," he said. "You're doing a great job, and your aunt would be proud of you. I talk to ninety-year-olds more often than most, and the thing they really want is to know somebody's going to care about what they left behind. You care. That means a lot." He gave her another copy of his business card. "Drop by the shop anytime, okay? And I'll talk to you soon."

Laurie tried to keep the pity party short, with minimal fuss: a little wine, a little Julie London, and one of Dot's feather boas wrapped around her neck while she stretched out on the sofa and tried not to think about any of it. No Nick, no duck. Just a lot more boxes, and a lot more books.

She was only one sip into the wine when she saw the paper from Wesson & Truitt out of the corner of her eye. It seemed very unfair that she had been taken in by the sheer coincidence of Kittery having a Bar Harbor studio. It seemed very unfair that Dot had not actually known him, that clearly the Polaroid was not of him, that the loveliest night she'd spent in probably two years had been a wild-goose chase (duck chase, perhaps) that had been a misadventure before it even began.

People raised in places like Calcasset developed a healthy lack of regard for tourist objects. They clicked their tongues at little lobster-trap Christmas ornaments, lobster cookie cutters, and dish towels printed with colorful buoys. These things were part of the economy, but it was undignified to have feelings about them. Or keep them. Or collect them. To confuse a mass-marketed gift-shop throwaway with a piece of art was something close to sacrilege to those who had seen their towns full of working boats become homes to Airbnbs and day spas and people who held clambakes ironically.

This was a profound failure. She couldn't not ask more questions. Just how cheaply made was this? How could it possibly have made it into the possession of a woman who lived on the coast for ninety years, through the ups and downs of halibut and cod and the hipster interest in wild blueberries? Laurie picked up her phone and looked up the number of Wesson & Truitt, and she dialed.

"Wesson & Truitt."

"Hi, I'm wondering if you can help me with some details from a consultation you recently were kind enough to do on a duck decoy from my aunt's house. Well, my great-aunt. It turns out it's not really valuable, but I was wondering whether whoever did the assessment might know anything that would give me a little bit more detail about how the piece got to my aunt. My great-aunt."

"Okay," said the cheerful woman on the phone. "Can you give me the document number from your copy of the consultation record?"

Laurie leaned forward and grabbed the paper off the coffee table. "Yes, hang on." She pushed the boa out of her face. "Sorry. It's 283491."

"Huh," the woman on the phone said. "Does it have a letter in the front? All our document numbers start with a letter. If it's a decoy, it would be an S for Sporting. Can you look up in the top left corner?"

"It just says 283491." What a pain in the patoot this duck had turned out to be.

There was a pause on the phone, and Laurie could hear the muffled sound of the woman talking to someone while holding her hand over the receiver. Then she was back. "I'm going to put you on the phone with our decoy expert, okay?"

"Okay, thank you."

The next voice was a man. "This is Jim Baines. Can I help you?"

"Yes." She twirled the boa in her hand. "I have a consultation report here, the document number is 283491. It was a replica, a Carl Kittery replica. You did it sometime this week, and I'm just wondering if you know anything else about it. It was my aunt's. My great-aunt."

He was quiet. "I'm a little bit at a loss. As Debra told you, that's not our document number, and I haven't evaluated anything from or related to Kittery in at least a few weeks."

Laurie felt something very, very unfortunate happening in the pit of her stomach. "Well, my—a guy I know brought it in for me. I'm looking at the report right now. It's on your letterhead, dated yesterday."

"It says Wesson and Truitt on the top? Blue lettering?"

Did he think she couldn't read? "Yes, of course."

"Ma'am, I have to tell you, I'm stumped. If you can, go back to your friend and double check that what he gave you is our document, and that he didn't maybe put together his own report referencing ours? Have him give you the original."

"I'm sure it's the original." She was not sure it was the original. She cleared her throat. "I'm going to check and get back to you." After she hung up, Laurie sat on the couch, staring at the report. Letterhead at the top looked right, the same logo that showed on their website. The phone number was different, though, from the one she'd just called. Not unusual—lots of places have more than one number. She dialed the number on the report, but the phone just rang and rang.

Something is wrong, but I don't know what. Something is wrong. What's wrong? Am I confused? She had that feeling that you get when you're searching the parking lot and you're briefly certain that your car has been stolen, until you turn around and it's there. Her car was going to be there in this case, she was sure of it. It was just, there was something confusing, what was it? She had been looking the report up and down for close to a minute when her eyes fell on the tiny, tiny footer type at the very bottom of the page. The address was listed as 1234 Bluebird Way. And under that, there was a space for a motto, a little spot where you'd expect to see "Est. 1905" or "Best plumbers for the money" or something.

On this piece of paper, at the very bottom, under the fake-sounding address, it said, "Lorem ipsum dolor sit amet."

Oh no. Oh no oh no oh no oh no.

Laurie normally loved going to Camden; it was touristy down by the water, but there were sprawling houses not far away that she had admired when she was little, dream houses with acres of space spread out around them. And a couple of blocks from the road, there was a small building with a sign outside that was divided in two: the left side said SEA SPRAY ANTIQUES, and the right side said SAVE THE BEST. There was only one door. Laurie parked her car and went up onto the stoop to peek inside. It was neat and quaint, with long shelves full of dishes and clocks and lamps and vases, full but not cramped. She stepped inside, and a bell rang.

She didn't see Matt, but a woman with short dark hair and a Captain America T-shirt was sitting behind a counter in the back. She called out a greeting at the sound of the bell, and Laurie acknowledged her with a smile and a weak wave. She walked up a row of clocks, touching their bases even though the sign said DO NOT TOUCH, watching the row progress from small bedside models to tall living-room fixtures that probably had to be wound by hand. At the end of the row, she saw that there was a desk in the corner opposite where Captain America was, with two chairs out in front of it and one behind it. There was no one there, just a computer, an old-school yellow rotary phone, and a display of business cards. She went over and took one, and it was identical to the one Matt had brought to her when he came to Dot's house. There were two phone numbers listed. One had the words "business hours" next to it, and one—the one he'd called her from a few times that he'd said was his cell—said "anytime."

Laurie hid behind a row of shelves of twee figurines. She took out her cellphone and dialed the "business hours" number. The phone rang over at Captain America's station, and Laurie hung up after one ring, before the woman could even pick it up. The yellow phone was silent. Laurie pulled the Wesson & Truitt invoice out of her purse and dialed the number printed at the top. The one that she already knew was not the number for Wesson & Truitt.

The yellow phone trilled.

It rang and it rang, and Captain America paid no attention to it. Laurie let it ring for almost a full minute before she hung up. Then she ambled over to Captain America. "Boy, somebody had a lot of time to spend waiting for you to answer."

"Yeah," Captain America said, rolling her eyes. "My boss doesn't answer that phone. It's for decoration and spam calls. The only guy in the world with a rotary burner phone, right?"

Laurie could barely breathe. Fake number. Dummy template language on the document he'd given her, which the people who supposedly printed it swore wasn't theirs.

She stepped behind a shelving unit and texted June. The Grim Reaper pinched my duck.

June texted back three question marks, and then, Is that sex?

NOT SEX. PINCHED = STOLE. HE STOLE MY DUCK. DOT'S WOODEN DUCK. HE IS A FUCKING CON ARTIST.

Chapter Eleven

Unsure what to do next, Laurie flopped down on a bench with a PLEASE DO NOT SIT sign taped to it and put her head in her hands. She didn't have the original agreement that had said he would take the duck to be appraised. They'd transformed it into his receipt when she sold him the duck for fifty dollars. All he'd had to do was lop off the top and produce the bottom, and it showed that she willingly handed the thing over—which, of course, she had.

She had the appraisal that was forged, that she could show was forged, but nobody had any way of knowing that he made it or gave it to her, that it was his scam rather than hers. Will talk later, have to think, she had texted to June, but what was there to think about?

She heard the phone ring over at Captain America's counter and started to walk that way. "Sea Spray, this is Daisy." A pause. "Hi, Matt." *Matt.* "Not busy, no. Couple people in and out. Sold that clown lamp." Beat, beat, beat. "For sure, you bet. Will do. Yes, I remember. Yes. No, I know. Okay, bye." Laurie came around the end of an aisle just in time for Daisy to mutter "and fuck you too, chucklehead," then look up at Laurie in horror. "Oh. God, sorry," she said.

Laurie came closer. Daisy was sitting on a stool behind the counter, putting her straight black hair back in a short ponytail. "That's okay," Laurie said with a smile. "I've had some crazy bosses." She hesitated. "I'm not going to say anything." She made a lip-zipping gesture with one hand and threw away the invisible key.

Daisy smiled. "Thank you. Long day, that's all."

"Yeah." Laurie walked over until she was only a few feet from the counter and started to skim a couple of shelves of paperbacks with her eyes while ignoring them with every one of her brain cells. "So, have you worked here long?" she asked.

"Yeah, about seven years. Since I was in high school." Daisy started picking at her nails, which were polished blue.

"I see you like Captain America," Laurie said.

Daisy looked down at her shirt. "Oh, yeah."

"You took his side in *Civil War*?"

Daisy shrugged. "Oh, I don't know, but I go with Cap anytime it's him or Iron Man, who's just a rich arms dealer and doesn't belong with superheroes in the first place. I mean, if I had a bulletproof AI suit that shot lasers out of my hands, I'd be brave, too, right?" She pointed at the Claws shirt Laurie was wearing. "Are you from Calcasset?"

"Oh, yeah, I grew up there."

"I used to go to camp over there. Camp Smithson."

"The arts camp? My brother was a counselor there when he was in college. Probably about 2004 to 2008-ish? Ryan Sassalyn?"

Daisy broke into a grin. "Did he sing *Bye Bye Birdie* all the time?"

"That's the one."

"Your brother was Hot Ryan!" Daisy pulled her head back, like Laurie had just shown off an Olympic medal. "Not for me personally, since men are not my jam and weren't my jam even when I was twelve, but everybody liked him. Tell him Daisy Sun says hi. I was into painting, so he didn't work with me as much, but one of my cabinmates fell off a bench in the dining hall trying to squeeze in next to him."

"Yeah," Laurie said, "that sounds like Ryan." She took a step away from the books and toward Daisy. "Do you still paint?"

"When I can. My girlfriend is a musician—she plays at a bar that's down on the water—so sometimes she writes music and I paint and we drink green juice with chia seeds and shit and it's just hippie-dippie-skippy. It's how I unwind after a long day dusting the clocks." Daisy picked up an apple that had been under the counter and bit into it. She chewed and watched Laurie stand by the books, clearly not actually looking at them. "Is there something else? I'm really sorry about before."

"No, it's funny, because, I actually—" Laurie gave a dry laugh. "As it happens, I actually came here looking for your boss. The chucklehead?"

The effort Daisy made not to roll her eyes was visible. "You're looking for Matt?" She was nervous again. "Do you know him?"

Laurie shook her head. "No. I definitely don't. I thought I did."

Daisy raised her eyebrows. "Uh-oh."

"I—he did some work at my aunt's house. She died last year. He's been helping with her things. You know, over at the . . ." She gestured in the general direction of the yellow phone. "Do people complain about him?"

"A few," Daisy said noncommittally. "And he's only owned the place three years," Daisy said.

Three years. Not fifteen, like he had told her. "Oh yeah? Who owned it before that?"

Daisy smiled. "The Brewsters, Mary and Emile. They opened it in 1965."

"And they sold it to him."

She nodded. "Mary died about five years ago. Matt swooped in after that. And the Brewsters were *not* running a . . . whatever that bereavement thing is. That's all him."

Laurie came right up to the counter. Daisy had one earring in one ear and four in the other, and on the inside of one forearm was a simple tattoo of a sun, surrounded by wiggly rays. Laurie took a breath. "Is he, like, very bad?" she asked. "Your boss? Like *really* bad?"

Daisy froze. Then her eyes slid up to meet Laurie's. "You're asking if he's bad?" Laurie just nodded. Daisy narrowed her eyes just so very slightly. "He's not great."

Just then, the bell rang on the door, and a couple came in chattering about how adorable everything was, in that unguarded voice people only use in places where they think everyone else present is part of a simulation. They should bring something back for the woman's mother, they agreed. They should tell her about how cute this place was, they agreed. They should swallow a lobster whole, Laurie thought. The woman started admiring a table full of extremely tacky knickknacks.

"I can't really talk about this here," Daisy finally said. She flicked her eyes toward the couple. "But I'm interested."

"Right. Well, my name is Laurie Sassalyn. Like I said, I'm staying out in Calcasset at my aunt's house." Daisy nodded. "Maybe this is weird, but it's supposed to be a nice night, and I have a deck there. Do you want to come out and have a drink with me and maybe a couple of my friends later? It's nothing cool, it's just me and a librarian and a nice soccer mom, probably. Bring your girlfriend if you want? Maybe eight o'clock or so?"

"Sounds good." Daisy scribbled on the back of one of the store's cards and handed it over. "Text me your address." It said *Daisy Sun* and her number, and then in Sharpie, it said, *He's the worst.* "Worst" was underlined twice. Laurie looked up at her, and when their eyes met, Laurie mouthed, *Oh, I know.*

. . .

To say Laurie was nervous that things were going to be strange with Nick after the library was an understatement; it was more that she was nervous that they were going to be ruined entirely. She knew they were both right that there was no point in getting involved in anything complicated when she wasn't staying—and she *wasn't* staying—and he was probably specifically right that anything uncomplicated might well be a lot to expect from this situation.

Why couldn't he just have been hot and boring? If he were hot and boring, she could do a little itch-scratching, a little rebounding, a little nostalgic tour of something nice from her past, then go back to Seattle. To come here and have something fall apart with someone she never even meant to pursue *on top* of being charmed by what now appeared to be an actual criminal was not a good start to life after a broken engagement.

Never trust a guy who's leading with his feminist T-shirts. How had she forgotten such a simple rule? She'd known this since the guy with the Sleater-Kinney shirt who turned out to be married.

But the best way out was through, so she texted Nick about her impromptu party before she even texted June: The thing with the duck has gotten WILD. There is a whole story. Can you come over and have drinks tonight with me and Junie and my confidential informant?

It only took two minutes: How can I say no?

Just after he responded, the phone rang, and it was June, calling to follow up on the frantic texts Laurie had sent from Sea Spray. The kids made it harder for her to make plans on the fly, but she said that they were at her mother's and Charlie was working, so as it happened, she was available.

"June," Laurie said, with all the gravity a wooden duck could possibly deserve, "I promise I am going to make this worth your while."

. . .

It really was a nice night. Maybe Dot had used the deck this way, for parties with friends. Or maybe she'd used it for dates, or for reading, or for moderately scandalous makeout sessions with the scientist and the journalist and the rest of the people whose letters Laurie had been so careful not to open. Maybe with a man who carved ducks out of pristine cedar or leftover lumber or a downed telephone pole. People could have gotten drunk out here before, gotten sloppy drunk and kissed inelegantly while fumbling with each other's buttons, or they could have talked about fishing or the breeze off the water or who was going to be mayor. When Laurie was little, she'd never cared about the deck; it was a bunch of grown-ups chatting and laughing and being much too tall. She just wanted to root around in the back-yard for whatever was moving, eyes peeled for worms and bugs and squirrels and butterflies and things. She was a gatherer of interesting life then, just like she was now.

She got settled with Nick and June out back on the deck about an hour before Daisy was set to get there. When they all had drinks in their hands and the sun was low, she explained it to them in as much detail as possible: how she'd concluded that Dot might have known Kittery, but how Matt had shot her down with the appraisal that said it was some kind of dime-store piece that circulated in the aughts and was sold at the airport, which she now understood was a detail added by a skilled jackass who knew it was embarrassing to like airport stuff.

And then she recounted her call to the auction house and the series of revelations that had led her to conclude that Matt wanted the duck and knew she didn't want to part with it, so he had faked a document that would not only convince her to give it to him but make her feel like a fool for thinking it might be important. "And," as she said, "just as he expected me to, I got so embarrassed that I let him walk off with it." Just saying it still pinked up her cheeks.

Nick exhaled in a low whistle. It was distractingly sexy. Of course, everything he did seemed distractingly sexy now, for which she knew he couldn't be blamed, but on some level, it seemed like it had to be willful. How could such a thing be an accident? He had to know he was doing it. She briefly wondered if she was doing anything he found distractingly sexy, but such inquiries were very much beside the point. "So do you think this means he knows it really is worth something?"

"Well, that's the question, right?" Laurie said. "Why would he go to all this trouble if he wasn't pretty confident he could sell it for more than fifty bucks? That wouldn't really make sense. So he knows something about it, or he thinks he does." Just then, a text from Daisy rang out. I'm out front.

When Laurie opened the door, Daisy was there, still in her Captain America shirt, but beside her was a young woman with short blond hair, wearing a white tank top, camo pants, and black sneakers. "Hey, Daisy," Laurie said with a smile. "I'm so glad you could come."

Daisy pointed to the woman next to her. "This is Melody. Thank you for inviting her to come along so I didn't have to come alone and trust you not to turn me into a lamp."

Laurie smiled. "Happy to have you both. Nice to meet you, Melody. If anything, I'm trying to get *rid* of lamps, so you're very safe. Follow me through here, we're on the deck." On the way through the kitchen, Laurie grabbed an extra chair, and something about the extra chair pleased her. The act of making room made the house seem full, like she was transitioning from having friends over to *hosting* something.

When they were all settled outside (with wine for Daisy, fizzy water for Melody), she took a breath. "So. Daisy, I am dying to talk to you about your boss." Once again, she ran through the story, and Daisy not only didn't look surprised, but nodded several times in the way you would if someone was describing a movie you'd already seen. Which, in a way, maybe Laurie was.

When she was finished, Daisy and Melody exchanged a look. "Based on what I know," Daisy said, "this checks out. He's one of those guys where you always have questions he can't answer, you know? Where did this thing go, why does this angry lady keep calling, why did this person think you had an appointment when you say you didn't?" Daisy refilled her wine from the bottle on the table. "People get mad, it happens. But with him, it's constant. It's the most WTF job I've ever had."

"There's stuff he doesn't keep in the store, right?" June asked. "I feel like he wouldn't put the really expensive stuff out if he's not just selling it on the level."

"Right," Daisy said. "He's got lots of stuff he holds back, looking for particular buyers or waiting to sell to particular places. Your duck is a good example. He wouldn't put it on the shelf with an eighty-thousand-dollar price tag or whatever. He could go to Wesson & Truitt and auction it through them. But if it's shady, he'll probably go to somebody privately."

"I just feel like he gave me such a hard sell," Laurie said. "He came over here in his band shirts—"

Daisy and Melody both cackled. "I call him Captain Lilith Fair," Melody said. "I bet he's been wearing a supposedly feminist shirt every time you've seen him."

"Other than The Decemberists, which he was wearing when I met him."

Daisy nodded. "You said something that made him think the feminism was going to work on you."

"He seemed really, really nice," Laurie said. She pointed at her friend. "June wanted me to ask him out!"

"Hey, I didn't know," June said. "He was cute."

"Well, you should be glad you didn't ask him out, because he's a complete jackwagon." Daisy settled back in her chair. "The first thing he told me about himself was that he was thirty-six and he wanted to be a multimillionaire by the time he was forty. I was like, 'By buying an antiques store?'"

"It does seem like the long way to get there," Nick said.

"Apparently, he'd read an article that said Maine was a hot region for tourism and had a lot of potential." She pulled down the finger-quotes around "potential" in the way you do only when contempt is running hot in your veins. "He showed me this newsletter from some business asshole that said if you go to a distressed area—that's what it said, a 'distressed area'—you can buy cheap and soak both locals and tourists by getting into used stuff. The locals would sell you junk for cheap, and the tourists would buy it."

"That sounds upsettingly familiar," Laurie said.

Daisy nodded. "There's a lot of *caveat emptor* with old stuff, right? You're not very well protected if somebody buys something from you and they know more than you do about how much it's worth. If they just have better information, that's fine. If you don't know some comic book is valuable and he does, he's allowed to buy it for whatever you'll sell it to him for, and maybe he makes a ton of profit, and good for him. But he can't tell you he's going to get an appraisal for you and not get it, and he definitely can't forge documents. That's fraud. There's no special exception for people who are lying about old stuff or dead people's stuff."

"Sounds good so far," Nick said.

"I think you should just go confront him," June said. "Go over there and tell him you know he was lying, you know he forged the thing, you know all about it. Put the fear of God into him."

"He'd just freak out, though," Daisy said. "I remember a guy coming in one time and raising a fuss about some baseball jersey Matt bought off him, how he wanted it back, and Matt sold it practically right away. As long as he's got a remotely plausible claim that he bought it off you fairly, once he knows you're after him, he'll sell it, throw up his hands, and say he's not part of it anymore. You could sue him, but if you really want to get the thing back, that's not the way to go. It will vanish even faster."

"Maybe do it nicely," Nick offered. "Not to be a cliché of a librarian, but just go and ask nicely. Don't tell him you know he's a thief, just tell him you changed your mind."

"Not to be a downer, but if he thinks it's worth money," Daisy said, "and he thinks he has the option of keeping it, he won't just give it back. He bought a ring one time that turned out to be a family heirloom the husband wasn't supposed to sell, and when the wife came in and said it was a mistake and asked for it back, he told her that if he gave back one thing, he'd have to give back everything. He won't give it back to you."

"But you said it was fraud," Laurie said. "That's illegal."

"It's definitely illegal. The problem is proving it. And it's hard to prove what he did, given the paperwork. And once it's gone, you're not going to get it back."

"That's why he took back the sheet where he promised me the appraisal." Laurie kept thinking about that sheet of paper, that stupid sheet of paper. "I still can't believe I let him do that."

"Yeah." Daisy shook her head. "The fraud is in the fake appraisal, and I don't know how you would prove he made it. He'll claim you did, to try to get it back, because you had regrets."

"I truly can't believe I was this dumb," Laurie said.

Daisy shook her head firmly. "Hey, you're not dumb. He's just really good at making people feel guilty for hiring him, and then they're easy pickings."

"Why do you still work there?" June said.

Melody stage-whispered, "That's what I keep saying."

Daisy rolled her eyes. "I've been suspicious, but I haven't been sure."

"So I have to get it back," Laurie said. "And he's not going to give it to me."

Melody shrugged. "You could steal it."

Laurie shook her head. "I don't know where it is."

"Even if you did," Daisy said, "that would just make it look more like it was your fault. Like you were the con artist, not him. That would almost make it easier for him to go on the offense, if you took it."

June nodded. "You really need him to con himself."

Nick frowned. "Meaning?"

"Well," June continued, "you need him to return the duck in a way that takes advantage of the fact that he's a trash can. The fact that he's a trash can has to be how he winds up giving it back."

Laurie started tapping her fingers on the arm of the chair. "Something where he does something dishonest, so that he can't report it to anybody."

"It shouldn't be too hard to get him to do something dishonest," June said.

Daisy nodded. "It won't be. I sat there once while he called and extorted a Taco Bell for a free lunch by claiming he found a nail clipping in a quesadilla."

"Gross," Melody said with a full-body shudder.

"I have to think about this," Laurie said. "I have to think about what to do. I also have to figure out whether Dot actually knew this guy and whether he really made the duck. The only thing worse than what's already happened would be going to a lot of trouble to get it back and finding out she really did get it in an airport. I also have to try to figure out what he's going to do with it. I mean, sell it, obviously, but I don't know where."

"You know," Daisy said, "he keeps all his messages on that iPad. If we could look at it, we might be able to figure out what his plan is. He knows all kinds of sketchy dudes, but I don't know which one he would go to for this. I don't know that he specifically has a sketchy duck dude." She stretched out her leg, and Laurie saw that on her ankle, there was another tattoo, a simple line design, just like the sun on her arm.

"Is that a . . . daisy?" she asked, nodding toward it. "It's gorgeous."

"Yeah. Daisy Sun, get it? People think it's basic." Daisy rolled her eyes. "Whatever."

"It *is* basic," Melody said. "But it's also cute, so who cares?"

"I ignore people with opinions, generally," Daisy said. "Particularly opinions about the way I should look."

"Me too," Laurie agreed. "Believe me, if you walk into a sporting goods store and tell them you want a piece of gear in a women's eighteen, they look at you like you just asked for a scuba suit for a horse."

June looked at Laurie. "How do we look at that iPad without him freaking out?"

"I don't know." She took out her phone. "But I'm going to make an effort."

Hi Matt! It's Laurie Sassalyn. Would you have any time in the next few days to help me with something else over here at Dot's?

"Well, now I guess I'm committed," she said, putting it back down.

"Committed to being a spy!" June nearly chirped. "It's exciting!" She paused. "I have small children," she said. "I get very amped up about things that aren't related to *Bluey*."

"Hey, *Bluey* is boss," Daisy said. "We watch *Bluey* all the time. And I'm amped up about anything that's going to cost this stink-rat a lot of money."

Laurie's phone gave a ding. *Oh, hello, Matt.* Of course! Monday okay? Around 3PM?

Perfect, she texted back. She turned to her team. "We're on."

The gathering lasted until almost midnight. Daisy nudged Melody until she sang a bit of a song she had written that sounded a little Joni-Mitchell-y, while Daisy mouthed all the words. Nick rattled off stories of his favorite moments spent interrupting library patrons who were having sex (alone or together) or surreptitiously researching what they considered taboo subjects. ("Kids google sex stuff so much," he said. "Just *so much*. And they always, always think I'm going to be surprised.") June and Laurie shared the cat-skeleton story with their new allies. And eventually, when someone looked at their phone and said it was 11:40, there were quick hugs and promises to talk soon. And when they were all gone, Laurie sat on the chaise alone, looking at the stars and finishing the last half-glass of wine. "Okay," she said into the blue-black night. "Okay."

Chapter Twelve

Ginger Buckley, Nick's grandmother, was eighty-six. She'd grown up in western Massachusetts, but she married a man from Lexington, Kentucky, who made a success of a very special product called Smokewater Whiskey. After he died, Ginger followed one of her daughters to Maine, where she'd settled with her husband to raise their kids—including future librarian Nick Cooper. Ginger moved into a decommissioned lighthouse, started adopting greyhounds, and bought a minor league baseball team. Her nineteen grandkids, now ranging in age from high school to Nick, came and went from Calcasset and from her house, kissing her cheeks and bringing her gifts and taking her out to eat, and she helped with college and down payments for houses, and sometimes even travel when she could. She'd sent Nick and Becca on their honeymoon to Melbourne, according to June.

Ginger didn't have a favorite grandchild, but Nick had been her first one, and he'd brought Laurie over to her house for dinner a handful of times when they were dating as teenagers. So when she invited Laurie and Nick for brunch, there was no question they'd go.

The house was at the end of a jetty, and it made for a windy walk on Sunday morning. Windy enough to ruffle a jacket, but not so windy you had to lean forward to walk. "She's going to be so excited to see you," Nick said, bumping Laurie's shoulder gently with his.

"I haven't been here in such a long time. I'm impressed she's still so independent, especially since she basically lives in a cartoon house that goes straight up."

He laughed. "I have to warn you, even though she's owned it for like twenty-five years, she still might tell you how cheap it was and how much work she put into it."

"Do you think she ever thinks about moving? Since the entire thing is a giant circular staircase?"

He gestured toward the smaller part of the house attached to the lighthouse tower. "She can live on that main level if she has to. She did it when she broke her foot. Her bedroom is down there, and her kitchen. I kept trying to get her to come stay with me or with somebody, but as you can imagine, I didn't get anywhere, especially since I didn't have a way to contain the dogs." He pointed at a tall wooden fence that surrounded the base of the house and opened at a wide gate.

"I know you—it must have driven you nuts, not helping."

"She let me drive her to Claws games. She had an aide who came for a few weeks. Most important, she had somebody make a boot for her that was covered with pink rhinestones, and that's what she'd wear when she was at the ballpark. She also had bright pink crutches."

"There's something very comforting about the fact that Ginger is still very, very Ginger," Laurie said. The water was slapping the rocks on the jetty, and two fishing boats going in opposite directions motored by in the middle distance. "I still like it here," Laurie said as she tasted salt on her lip. "I like it a lot."

"You can come back anytime," he said, not looking toward her, keeping his hands in the pockets of his jeans.

When they got up to Ginger's door, Nick went to knock, but it flew open before he could make contact. She wasn't anywhere near as small or as frail as Laurie realized she'd been imagining. She was dressed like an ad for a lush senior living facility, in white pants and a navy blue top. And as had been the case every time Laurie had ever seen her, her hair was perfectly curled and brightly colored. It was often some shade of red—sometimes more auburn, sometimes more pink—but right now, it was a robin's-egg blue.

"Well, come here and put your arms around me, Laurie Sassalyn," she said. Ginger's arms were thin, but her embrace was emphatic, and Laurie could smell vanilla and lavender that lingered faintly around her hair and her shoulders. "You look just beautiful, my love," Ginger said to her as they pulled apart.

"You do, too. I'm so happy to see you," Laurie said as she and Nick followed Ginger inside.

"Now, darlings," Ginger said, "I'm afraid my babies are on a playdate with their besties, but I'm sure they'll be sorry they missed you."

"The . . . dogs?" Nick said. "The dogs are on a playdate."

"Of course the dogs," she said. "They play down the street with Mr. Waltham's pugs. Otherwise they get lonely. Chrissy especially."

"Oh, tell Laurie what the dogs' names are. She hasn't met them." Nick looked over at her and raised his eyebrows. "You're going to love it."

"They're named Jack, Janet, and Chrissy," Ginger said. "Like on *Three's Company*. But Jack isn't gay."

"Jack wasn't gay on the show," Nick said.

"I know that." Ginger scowled. "But they said he was."

"I love the fact that you introduce your dogs by telling people, 'My dog's name is Jack, but he's not gay.'"

"Oh, go ahead," Ginger said, "come by to drink a lady's coffee and tease her about her heterosexual dog."

When Laurie was a teenager, she had loved coming with Nick to visit Ginger. There were people who would visit the house and expect that it would be rehabbed in some basic-cable way that would conceal its origins, so that you wouldn't know it had ever been a lighthouse except perhaps for a tasteful oar mounted on the wall. This was not that kind of home.

The entrance opened into a round living room surrounded by a winding staircase that, if you climbed it, led you through a series of round spaces: a bedroom, then the dining room, then a library with enormous windows that looked out at the water. (That was the *first* library in which Nick and Laurie had awkwardly made out while the sun was going down.) In the boxy section beside the tower—the part that looked like a regular little house—were Ginger's bright yellow kitchen, her primary bedroom suite, a powder room, and a small sitting room that unofficially belonged to the dogs.

As long as Laurie could remember, she'd never been able to find so much as a dust particle on a surface where Ginger was in charge. Having spent so much time in Dot's cluttered house with half-empty boxes and stacks of photos, Laurie could have been self-conscious in this bright oasis. But Ginger gestured at a cream-colored couch—Cream! In a house of dogs!—and Laurie and Nick sat together, much as they would have when they were seventeen. On the coffee table, there was already a glass carafe of orange juice and an opened bottle of champagne in an ice bucket. "I'm not telling you what to do," Ginger said over her shoulder as she headed into the kitchen, "but I'll be right back, the glasses are right there, and you can follow your bliss."

"Follow your bliss," Nick whispered as he poured orange juice into a tall glass and topped it with a glug of champagne, then did the same for her. "What are you making in there, Gran?" he called out.

"We're having some fruit, and some very delicious pastries and coffee," she answered, "because I couldn't get the good eggs this week. They mob that farmers market, I tell you. I get there fifteen minutes early and the tourists from the cottages clean out the eggs before I get to the front of the line. I don't know what they're even making. Who eats that many eggs on vacation?" She appeared with a tray that held a plate of croissants and muffins, plus a pot of coffee and two white mugs with photos on them of small children grinning to show off mouthfuls of teeth that sported a few gaps. "Now, do you know who these beauties are, Nick?" she asked as she set down the tray.

"Oh boy," he said, picking up one of the mugs. "These are the children of . . . one of my cousins."

She clicked her tongue. "One of your cousins. Shame on you. These are Betsy's boys. That's Clayton with the bat on his shoulder, and that's Calvin with the cat in his lap."

Laurie poured herself coffee in the Calvin mug. "Betsy is John's daughter, right?"

"Show-off," Nick muttered as he filled the other one.

"That's right," Ginger said. "John's got Betsy, she's a nurse, and Brian, he's a dog trainer, and Tracy, she works at a coffee shop in Bangor. I supported her at the Pride parade, you know." Ginger got up and went to the mantel, where she took down a small framed photo. In it, Ginger had a full rainbow of colors in her hair, and she was wearing a shirt that said BI BI LOVE, and Tracy, a brunette with a short bob, was grinning and kissing her cheek.

"That is a beautiful picture," Laurie said, handing it to Nick. "How's your team doing, Ginger?"

"So far, so good," she said. "They lost to Freeport the other day, but only because some lucky bastard put a little grounder past my

David. Utter luck, it was a terrible bounce. You have to come to a game, Laurie. They're just such fun."

"Do they still run the cereal-box race?"

"Oh, yes." Ginger sat in a green wing chair. "You know, they added a box. There are four now. There's one for Raisin Bran. Raisin Bran hasn't won yet, but people are going to go crazy when it happens. The little girl, Lily, who's running in Raisin Bran next weekend, is supposed to be a real pistol, so we'll see. How are things at Dot's, my love?"

To her own surprise, for the briefest moment, Laurie thought she might burst into tears. God, how *were* things at Dot's? She had cleaned out maybe a third of the closets. She had stacked books. She might have given away a priceless antique after being swindled by a man who somehow understood precisely the variety of kindness to which she would immediately overreact. "I'm doing my best," she said, running her finger along the rim of the mug. "I'm afraid I'm going to miss something important that my mom or my aunt would want. I don't know if it's enough, what I'm doing, but I'm really trying."

"It's plenty," Nick said. "Gran, she's touching every piece of jewelry. Tell her it's enough."

Ginger frowned. "Of course it is. She knows it is. She just isn't sure if I know it is, because I'm an old lady, and someday you and your cousins and whoever else are going to be looking at my stuff, too." She leaned toward Nick. "You listen, the last thing on my mind is what's going to happen to the spoons when I die. Now, my baseball team? That, I care about. You make sure somebody takes that team and treats them just as nice as I do now, okay?" Nick nodded. "But spoons are spoons, and you can keep them or throw them in the ocean."

"You should see all Dot's pictures," Nick said. "Boxes and boxes and *boxes* of them."

"Oh, I imagine," Ginger said. "Dot and her cameras, clicky-

clicky-click. I'm not sure I ever saw her without a camera in her hand. I think I have a Polaroid on the refrigerator that she took at my friend's daughter's wedding. All those boxes, but I tell you, she probably gave away as many as she kept."

"Were you friends?" Laurie asked. "I feel like you would have been friends."

"We were friendly. We didn't go to the same church, of course, since she was a Methodist and we're Baptists. And by the time I moved here, she was near retired, and she traveled so much after that. We used to make jokes that she'd show up with a sticker on her behind that said PARIS. It wasn't mean, of course, we were just jealous. I don't think I ever knew a lady my own age who had so many adventures, not even me. And boyfriends, of course. She'd go out to dinner with somebody she met at a play or a talk or something—I set her up with my first-base coach once. She was just a beauty, had a nice figure until her very last day, and she was just so funny. And wild."

"Tell me about her boyfriends," Nick said, sliding back in his seat. "Maybe we saw their pictures."

"Oh, well, she had a little thing with Frosty, you know."

Nick's eyes widened. "From the hockey rink?" He turned to Laurie. "Frosty rode the Zamboni."

"His real name was Felix," Ginger said. "They called him Frosty because he got gray hair when he was thirty."

"Wait, they didn't call him Frosty because he rode the Zamboni at the hockey rink?" Nick said.

"No, no, that was a coincidence. And oh, she had a fellow for a while who worked at that bar, that tourist bar with the buoys out front where Betsy's husband got arrested that time." She looked at Laurie. "He popped a young man in the mouth for what I'm sure were very good reasons." Ginger paused as if she were considering her next move. "I did hear a bit about another boyfriend of Dot's, maybe. I don't know if I should say, though."

Nick rolled his eyes. "Well, if you weren't going to tell, you wouldn't have started to tell, so you might as well just go ahead and spill it."

"Do you hear how he talks to his grandmother?" Dot asked Laurie, who nodded sympathetically. "Well, I did hear," Ginger said, smoothing the fabric of her pants over her knee, "that she might have once been involved with someone who was married, but that did not seem like Dot at all. I think it was just gossip, honestly. Like I said, a single woman who can take herself to Paris attracts a lot of attention from a lot of people who have to wait around to be taken places, and not all of it is positive."

Laurie leaned forward a little bit. "Did you hear anything else about this guy? Was he from here, or out of town, or what?"

"Well, this would have been a long time ago if it even happened, before I lived here. And I let those things sit, mostly. If everybody in this town who ever had an affair had to talk about it with their grandchildren, I will tell you right now, they would not recover."

"You think it's that hard for people to talk about something like that even when they're so far past it?" Nick asked.

"No, I'm saying their *kids* wouldn't recover. Look at Laurie's face, she knows what I mean."

Laurie had not read the letters. She did know what Ginger meant.

"Dot was hardly sitting around waiting for somebody to call her for the last thirty years," Ginger went on. "It may come as a shock, but nobody shows up on your porch when you turn sixty-five, gives you your Medicare card, puts you in a housecoat, and puts a rubber band around your knees. I had my last boyfriend when I was seventy-eight. Nick knows. I was seeing a man from church."

"Why did you stop seeing him?" Laurie asked.

"Oh, honey, he drank beer, and I can't stand beer. A man who drinks whiskey, or wine, that's perfectly okay, I'm not square. But I cannot kiss a beer-drinker."

"Gran, you own a baseball team. You spend half your summers at the park."

"And I do not kiss the beer-drinkers there, either."

"Nor should you," Laurie said. "Can I ask you one other thing, though? It's about Dot, about the house." Ginger nodded, and Laurie gave the shortest summary she could muster of what had happened: found a duck, lost a duck, not sure how to get the duck back, still not sure what the duck even is. "Does any of this sound at all familiar to you?"

Ginger shook her head. "Darling, I'm sorry, it really doesn't. But I'll tell you what it does make me think of. I did know a lady from my church group who said when she downsized, she used a guy just like this, and he stole from her. We all figured she was probably mistaken, you know, everybody loses some things when they move, and half my friends are just sure they used to have all kinds of valuables they can't find. But now I have to wonder if she used the same man you've been working with at Dot's." Ginger wrote the woman's name on a sheet of paper and handed it to Laurie. "Betty Donnelly, that's a nice lady. Said a clock she had just vanished. It was very special, in the shape of a tiger. Worth a lot of money. I wonder if it was the same fellow."

Laurie tucked the paper into her pocket. "It's a good question."

When she got home from brunch, Laurie had an email from Erin, whose wedding fortunes were continuing to spiral downward. The latest disaster involved her dress: Her cat had gotten into her closet while she was working and had destroyed the bottom of her dress. "LAURIE THIS IS A CURSE, MY WEDDING IS CURSED, I HATE THIS, I DO NOT WANT TO DO THIS," Erin had tapped out, then she had followed this with ten skull emojis, three knives, and a little black cat.

"Wait," Laurie wrote back. "Your dress was an eighteen, right?"

Chapter Thirteen

You absolute weasel, Laurie thought as she opened the door the next day to Matt, standing on her doorstep in an Indigo Girls concert shirt. "Hi there," she nearly chirped. "It's so good to see you again. Thanks for coming."

He smiled. So many teeth. "Oh, I was glad to hear from you. I wondered if there were more treasures over here, and I knew if there were, you'd spot them."

He had a messenger bag over his shoulder, and as he moseyed into the living room and sat on the sofa, Laurie eyeballed it, figuring that was where the iPad was. Somewhere in there, probably kicking around next to a book that was vaguely Machiavellian—like maybe Machiavelli—and a leather wallet and a ChapStick and something he stole. Somewhere in there was the first answer she needed. "Can I get you something to drink? I'm working on a nonalcoholic cocktail, want to try it? It's cranberry and lime. I'm calling it the Lilith Fair." Too much?

"Sounds great." He grinned.

Of course it wasn't too much. She could probably have told him she was calling it the ERA Yes, and the only thing he would have thought was that he had her number even more perfectly than he realized. She went into the kitchen and took down two tall glasses. She mixed some seltzer with cranberry juice, lime juice, and a sprig of mint. Would it be good? It didn't really matter. She didn't spit in his drink; that was her gesture of goodwill toward her fellow man. "Here you go; tell me what you think," she said as she sat on the green chair across from him.

He took a sip. "Delicious, you're talented." He grinned again. "So what can I do for you?" he asked, because yes, he wanted to know immediately where the treasures were, if there were treasures.

This was the moment in which she had to try to be as adept at lying as he was, and she wasn't sure at all she was up to the challenge. But there was nothing to do but start. "Well," she said, "I found this letter."

He nodded. "Okay."

"And I'm not sure whether I can believe it is what it says it is. But I figured you were the right person to talk to first."

"I'm honored," he said. Oh, she hated him. But she had chosen the right way to get him over to the house. All she had to do was dangle something else he could steal from her, and he was over here with his stupid face and his stupid bag and his stupid shirt and his stupid iPad, and it made her feel so stupid. She took a breath anyway.

"So, Dot had this letter in her writing desk, tucked inside her address book. And, I mean, I have no idea what to think, but it said it was from . . . someone kind of important."

His eyes were greedy, right away. "Oh yeah?"

She smiled a little and nodded. "Yeah. It said it was from Andrew

Wyeth." Earlier in the day, unsure whom the letter should be from, Laurie had googled "famous people from Maine" and chosen the painter, who had lived until 1985 and could theoretically have written to Dot. She had read that there weren't that many letters from him available, and that they were potentially valuable if they mentioned any of his paintings. "The letter talks about all these doubts that he had about his ability. How he wasn't really sure his landscapes were that good."

Matt nodded. "Interesting."

He needed more. "So I kept looking, and I found all these other letters. They were friends, I guess. They had a correspondence."

"Huh." He paused. She watched. He leaned over. He unbuckled the bag. *Yes!* He pulled out the iPad. *Yes!* He woke it up and punched in a code to unlock it, so quickly that she couldn't catch it. *Blergh.* Even if he walked away and left it on the coffee table, if it locked, she was toast.

"What magic are you doing over there?" she asked.

"Just a little quick peek at a couple of things, hang on," he said, tapping away at the tablet.

"Can I look?"

"Of course."

She came over to the couch and sat next to him, carefully setting her drink on the coffee table. He had pulled up the same memorabilia auction site she'd checked out herself earlier in the day. It was the same place she'd learned about the rarity of his letters. "How the hell did you find this?" she asked, leaning over slightly. "I can never figure out what I'm even looking for. I don't understand this stuff at all." She was a journalist. He could not possibly believe that this portrait of incompetence as to first-grade-level research was true—but he did. She had found the weakness in him that she needed, which was that she had inadvertently lulled him into thinking she was comically, persistently, and thoroughly dumb.

"You just need to have a little experience," said the guy who probably was one of those "why isn't there a Netflix for books?" people right up until he read about the fortunes available to a young man willing to rip off tourists and the recently bereaved. "So, as you can see here, it's certainly possible it could be valuable. Can we take a look at the letters?"

"Well," she said, scrunching up her face in an imitation of what she assumed all his girlfriends had done when he tried to kiss them in public, "I kind of don't have them here. I took them and put them in a safe deposit box at the bank, because I was afraid I'd start a fire or something."

"Ah, that's smart." He nodded. He turned toward her, and their faces were very close, and she blinked like she was nervous instead of kind of repulsed. He would definitely expect her to be made nervous by his grimy mug—spiritually grimy, emotionally grimy—invading her personal space. She picked up her drink and, as faux-flustered as she could manage, she poured some of it on the knee of his jeans.

"Oh no!" she said. "I'm so sorry!"

Through gritted teeth, he said, "Oh, don't worry, don't worry."

"The bathroom right down the hall has clean towels if you want to wash it out before it stains." She crossed her fingers that these casual jeans cost at least a hundred dollars. She should have added more cranberry juice.

"I'll be right back," he said with that little demon smile. "Don't go anywhere." But where a normal human being would set down his iPad instead of toting it to the freaking restroom where he was going to get a stain off his pants, he tucked it under his arm and took it with him. *DAMMIT*.

She'd listed the options earlier in the day in order of preference: *1. He leaves it on the table and I look at it while he's gone by using the code. 2. He leaves it on the table and I look at it while he's gone by getting to it before it locks.* She had now reached 3, which was *He hands it to me and lets me look at it.* But why? Why would he do that? What would be so important to him that he would just hand over his most important possession—his most personal item—just because? What could he possibly care about that much?

Remembering that one of her bosses had once told her that the email signature was the window to the soul—back when email was more widely used—she picked up her phone. She pulled up an email he had sent her right before she figured out he was a snake. At the bottom was his name, and his business information, and then this: "'An entire generation pumping gas, waiting tables—slaves with white collars.'—Tyler Durden." A *Fight Club* quote? On a business letter? Quoting a vengeful, violent weirdo? *Oh, you clichéd little creep,* she thought.

It took a few minutes for Matt to emerge from the bathroom. He had a large wet patch on his knee, but it wasn't too pink. "You think they're salvageable?" she asked, sort of hoping the answer was no.

"Oh, definitely. It's no big deal."

"Whew. I try not to get too attached to my stuff, but it's like . . . not to be the 'capitalism is a prison' person, but it's kind of true." Laurie resettled at the opposite end of the couch where he had been, just as he returned to his place there. She leaned back against the end of the couch and pulled her feet onto the cushion so her knees were up like a contemplative teenager on *My So-Called Life.* "Have you ever seen *Fight Club*?" she asked.

She said this knowing that even a smidgen of self-awareness would have led this man to take note of the fact that she had just asked him whether he had ever seen the movie that was quoted at the bottom of his every email. The slightest sense that he might not be the smartest, the most savvy, the most calculating son of a bitch in the room would have caused him to catch on instantly. Of course, he had no smidgens to speak of, no sense of the potential for him to be outwitted, and probably no memory of what was currently in his email signature, since it seemed likely that he rotated it between

Fight Club, Jonathan Franzen, and perhaps Walter White. Ironically, of course.

"I love *Fight Club,*" he said. Not one smidgen. Smidgens were absent.

"Me too," she answered, widening her eyes. "You know the part where he goes to lunch with Matthew McConaughey, and McConaughey starts pounding on his chest? It's, like, amazing."

Matt frowned a little. "I think that's in *Wolf of Wall Street,*" he said.

"It is not!" she said, trying to be put out but endearing, the way people on awards shows do when they have to banter. "It's in *Fight Club!*"

"I don't think so," he said.

"Give me your iPad!" she said. "I'm going to show it to you."

She didn't usually believe in self-congratulation; she really didn't. But in her head, she did hear "Ode to Joy" playing, just like in *Die Hard,* as he handed the tablet to her. "Suit yourself," he said with a little smile.

"You are going to owe me such a huge apology," she said, narrowing her eyes as she went directly to his iMessages, facing his tablet resolutely in the direction that didn't allow him to see the screen. She quickly scanned them until she saw one that said, "pretty sure it's real, man." She opened it, still grinning and screwing up her face like she was confused by the multitude of buttons. She gave him a giggle. "Sorry, I'm having a blond moment."

"When I'm right, I might make you buy me dinner," he said.

"Not if I make you buy me dinner first," she said, opening the message, which was an exchange with a guy listed in Matt's contacts as "Rocky." Time was limited, but she was able to spot a mention of what Matt called "the bird we talked about," and to see that Matt was planning on meeting up with Rocky at Sea Spray on Saturday at 6:30. *Rocky, Saturday, 6:30,* she chanted to herself. Then she opened up YouTube and searched "Matthew McConaughey chest beating." She allowed her face to dramatically fall. She even opened her mouth a little, and she hit Play. The scene started. She looked over at him.

"*Wolf of Wall Street*?" he asked, with all the humility of a man growing intellectually aroused by the experience of being right about *Fight Club*.

She nodded. She handed him back the iPad and covered her face with her hands. "I'm so embarrassed."

"Don't be embarrassed," he said. "Nobody knows everything."

Except meeeeeee, she imagined him saying. But only to himself. But gleefully. And not for the first time.

Matt carried himself with the unshakable confidence, she realized, of someone who had never really had to worry about anyone thinking he might be full of shit. This was his superpower. And there had probably been a time when he was not full of shit. There had probably been a time when at least some part of this was genuine, perhaps a time in college when he was sleeping with various feminists and listening to them talk about the music that they loved, and then he just started exaggerating his level of interest in Ani DiFranco a *little* bit to get them to like him a *little* bit more.

And maybe he thought he *could* just have a cozy antiques shop for tourists, and the clean-out and downsizing business was just "synergy." And maybe at some point he found out some little item was more valuable than the person who sold it to him had realized. And before he knew it, he had decided that people who didn't know what things were worth didn't deserve to have them and wouldn't miss the money anyway. He had probably eased into forgery the way he eased into owning Gen-X feminist heroine T-shirts: He used what was at hand. These shirts pleased the women who could give him things that were worth money. They were the ones cleaning out their parents' places, their grandparents' places, the houses that had once belonged to their world-traveling great-aunts who maybe knew famous artists even if they did not, admittedly, actually know Andrew Wyeth.

"Okay, now that I've completely embarrassed myself," she said, wanting to get him out of the house as soon as humanly possible, "what should we do about the letters?"

"I'm going to make some inquiries," he said. "Call around. Do you think you could grab them from the bank so I could get a look? I could take pictures and send them to some of the people I know who might be able to give us a head start."

"I can do that." She grinned. "You're so helpful, I don't know what I'd be doing without you." She suddenly recalled those cartoons where two characters were stuck on a desert island and kept seeing each other as a giant ham or a trussed turkey. When Matt looked at her, she had a feeling that he saw those little white paper decorations that you put on turkey legs sticking out of the ends of her fingers. And it didn't even occur to him that he, in fact, was the whole ham.

Rocky, Saturday, 6:30.

"Oh, I know Rocky," Daisy said over breakfast the next morning at the Compass Café, known for its fluffy pancakes and blistering local gossip. "Rocky is one of his dirtbag friends. He looks kind of like the Green Goblin from *Spider-Man*."

"Willem Dafoe?"

"Yeah, yeah. Rocky looks like that, with the gap in his front teeth. I always assumed he was, like, one of those guys who sends out twenty emails a day about cryptocurrency. I'm pretty sure he's shady, but I don't know for certain. Matt is probably trying to get the duck sold ASAP in case he gets caught. And he would probably rather sell it to somebody he knows, who won't ask too many questions, just in case it's not real. For all I know, they could be faking up some kind of documentation. I mean, he already forged your appraisal."

"What do we do?" Laurie couldn't stop remembering the feel of the painted wood under her fingers, the sharp tail feathers and the smooth green crown. "At least it seems like he still has it. It's not gone yet."

"Right," Daisy said. Just then, their waitress, Marnie, walked past with a huge tray that held an omelette and a stack of blueberry pancakes and signaled that she'd be right back. "Man, I'm over here planning to order the veggie scramble, but I can't lie, I want *that*," she said, pointing to the pancakes. She shook off her carbohydrate lust. "If they're meeting at the store, they'll meet in Matt's office, which is at the back, through the little door behind the counter."

"I think I need to know what happens at that meeting."

Daisy tapped her fingers on the table. "Right, right. Well, there's a closet back there. In the office. You could hide in there. It's tight, but you'd hear them."

"You think I should hide in the closet?"

"In for a penny of spying, in for a pound," Daisy said, adding cream to her coffee.

"I guess you're right. How would I get in?"

"There's a door in the back," Daisy said, "that leads out into this tiny little parking area we have off the alley that holds like two cars. The bigger problem is figuring out how to get you in there without Matt seeing you, and I have no idea how we would do that." She picked up her cup of coffee. "How did this all end up being your problem anyway?" she asked. "Don't you have a bunch of brothers? Didn't Dot have friends?"

Laurie smiled. "Everybody does what they can."

Daisy nodded. "It's like you're at the bottom of the funnel. Everything swirls down, down, down, and then at the bottom, there's you. I mean, it's not so bad. Somebody has to do it. I think every family has somebody. I do it in my family, too. But they should say thank you. I mean, damn. You're really going to the mat for this duck."

Laurie laughed. "I just can't help thinking . . . if it was my mom's, there would be five of us, you know? Five of us trying to make sure everything was accounted for, everything was looked after. She should have the same."

Daisy nodded. "My aunt told me once that I should have kids because if I don't, there won't be anyone to take care of me when I'm old. She was kinda saying it because I'm a lesbian, but either way, that's messed up. First of all, I know my cousins, and none of them would be spending this kind of time on a duck. She'll be lucky if they take her out on her birthday."

Laurie looked dubious. "I bet they would."

"You'd be surprised. Plus, not taking care of anybody when they're old unless they're your mom or your dad is some crazy-ass capitalist boomer shit. I took care of Mary Brewster when she was sick. I even lived with them for a while. You don't have to be somebody's kid to be their kid, if you know what I mean."

"Can I ask how you ended up living with them?"

Daisy smiled. "I bet you think it was when I came out, right? Nah, my parents didn't care about that too much. I was just being an asshole, honestly. I was seventeen and I was kinda getting in trouble, and Mary called up my mom and just said she thought I needed a change of scenery. It was going to be a week or two, but I stayed six months. And she was right, because now my parents and I are fine. And it's not like I won't take care of them when they're old, but that's not why they had me. People who have babies don't go, 'Oh, welcome to the world, little one, I'm glad you'll be able to clean out my garage when I'm dead.' I don't think most people have practical reasons for having kids, they just want them. Besides, who says kids are going to take care of you when you're old anyway? Who says you won't still be taking care of them?"

"I have to tell you, Daisy, you are a lot smarter about all this than I was when I was in my twenties."

"It's just different. Life is long, et cetera, amen. I go for balance. That's why I drank some of Melody's green juice this morning, but now that I'm here, you know what? I'm definitely getting the pancakes."

Chapter Fourteen

Laurie and Nick waited in his car, down the street from Sea Spray. The air was hot and salty, and they rolled down the windows just so they could breathe. "What time is it?" she asked as she saw him look at his phone.

"It's 6:18," he said. "Two minutes." He rubbed one hand on his thigh.

"You don't have to come in with me, you know," she said. "I can do this myself."

"We decided," he said simply.

When they were seventeen, Laurie had gotten her first speeding ticket while driving her mother's Toyota Camry home from June's house. Convinced her parents would ground her for life or simply gaze upon her with disappointment forever, she had agonized for fully two days before she could bring herself to tell them. When she did, Nick had sat in his car in front of the house while she did it, just so she would know he was there. She got a stern but easily survived talking-to and agreed to pay the ticket herself, and then she pulled the curtain back on her bedroom window and gave him a thumbs-up, and he drove off.

Laurie listened to the birds, the occasional car going by, and the sound of her heart in her ears. "I'm nervous," she finally told him.

"Are you sure you want to do this?" he asked.

"Well," she said, "I'm almost forty and I've never been part of anything scandalous, so I guess it's about time."

Nick looked at his phone again. "Okay," he said. "6:20." Just a moment later, his phone pinged, and so did Laurie's. There was a text from Daisy addressed to the two of them and to June.

I'm ready, it said.

Farther down the street, June's hand, easily recognizable from her bright red nail polish, emerged from the passenger-side window of a pure white Cadillac and gave a thumbs-up. The Cadillac pulled away from the curb, crept down the street, and turned in to the front lot at Sea Spray Antiques. When it was parked, the driver's-side door opened, and a petite woman in her eighties emerged. She wore a bright blue dress and carried a purse that looked like a slice of watermelon. Her hair was an arresting shade of blue. She went up to the front door, then disappeared inside.

"Do you think this is going to work?" Laurie asked.

"Of course. You've heard how it goes when she starts asking questions."

"I probably haven't heard it as much as you have. She's not my grandmother."

He nodded. "Believe me, you have nothing to worry about. She's been training for this her whole life. She's going to eat lunch off this story for the entirety of her remaining days."

It took about another two minutes to get the next text from Daisy. It was similar to the last one: He's secured. Ready.

"Okay," Laurie said. "Let's go." They got out of the car and shut the doors as quietly as they could. They walked a wide path around the back of the building until they found the parking lot where the rear door wasn't quite closed, but was instead resting on a brick. Nick moved the brick Daisy had put there and opened the door, and they stepped into a small, dark passage with an employee bathroom and several stacks of dusty boxes. "Oh God," Laurie whispered, grabbing Nick's arm.

"What?"

She pinched her nose. She tipped her head back. Finally, she relaxed. "I thought I was going to sneeze."

"Don't sneeze," he barely breathed. A closed door to their left led to the small office, where a dingy metal desk and a couple of file cabinets shared space with a mini-fridge and, for some reason, a standee of James Gandolfini.

"This fuckin' guy," Laurie muttered. When they got into the office, she spotted in the corner a tall and narrow door. She pointed to it and mouthed "Closet." They crept across the office and opened the door. Fortunately, there wasn't much inside; unfortunately, there couldn't have been. It wasn't more than a cubby for brooms, a tiny box that might hold a stepladder, and a mop bucket. But at the moment, it was empty except for what looked like furnace filters standing against the wall. "After you," she whispered, and Nick stepped in. She followed behind him and closed the door. There was a square vent in the door near the bottom, but it still felt like the same air molecules had been in this closet for, conservatively, thirty years.

"It smells like wet cardboard," Nick whispered. He was so close that she could feel his breath on her ear. If the light went on, she'd be able to see the texture of his cheek, the mole she'd forgotten about until the library, and the crinkles by his eyes that were just like the ones she had started to see in the mirror herself.

Total darkness was an unfamiliar sensation, and she instinctively reached out and felt for his arm, so she could rest her hand there. "It smells like several generations of spiders lived and died in here."

"No no no," he whispered back in the blackness. "Don't say 'spiders.' You'll make them come out."

She felt him moving, then his hand was resting on her waist. She flexed her hand against his arm. One of his fingers sneaked under the bottom of her shirt and gave a reassuring scratch to the skin above her hip. It was quick. Scratch-scratch-scratch. *I'm-right-here.* Then they didn't move. She could hear herself breathing. Was she breathing too loud? Did it sound like she was panting? Why did it seem like the air was whooshing in and out of her lungs? Could he hear it too? Then she twitched with surprise when his voice, more like a shaped exhale, came from just beside her ear: "It's going to be fine."

It got so quiet that she could hear voices coming from the store. One of them, unmistakably, was Ginger. The other was Matt. Ginger's tone was patient, curious, friendly, unrelenting. His was practiced, polite, and under that, just a little tense. Just a little. "Okay, ready?" she whispered to Nick. He answered with a pat on her arm. She took out her phone and briefly flooded the closet with light long enough to text Daisy: We're ready. Then she put it on Do Not Disturb.

While they waited, Nick's hand stayed on her waist, and eventually he hooked his thumb through the belt loop of her jeans. He had done this when they were younger, when they were dancing or leaning against his car, or when they were kissing in front of her house while her mother pretended not to peek out the window. She slid her hand up until it was resting on his elbow. He leaned over until his face brushed the hair by her ear, and she jumped again, and he said, maybe as quietly as anyone has ever said anything, "I'm hanging on to you because I'm afraid to touch anything else."

If someone had flipped the light on right then, she knew exactly what they would see. She and Nick would both be grinning, both looking at the ground, leaning toward each other like they were slow-dancing, their eyes closed because it somehow felt like you could hear better that way.

Then there were voices, much closer. Matt. Someone else. Some guy. The first words Laurie could make out were "thought she was never going to shut up." Then the door opened, and Laurie tried to breathe even more quietly, to barely breathe at all. It was really happening: She was in a closet, with her high school boyfriend, listening to a man talk to another man about an ill-gotten duck.

"So, tell me," the other voice, which had to be Rocky, said. "Why am I here?"

"Like I told you on the phone," Nick said, "it's a Kittery, I'm positive. And I know you know guys in that market. I need a collector." This Matt voice was mostly the same as the one Laurie knew, but a little more relaxed. A little more naked.

"Why don't you find a buyer yourself? Or just take it to an auction? What's this all about?" Rocky asked.

"I'm trying to keep this low profile," Matt said, "and ideally I'm trying to keep myself out of it, you know, publicly."

"And why's that?" *Good question, Rocky!*

"I bought it from this woman, she didn't know what it was worth. I offered to have it appraised for her and she turned me down. I told her what I thought it was, and she said she didn't care, she just wanted to get rid of everything. I don't want her to be pissed off after I sell it if she finds out, and I don't want her to come back to me and complain." Laurie tightened her hand again on Nick's elbow. *He even lies to his co-conspirators! This fuckin' guy!*

"Why am I not buying this?"

"How many questions do you want to ask?"

A little pause, maybe while Rocky considered how deep to get in. "What makes you think it's real?" Rocky asked. "What do you have as far as provenance?" Provenance, Laurie had not known before but knew now, was the known history of a thing. It was the proof that the thing was what you said it was, and not, for instance, a souvenir bought in an airport.

He doesn't have anything, Laurie thought. *He doesn't have any proof at all, and he's going to skate through this anyway.* But the next thing she heard was papers shuffling. And then Matt's voice: "Here you go." She squeezed Nick's elbow even harder.

It was so quiet, she could hear that Rocky was holding at least two pages. *What the hell?* she thought. And then he said, "Huh. Okay."

"Good enough, right?" Matt was very impressed with whatever documentation he had just provided. It took everything for Laurie not to throw the door open and grab it.

"Let's say it is. If I find the buyer, what's my fee?"

"Ten percent?"

"Come on, man. More like twenty-five. You don't know shit about this market and you're trying to keep a secret. It's going to take me at least a few days of work to find your buyer. You don't want me to ask questions, and you don't want anybody else to ask them either. I'm taking all the risk."

"Don't be a hard-ass. I found it," Matt groused, in precisely the put-upon tone of an outright con artist who thinks he's being over-charged. It was his sincerity that was disquieting. It was his conviction that his biggest problem was that nobody would cut him a break.

"If you knew what the hell you're doing, you wouldn't need me," Rocky said. "If you knew anything about anything, you could do this yourself. But you don't, because you don't have any experience, and because like I've told you a million times, it's pretty obvious you don't actually care. You try to deal with this, you'll wind up with nothing. You might even get sued or arrested or haunted by some old lady's ghost. Seventy-five percent is better than nothing. Give me the twenty-five and I'll take care of it."

"How about fifteen percent? I can give you fifteen percent."

"You can give me twenty-five and a half."

"You're a shit."

"Take it or leave it." Rocky might have been a dirtbag, but Laurie got a tiny thrill from the fact that he was a better dirtbag than Matt. He was winning.

"Fine. I'll give you twenty." *Never say die, asshole!*

"It's twenty-five, Matt. It's twenty-five percent, you give me the thing, I'll bring you back the money. We can both do well here. Don't be stupid."

There was a pause, and Laurie kind of enjoyed imagining Matt's miserable, defeated, helpless expression. He'd gone to all this trouble to steal from her, and because he was such an ignorant lunkhead, he had to give 25 percent to somebody else just to make any money. She hoped he looked like a disappointed little troll. Specifically, like a disappointed little troll right after somebody punches it in the face.

"All right," he said. "Fine. We'll do twenty-five percent. But keep me out of it." There was the sound of a key in a lock, and then of a drawer in the file cabinet sliding open. Of course that was where he was keeping it. In her mind's eye, Laurie could see him picking up the duck—her duck!—out of the drawer, putting his grubby hands all over it, handing it over, a creep-to-creep transfer.

"Nice piece," Rocky said. "Could use a cleaning."

"I've got some stuff in that closet, just give me a second." This last word—"second"—came from so close to the door that Laurie imagined Matt speaking it directly into the vent. She clutched Nick's arm. Her heart started to pound, and she ordered it to settle down, because it seemed like the rush of blood might be audible through a door, through a room, on the other side of a hockey arena. She heard Matt's hand on the knob.

Rocky interrupted. "You don't just spray this thing with Windex, man. I've got stuff at home. I'm going to throw in a cleaning for free. I think it's going to look pretty good when I'm done."

"I told you," Matt answered, and his voice receded from the door. "Knew it the minute I laid eyes on it, even though it took a little doing to get it." Laurie went back to breathing.

A pause. "I thought you said she gave it right to you."

He really was dumb. Scheming, but dumb. "She did. I just had to work on her a little bit. She appreciated the attention. I don't think she gets much. I bet she dies alone in that house just like her aunt."

Knowing he was a crook, knowing he was a scammer and a jerk and a liar, knowing he was bad at his job and didn't know anything about antiques and had probably never cleaned out this closet ever, Laurie was particularly horrified that she felt this right in her chest. Nick's fingers on her waist tensed. Her hand dropped limply from his other elbow, but he reached down and picked it up. He gave her two quick squeezes.

"All right, man." Laurie heard the zip of some kind of a bag as Rocky tucked the duck out of sight, so close to her but so very far away. "I'll get back to you in a week or so. I have a few ideas, but I've got estate sales I'm hitting all week, so it's not going to be right away. I'm going to be in Damariscotta in a couple days, and I have a guy out there."

"Okay, I'll wait to hear. I'll walk you out." The door opened and closed, and Laurie took her phone out of her pocket. After a moment, a text arrived, silently, from Daisy. They're bullshitting by the front door. All clear to get out.

"Okay, now," Laurie whispered. She and Nick slipped out of the closet and she blinked in the bright fluorescent light. They left the office, crept out the back door, and found themselves in the evening sun. They made their way around the side of the building and out to the street, and they climbed into Laurie's car. She opened the text thread with June and Daisy. We're out. Everybody okay?

From June: Ginger and I are on our way back to her place.

From Daisy: Rocky's gone. Matt's in his office.

Laurie, to them both, wrote: You're all superstars. We'll see you at Dot's at 8:00. We have lots to tell you.

That night, Laurie ordered Thai food, and Nick, Daisy, and Melody sat around the table in the dining room. June was at home with her husband and her kids, but she FaceTimed into the meeting while they dissected the events at the store. Nick relished the story of the hand on the door, the risk of being caught, and the fact that they had almost been busted because Matt didn't know how to clean a collectible duck. He imitated Rocky's voice, low and more menacing than it had in fact been, barking "Windex" as if it were the word "asshole," because, let's face it: It was implied.

According to June and Daisy, Ginger had come strolling in the front door with June and immediately engaged Matt in a long conversation about a collection of basketball cards that one of her grandsons allegedly owned. (He did not. None of the grandkids collected basketball cards, and neither did any of the greats, but Matt was not willing to risk blowing her off, seeing as how sports cards had recently become so popular they'd stopped selling new ones at Target for security reasons.) She had told him that she was quite sure there was a signed rookie card from someone named LaBob James. Matt kept asking her if she meant LeBron James, and she kept saying no, no, it was definitely LaBob James. She explained that this was a player who went directly from high school to professional basketball. He said yes, that man's name was LeBron James. She said no, she meant the one who moved to Florida. He said yes. Yes, the one who moved to Florida—LeBron James.

At this point, according to Daisy, Ginger had seamlessly transitioned into a series of questions about Floridian kitsch memorabilia, including some postcards she believed she had somewhere that were from a place called Marineland. Matt knew of it. She wanted to know if he had ever had the chance to swim with dolphins. Dolphins, she'd told him, were more intelligent than humans. She had heard that they could follow a book if you read it to them. He said he had not had the pleasure.

At one point, Matt tried to pass her off to Daisy, saying that he had a meeting to prepare for, but Ginger had stopped him in his tracks by recalling that she'd also meant to ask him about her son's *Star Wars* toys, none of which had ever been opened. She had, she told him, an original Darth Vader, with the bicycle. Darth Vader did not ride a bicycle, Matt told her. Ginger asked him why, then, was there a bicycle in the package with her son's original Darth Vader?

"I have never seen improv that intense," Daisy said, "and I dated a woman who was a member of three experimental comedy theaters."

"Did you feed her any of this material?" Nick asked June. "Like in the car?"

"The only thing I told her," June said over FaceTime, putting her hands up defensively, "was that she had to keep him completely occupied until his appointment showed up and he went back to the office. Everything else was just Ginger's genius in full flower."

"The real question," Laurie said, "is what the hell Matt gave him that convinced him this was real. He found something I didn't, maybe. Some record, or some evidence, something."

"I don't know," Nick said. "Remember, he faked up an appraisal for you, so he could have faked this up, too. For all I know he's got a letter from Richard Nixon about what a completely real Kittery duck this is, but he made it in Microsoft Paint and misspelled 'Richard Nixon.'"

"But he gave him something," Laurie said. "He definitely gave him something."

At the end of the debriefing, Nick turned to Laurie and took a breath. "So," he said. "What now?"

Laurie swirled the red wine in the bottom of her glass and

tapped her finger against the side. "I'm starting to put something together in my head. Just starting. But as good as all of you are, I think I need a little bit more help."

"What kind of help?" Daisy asked.

"The kind I'm related to."

Chapter Fifteen

Laurie was one sister to four brothers, and she believed that made her position among her siblings the worst. But Ryan had always insisted that, actually, being the youngest was the worst. At least she was smack in the middle, where she had siblings she outranked instead of exclusively people who outranked her. "I was on the end," he'd once told her. And she asked on the end of what, and he said on the end of everything.

Their house had had only three real bedrooms, so for a good stretch of Laurie's childhood, all four boys had shared a large room with two sets of bunk beds, and Laurie had one all to herself. This engendered no shortage of resentment on the part of her brothers until an attic room was added for Patrick and Scott, and then eventually, the basement was (mostly) finished and Ryan moved down there. But the truth was that when they were young, she would sit in her reading chair or lie in bed at night and hear the four of them talking, or playing Uno, or playing with the handheld games they fought over constantly, and she would desperately want to block out all the noise while simultaneously wondering what it would be like to be in the middle of all that. She rarely got to spend a lot of time with any of her brothers by themselves; so much of the time, they traveled in pairs, or in a pack, when they weren't running in or out the door with friends or dates or hockey sticks.

But all the kids used one bathroom, sat around one table, fought over one set of leftovers, and sometimes rode in one minivan. Four boys were an often unmanageable cacophony for a girl who was mostly an enthusiastic reader. Scott's mood was unpredictable because of what their mother called his "temperament," which Laurie now knew had more to do with depression and ADHD and some other things it had taken until adulthood for him to treat. He never hurt anybody except himself, but he would rage and cry and with some of his first full sentences tell people he hated them. Patrick was the oldest; he tried to be in charge. Joey was between Laurie and Ryan; he tried to be charming. Ryan just tried not to be last all the time.

He was pursuing a girl in tenth grade when he tried out for the high school production of *Bye Bye Birdie*. He thought it would be fun to be part of a group, part of a dancing crowd onstage in matching costumes, and maybe to spend a lot of extra time around Lorelai Page, the killer mezzo-soprano of Calcasset High. From when he was little, singing Christmas carols in the backseat of his parents' car, Ryan had been told that he had a very nice singing voice. And from when he was a little older, doing puppet shows behind the couch with socks on his hands, he had been told that he was a ham. And so, only partly because trying to get teenage boys at small schools in some communities to audition for musicals can be a grind on par with climbing K2, Ryan found himself cast as Conrad Birdie, the Elvis-like figure who hypnotizes a small town with his rock-and-roll stylings and brings down the house—pretty much always—singing "Honestly Sincere."

One of the mothers—someone's wonderful mother, they didn't remember anymore whose mother—sewed him a jumpsuit out of shiny gold fabric that gave him a pronounced ass and a bit of a rash. But it didn't matter. He had scraggly grunge hair then, and one of the girls in the chorus helped put gel in it until it stood up six inches. He learned how to throw his hip out to the side when he said, "Suffer!," and all the parents laughed, and the girls screamed, and it was only partly a bit. When the song was over, the entire cast playing the townspeople would be flat on their backs on the stage, having fainted from Conrad's sheer charisma. And at every one of the three performances—Friday night, Saturday night, and a Sunday matinee—the ovation was so overwhelming that it took quite a while to get the show back on track. At least this was how Laurie's entire family remembered it.

Laurie was a year into college then, but she was home on break and she went to all three shows. When he got home the first night, Ryan knocked on the door of her room. He thanked her for coming. "I'm your sister," she said. "Of course I'm going to come, dummy. Did you have fun?"

He looked at her with such utter seriousness that she almost thought something might be wrong. But nothing was. He said, "Laurie, they screamed."

"I know," she said. "I was there."

"Not the people in the show," he said. "The audience. They screamed."

She nodded. "I know."

His eyes widened. "It was the best thing that's ever happened to me."

To say he never looked back would cover only part of it. He never looked up, down, over, under, anywhere except at stages to leap onto.

He played Tony in *West Side Story* and one of the jurors in *Twelve Angry Men* before he graduated, and in college, he studied Shakespeare and Pinter and Beckett, and he played Torvald in *A Doll's House* and Herod in *Jesus Christ Superstar* (in which he wore red satin pajamas). He played Ado Andy in a cross-cast production of *Oklahoma!* directed by his roommate. Their mother used to say, "Point him at anything where people clap for you, and off he goes."

New York had not gone well at first. He was broke, working several jobs that were not acting, living in a series of roach-filled apartments with weird roommates, and constantly flirting with abandoning acting and becoming an English teacher (the irony was not lost on people who had first seen him in *Bye Bye Birdie*). But then he was cast on one of the *Law & Orders*, playing a waiter who isn't a murderer, and then he was cast on another one of the *Law & Orders*, playing a bartender who *is* a murderer. It got a little bit easier. A series of ads for a bank put some money in his pocket. He played a congressional aide in two episodes of *Halls of Power,* a raucous political soap that had run for seven seasons and killed off half its original cast.

By the time Laurie FaceTimed him from Dot's house, he'd done a decent amount of recent theater work and completed a short run in an off-Broadway play. He was between jobs, and his wife was part of a Broadway costume department for the first time. When he answered the call, Laurie was sitting at Dot's dining room table in front of her laptop, and he was sitting on the sofa in his apartment, looking at his phone. "Hey," she said, smiling as the video connection stabilized.

"Hey, Laur," he said. "How's it going up there?"

She shrugged. "The same."

"I heard you saw Nick."

"For heaven's sake, where did you hear that? Who is *talking* about this?"

"I heard it from Mom, and I think Scott had a text from one of Nick's cousins."

"There are way too many people in this town for a town with so few people in it. How are you?"

"I'm good, I'm good." Just then, Lisa crossed behind him, carrying a garbage bag toward their front door. "You need me to take that, babe?" he asked.

"No, thank you," she said. "Hi, Laurie," she called out as she disappeared from view. "I'm making a glamorous trip to the trash chute, back in a minute."

"Tell me how it goes," Laurie called back. "Are you working?" she asked Ryan.

He nodded. "Not this second, but in a couple of weeks I'm doing something, and I'm up for a few new things that might pan out. One small TV thing on a show you don't watch."

"Well, then," she said. "You're free over the next couple weeks, possibly?"

He raised his eyebrows. "Do you need something?"

She was getting pretty good at the short version: *Found a duck, might be important, guy ripped me off and stole it, I'm trying to get it back.* She gave it to him in as few words as she could manage, and by the time she was done, Lisa was back and sat on the couch next to Ryan, waving. "I'm back!"

"I was just telling my brother I might need to borrow him for a little while."

"For what?"

Found a duck, might be important, guy ripped me off and stole it, I'm trying to get it back. "So," Laurie finished, "I have a plan to get it back, I think. I think. And Nick's helping me, and June's helping me. Daisy, who works at his store. Possibly other people. But I could use your particular genius."

"What do I have to do?"

"Well," she said, "it's a little bit hard to explain. I'm trying to figure out a way to get hold of the duck . . . through various methods. It's kind of a complicated thing. It's just, he has this thing, or his guy has it, and I'm trying to get it, and—"

"It's a heist!" Lisa said, bouncing up and down with excitement. "You're doing a heist!"

"I guess that would be one way to put it."

"Heist!" Lisa repeated. She started clapping her hands. "Heist! Heist! Heist!"

"I have to tell you, Laur," Ryan said, "it kinda sounds . . . heist-y."

Laurie nodded. "Okay. Well, either way, can you come up on Tuesday? Maybe stay until Friday or so?"

"For the heist! The weekday heist!" Lisa contributed, and Ryan and Laurie both laughed, because how could you not?

"You can come with him if you want, Lis. I'd love to see you."

"You know I don't go places where I singlehandedly increase the Black population by more than ten percent," she said. "But you better keep me updated. This is very exciting. And if you don't let Ryan wear a costume and take a picture of it, I might not forgive either one of you."

Chapter Sixteen

Ryan's plane was already going to be late, and then it arrived late, and it was almost not worth anyone dragging themselves over to the house to say hello. But when Laurie got him back to Dot's at 10:30 on Tuesday night, they found that Nick and June had both come in the unlocked back door just as they'd been invited to do, and were sitting at the kitchen table, sharing a sleeve of Girl Scout cookies. "Can't resist the Thin Mints, huh?" Laurie asked as she slung her purse onto a hook by the door.

"They set up outside the library every single year," Nick said as he pushed his chair back. "I'm helpless." He put out his hand and took Ryan's, and then they pulled each other in. "Good to see you," Nick said.

"I love a bro hug!" June cooed, and then she hugged the thirty-six-year-old actor, now handsome and married, who had had the most devastating crush on her when she was eighteen and he was fourteen.

He just said, over her shoulder, "Junie."

Dot's square kitchen table now seemed like it had four sturdy chairs in it specifically for this night, for this reunion between these four people who had not all been in the same room at an event that was not a wedding full of strangers for close to twenty years. Laurie sat directly across from Nick, and if asked, she would have denied that it was so she could look at him while she drank her iced tea. Ryan had a pack of gum in his hands and he kept turning it over and over, end to end, fiddling with it on the table, as he told them about the TV job he was auditioning for and the play he was hoping to star in that his friend was writing. "And of course," he said, "we're trying to have a baby on top of everything else."

"Oh boy," June said sympathetically. "How's that going, bub?"

"Right now," he said, "it's not really going. We're trying to figure out whether we're doing one more IVF round or not."

"What's that going to come down to?" Laurie asked.

"Whether Lisa wants to go through it and whether she wants to take any more money from her parents," he said. "It's the hardest goddamn thing. I don't know how much you guys know about this, but it's this series of, like, gambles where the odds keep getting worse. It's basically like you start with twenty-five coins and three have to come up heads, and it sounds like it could happen. But then they keep checking and checking, and you're down to fifteen coins, then ten, then eight, and then it's just . . . you know, 'Sorry, you're out of coins.' And she's getting shots and taking meds to keep things from happening too soon or too late or too much or not enough. And I don't have to do anything I haven't been doing since I was twelve, but she's sobbing and she's miserable half the time and she feels sick and hot, and I don't know if she wants to do it again."

June shook her head. "I don't blame her. Being pregnant isn't a laugh riot, and going through all this just to get to it, I can't imagine."

They were across from each other, and Laurie could see this thread stretching between them, even though June had kids and Ryan didn't yet. They were baby people, or wanting-a-baby people. They weren't baby-centric, but they were . . . baby-forward.

June had gotten pregnant easily every time she'd tried, but if she hadn't, Laurie felt sure she would have done this, too. The shots, the pills, the crying, whatever it was. June had been talking about having kids since she was old enough to know what it meant. She always wanted to hold babies and play with toddlers and baby-sit relatives. She never talked about when she would eventually get married to Charlie or what she would do about work without talking about how it would affect the kids she didn't even have yet. The first thing she told Laurie about Charlie that meant for sure that she was serious about him was that she'd watched him lean down to gently zip up his nephew's hoodie, and she'd felt like she was watching her future.

"Man, that's a lot," Nick said. "Becca and I didn't have kids, but we just . . . didn't have them, you know? I always felt like if we did it was fine, if we didn't it was fine. I think we thought we would. But we just had other things going on, and we put it off a few times, and then by the time we were done putting it off, we were getting divorced."

"Are you glad you didn't?" Ryan asked.

"Have kids?" Nick paused. "I was glad when we were getting divorced that we didn't have kids, yes. It certainly makes it easier. Not easier—simpler. It's one less thing. It's a completely different ball of wax getting divorced if you have kids. You get divorced with no kids, it's like . . . if you want, you just take your stuff and she takes her stuff and you go. Obviously, it's a lot more complicated than that in your head, but a week after you're divorced, you can choose to almost not have ever been married, you know what I mean? Which is easier, but also really weird."

"I used to worry so much about what would happen if we ever broke up," June said. "Especially since my kids are close together, when Tommy was a baby and Bethie was really little, I used to imagine myself trying to take care of both of them without Charlie. There was a night when he was out playing beer-league softball and he got in this home-plate collision, and his friends took him to the hospital. And I knew he would probably be fine, which he was, but there was this moment when I was waiting for him to get home and thinking, 'I have a three-month-old and a two-year-old. If something happened to him, what exactly would I do?' And it wasn't that big of a deal, obviously, but once I went down that road, I started thinking about what would happen if we broke up. I guess to me, we were less likely to survive being married to each other than he was to survive beer-league softball." She turned to Laurie. "I'm telling you, there's something to be said for deciding not to get married."

Laurie went around the table in her head. *Married, used to be married, married, and me.* "I don't think you mean that at all," she said. "I don't think any married people mean that. I've never met a married person who would tell anybody as a general principle not to get married, except, like, Andy Capp. Or Tim Allen."

"Andy Capp from the cheese fries?" Ryan asked.

"Well, yes, but not because of the cheese fries," Laurie said. "He had a comic strip before he was a mascot."

"A comic strip about what?"

"About how he didn't like his wife," she said. "I think the only person who's really happy I decided not to get married is Erin, my friend back home who's engaged. Her wedding is in a month, and her cat destroyed her dress."

"I don't understand what this has to do with you not getting married," Nick said.

"Remember I told you I had no choice but to keep the dress I had paid for? Well, Erin and I have very similar taste and wear basically the same size, plus or minus some alterations, so as we speak, she's retrieving it from my house, and she's going to wear it. It is hers to have and to hold, to give to her descendants, forever after."

"You gave away your dress?" Nick said.

"Yes. She needed it, and I don't."

"I guess not," he said, almost defensive, almost as if she'd insulted him to his face.

"You were happier when I said I was going to be buried in it," she said.

"I absolutely wasn't," Nick answered.

"Well, nevertheless. I decided not to marry Chris, and so now I don't have to be a supporting character in any dude's sitcom or comic strip."

"Or a brand of cheese fries," Nick offered.

"Precisely. Single lady house, single lady rules."

"You really brought the 'when I live by myself' ethos with you right up to now, didn't you?" A little smile brightened Ryan's eyes.

"What do you mean?"

He laughed. "You were designing your dream house when I was fantasizing about making the NBA. I didn't think I was even going to be allowed to visit you. When you left for college, I thought, you know, I hope she comes back home sometimes, because I don't think I'm going to be invited over."

"You thought you were going to play in the NBA?" June asked.

"Hey, we all had dreams," he said. "I wanted to be taller, and Laurie wanted a private villa made to her specifications where nobody would bug her."

"Well," Laurie said, "when Nick and I were locked in the office closet at the antiques shop, we heard Matt tell his buddy I was lonely and neglected and I would probably die alone in Dot's house, so if I cross my fingers, I might just get that ending after all."

When they debriefed about the meeting in the office and about hiding in the closet, they had not included this. Nick had yet to acknowledge out loud that he'd even heard it. One night, Laurie had lain on her back in one of the deck chairs and looked up at the stars and thought and thought and thought about it, writing comebacks in her head. She wrote stinging rejoinders about how Matt didn't know her and he didn't know what she wanted and it wasn't a matter of a lack of attention, because she could be married right now if she'd wanted to. She thought about how she could have thrown the closet door open and told him all about it. She had sat with the sensation of that moment, of what it was like being stuffed into a closet with Nick's sympathy—or maybe pity—until the memory stopped feeling like it was covered with thorns. Now his little jab at her meant much less; it was just a piece of a story, a story about Bad Matt, about a cheap con. But they all got pretty quiet when she mentioned it, and how quiet it got made it feel thornier again.

"Well, to hell with that guy," Ryan finally said. "We're getting back our duck."

They all stayed at the table for about another half hour. It was so late, but this mix of laughs was like a song she hadn't heard in years, and Laurie just wanted to keep hearing and hearing it. Still, eventually, June put her water glass in the sink, and Nick stretched his arms, and Ryan said he should probably get to bed. "Fortunately," Laurie said, "Dot's got five bedrooms, and two of them are cleaned out with almost no boxes left in them, so you should be able to get a good night's sleep without worrying that you're going to trip on something if you have to get up in the middle of the night." She gestured toward the stairs. "You're in the blue room where the rocking chair is."

Ryan nodded and yawned. "All right, I'm off to sleep, friends. I'll see you all very soon, I'm sure." And with a wave, he vanished down the hall, a duffel bouncing on his shoulder that read *Clone of Kong 2: Aped Again*. Straight to video, that one.

June left too, and then it was just Nick, standing in the kitchen doorway in his jacket, hesitating like he had when they were kids, when he wasn't ready to go, when he wanted to kiss her good night or kiss her good night again. It was on one of those occasions, two months before high school graduation, when he had eventually squared his shoulders and said, "I love you, Laurie," to which she had said, "I love you, too," and then he had slipped out the door and into his 1992 Honda Accord, the chosen transportation of so many great lovers through the ages.

This time, he didn't say that. He considered her, though, for so long that she walked over toward him, less like she knew what she would do when she got there and more like she was stepping into a circle he'd drawn on the floor. When she was close, he finally said, "Just so you know, that guy could be married, or in a club—hell, that guy could be in the middle of Mardi Gras, and he would still be alone. And you could float on a piece of ice at the South Pole, and you wouldn't be."

She thought about being in that closet with him, listening for his breathing, feeling his hand on her elbow in the dark. She thought about the first time they'd ever kissed for real, not over somebody else's sink but in the upstairs library at Ginger's during Nick's mother's birthday party. It had been the middle of the afternoon, with light coming in the windows from every direction. They'd sneaked up there with pieces of cake on paper plates, because everybody downstairs was impossibly old—though in many cases younger than they were now, of course. And sitting in the library, on the love seat in front of one of the tall shelves, they had kissed, still holding their plates in their laps, jumping apart when Nick's dad's voice carried up the stairs: "Nick, are you up there? We're giving Mom her presents."

So now here they were, in the doorway to Dot's kitchen, again sheltered by a woman who had been decades older than they were, who had made a home for herself. "Nick," she said. "Thank you."

He lifted his hand and tucked a piece of her hair behind her ear. "I always think about doing that," he said. "Whenever I see you."

"Because my hair is in my face?" She smiled.

"Because I haven't touched your hair in a really long time," he said.

She bit her lip, closed her eyes. Opened them again, and he was still there. She looked up at him and arched her eyebrow. "You better go. Unless you're going to come back in."

He broke into a grin and looked at the ground, nodding. "Your brother's in there."

"He is," she said.

"Should've gotten you to throw me down on the reference desk," he said. "I guess I missed my moment."

She shrugged. "You've got to stay sharp, Cooper. You never know when you might get another one."

The answer, of course, was *whenever you want one,* but that was hard to say out loud.

Chapter Seventeen

want my name to be, like . . . Bob Wanamaker." Ryan was gulping a cup of coffee the next morning on the deck as Laurie nibbled a cranberry scone and sorted another box of Polaroids.

"No," she said.

"Why not?"

"Because," she said, "this is not an episode of *Mad Men* and you are not the fictional president of Coca-Cola. You're just a guy who knows a guy. You're like him. Like Matt. And Bob Wanamaker doesn't sound like him; Bob Wanamaker sounds like his landlord. Or his landlord's landlord."

"How about Mutt? Mutt McClain? Mutt McClain, just your basic guy."

"That sounds like the star of a videogame. A kids' videogame where you're a detective. A dog detective. *Mutt McClain, Dog Detective,* rated E for Everyone."

"How about . . . Dave?" he said.

She looked up from her photos and narrowed her eyes. "Dave what?"

He looked up at the ceiling for a minute, then back at her. "Dave 'Hot Rod' Davington. They call him 'Danger Dave.'"

She swallowed a bite of her scone and nodded. "His name is Dave Davington, and his nickname is Hot Rod, and they also call him Danger Dave. So Danger Dave 'Hot Rod' Davington, that's your inconspicuous undercover identity."

Ryan spread his arms wide. "I think it's beautiful. I think it works."

"I'm naming you John. John No Last Name."

He sighed. "You're not making it very easy to get into this role."

"I'm just hoping he doesn't recognize you. Hopefully he doesn't watch *Law & Order* or *Halls of Power*."

"Or well-reviewed off-Broadway theater," Ryan said. Then he waved his hand. "Nothing to worry about. The closest I come to being recognized is that somebody thinks they knew me in college or I used to date their sister or something. My agent told me once, 'You have a face people can't imagine they haven't already seen.'"

Laurie looked at him. "That's awful."

He shrugged. "I'm like the weighted average of all the white dudes in New York who sometimes get work on TV. So when people try to remember who I am, they always slowly realize they're think-ing of somebody else. Sometimes they think I'm from *Suits,* that show Meghan Markle was on. What's amazing is that there are two guys from *Suits,* and people think I'm both of them. That's Holly-wood for you."

"Wow."

"Yeah. I mean, there are white dudes they know I'm not—they know I'm not, you know, Richard Kind. I'm not Paul Rudd. I'm just in there somewhere. The good part is that casting directors do it too. Intellectually, they're looking at my résumé and they know I'm not the person they're thinking of, but at some level, I *am* the person they're thinking of. And I'd love to be precious about my individuality, but I work a lot more than I would if I were not a guy people think they must have already seen on TV."

"For this," Laurie said, "I just want you to be blank. A big old blank slate. I don't want there to be any chance he's going to remember you. So you have to take your beautiful personality and pretty much stuff it in a suitcase," she said.

"Can I wear a hat?" he asked.

"Oh for God's sake, Ryan."

"Not a propeller beanie or anything. Like a regular hat. Just a hat. A Red Sox hat."

"You're going to wear a *Red Sox* hat? Isn't your scalp going to burst into flames?" He had switched allegiances after he moved to New York and fell in love with Lisa. It had been quite a conversation with their father.

"It's for a part," he said. "Other people lose eighty pounds or grow a beard; I can wear a Sox hat."

She eyed him warily. "Okay. John No Last Name can wear a Sox hat. He probably stole it." Just then, Laurie's phone pinged and she looked down to see a message from Matt.

Just wondering if you've had a chance to grab those letters. Still would love to take a look.

She groaned. "This guy."

"What?"

"Well, like I told you, I got him to come over to the house by telling him this story about finding these letters to Dot. I didn't really think about it beyond that. But now he's, like, obsessed with them, and he wants to see them, and I think I might have done a little bit too good of a job convincing him that I wanted his help and that he could definitely, absolutely rob me again. And he's very excited about it."

"So you're assuming he has not seen the Melissa McCarthy movie with the forged letters."

"I'm hoping he hasn't. I'm not sure he watches a lot of great women directors, plus I doubt he can fit it into his busy schedule of rewatching the special features on his *Joker* Blu-ray."

"As long as we're talking about fakes," he said, "what do you think our odds are here, assuming we get this back? Do you think Dot would have had some expensive thing in her house and she wouldn't have told us? She wouldn't have mentioned it in her will, or told anybody where or what it was? I'm not sure why she would do that. And I guess I don't want you to be upset if . . . if it turns out it's just a thing she had." He looked down into his coffee cup.

"I don't know," Laurie said. "But there's a story about this thing. I think she knew this guy, Kittery. Ginger said something the other day, and I just—I just think she knew him, maybe."

"And what if she did?"

"Well, what if this was a present from him? What if she really cared about him and this was what he gave her? I don't even care whether it's worth money, but if this was important to her, I want us to know the story."

Ryan thought about things in a very particular way. It was why he was a good actor. He could see in a lot of directions, Lisa always said. She said if he saw two people bump into each other going through the door of a coffee shop, he could understand how it felt for both of them. "Maybe she didn't want us to know," he said. "Or she would have told us."

Laurie felt the breeze getting a little warmer on her cheek. "Look, you put on a Sox hat and you want to be Bob Wanamaker. I try to figure out what happened," she said. "It's what I do, you know? I want to know why this bird doesn't live by this pond anymore, or why these wolves stopped coming back to this park, or why this flower died off. I don't want people to think she just took pictures of things. I don't want them to think she just stood outside of every-thing and watched and clicked her camera. I want to know what happened."

He nodded. "Okay. Fair enough." She was struck by the ease in him. He'd been skinny, really skinny, when he was younger. She used to say he had the A body and she had the B body in the family, and everybody else was somewhere in between. He'd had elbows with sharp corners like he was made out of Popsicle sticks. Now he was different. He went to the gym, which he said was a work requirement—which he wrote off on his taxes. He always had pro-level haircuts, and Lisa kept him in sharp ensembles, sometimes tweaking and tailoring for him. He was a good-looking kid, that was what people would say about him. He was a good-looking kid. He smiled at her. "If you say it's important, then we're going to get it back in your hands. I'm on board."

"Thank you."

"Can I ask you one other thing?" He paused for only a second. "I hear everything you're saying. But do you also want to get this thing back because you want to stick it to the asshole who took it away from you? Because if that's what this is about," he said as he put on his sunglasses against the morning glare, "then I'm really, *really* on board."

He had never gotten over the feeling of that shiny gold suit.

Chapter Eighteen

Rocky's last name was Sapwell.

This had not been hard to learn; would that everyone a reporter ever needed to track down was named Rocky and lived in a small town known for hooked rugs and its toy museum. Nick found him in about five minutes, smiling out from a Facebook profile that listed him as a "collectibles dealer" who lived in Waldoboro. When he sent the page to June and Daisy, both of whom had seen the guy while Nick and Laurie were breathing on each other in the closet, they said yes, that was him.

While Rocky's personal page was mostly private, he also had a business page under the name Fine Goods by Rock. There, he posted—or someone did—photos of quilts and vases, dolls and lamps and pitchers. There were before-and-after shots of a dresser he'd restored, and three days ago, this: "FGBR will be in Damariscotta this Thursday, joining forces with some of our faves at the Vintage Pop-Up at St. Mark's Church on Fairfield. Drop by to check out jewelry, textiles, small decorative items, and trading cards!"

"More freaking trading cards," Laurie had muttered when Nick sent her a screenshot.

There was never really a question that Laurie and Ryan would go together. She would have to stay out of the way, because she assumed it was possible that during some conversation she hadn't observed, Matt had told Rocky more about her or even explained who she was. Every avoidable risk was to be avoided, so Ryan and Laurie agreed that she wouldn't get too close.

"How am I going to know what's going on, though?" she said.

"You don't trust me?"

"Of course I trust you," she said. "That doesn't mean I don't want to know what's going on."

It was June who suggested the phone, while they were conducting a strategy session via FaceTime. The ubiquity of the Bluetooth earpiece—and especially the Bluetooth earpiece worn by an earpiece guy who didn't seem to have a reason to wear one—meant that Ryan and Laurie could surreptitiously be on the phone, him with a Bluetooth and her with her earbuds plugged into her phone, and nobody would know she was listening in. Asked where she got this idea, June admitted she got it from Jim and Pam on *The Office*. "That's a fictional show," Ryan said.

"Based on real phones," June said. "Also," she added, "Laurie should wear some big sunglasses or something."

"You are getting carried away," Laurie told her.

"No, she's right," Ryan said. "I'm going to be John No Last Name, and you're going to be . . . Big Sunglasses Instagram Mom."

"I have no idea what that means."

"Oh, I do," June said. And by that afternoon, she'd made a delivery of a large straw tote. Inside it were the aforementioned big sunglasses, a large-brimmed sun hat, a water bottle with the words

I WISH THIS WERE WINE stenciled on it ("It was a gift from my cousin," June said with an eye-roll), and a rhinestone iPhone case.

On Thursday morning, Laurie put on a yellow sundress and packed up the rest of her gear in the tote. When she came out to the kitchen, Ryan was there in his khakis and a plain white T-shirt. "I have to admit," she said, "you really look like a John No Last Name."

He whipped off his shades. "Just John. No interests. No history. No connections. Just a taste for vengeance."

"It's perfect."

Laurie drove her rented Civic. It took about forty-five minutes to get to Damariscotta following the curve of Route 1 as it wove around ponds and through quiet towns you could be into and out of within a few short blocks. "Does being back make you miss it here?" Ryan asked her.

"It makes me wish I visited more," she said. "You?"

He adjusted the vent so the AC was blowing more directly on him. "I don't think I appreciated it at all. That you could drive out and be by the water or get in a boat and be on the water, or . . . you know, when I was fourteen and I was playing basketball against Freeport, it's not like I thought about the fact that people literally took vacations here, just to be here."

"People take vacations to New York too, though," Laurie said.

"They do. But the people in New York know that, you know? But yeah, when I come back up here, I feel like I'm eating a really good sandwich I stopped tasting because I ate it every day."

"You like New York still?" she asked.

"Oh hell yes," he said. "I finally figured it out. The city. It's like a huge amusement park where you only want to go on a few of the rides, and you have to figure out how to get to just those things and where the bathroom is and how not to waste your time standing in all the lines for stuff you hate. Do you like Seattle? Are you used to the weather?"

Laurie let out a little sigh. "People think it rains so much more than it does. It doesn't pour all the time or anything. It's just gray for six months out of the year. But I can be in a gorge, or at the coast, or in the woods, or at a waterfall, you know, without doing more than a day trip. And I still get to be in a city where there's plenty of theater and music and more than three escalators. I get to know that I'm not going to run into people I know every time I go out to buy a bottle of wine."

"I'm sorry I haven't been out more since you bought the house."

She shrugged. "That's okay. You've been busy, you're working, and I've made it to where you are a handful of times, so I get it."

"Do you miss it?"

"My house? I do. I have the kitchen how I want it, I have the yard how I want it, I have everything where I want it. And not for nothing, I don't live around five hundred boxes of somebody else's stuff."

"Would you ever come back here?" Ryan looked over at her. "It seems like you're having fun seeing Nick."

She shook her head. "I told him I'm going home when this is over. I think he sees me here, he sees me in Dot's house. He envisions it, maybe. Or he did, for a second." She sighed. "I don't know. We like each other. But we always liked each other."

They'd been lying on their backs, on a blanket in the grass at Cobble Creek Park, talking about fall break, when she finally stopped rehearsing it in her head and just said, "I think we have to break up." It was fast after that; she didn't even say most of what she'd planned. She just got it over with. She had said she wanted to be friends—a hedge against a bone-deep terror at the thought of not talking to him practically every day. She didn't know at twenty that being friends was going to be impossible. He took her home. In the car outside her house, she asked if he wanted his hoodie back and his books. He said he guessed so, and two days later, she left them in a box on his porch when she knew he was at work.

They bumped into each other twice between that day and the day she went back to school, and both times they didn't talk, and both times, she came home after and went straight to bed and didn't come out of her room, even though the first time, it was three in the afternoon.

"We're here," she said to Ryan, pointing to a white church with a signboard out front that said POP-UP ANTIQUES EVENT!!! and, under that, TRUST IN GOD, AND NOT JUST ON SUNDAYS. There were cars parked on both sides of the street while tables, some of them with tents protecting them from the sun, ringed the parking lot. She parked a couple blocks down, and when she turned off the car, she faced her brother. "Remember, you don't have to be fancy. Ideally, we're going to get in and get out of this today. Don't make it more complicated than it has to be. Don't tell him anything he doesn't ask. This is only going to work if it's fast."

"Don't worry," he said. "I've got you."

"You still don't know what Matt gave him. You're going to have to think on your feet a little."

"Listen, whatever Garbage Dude came up with, I'm ready to deal with it."

"And you have the paper?"

"In my back pocket," he said. "Don't worry." He tucked his Bluetooth earpiece into his ear and slipped on his Red Sox hat. "I'll call you. Give me two minutes, then you can follow."

"Good luck," she said. "And thank you."

He grinned. "You're welcome. We never get to have fun together anymore."

Laurie watched as Ryan went up the sidewalk and then ambled

into the parking lot. He started to look at one of the tables, and then she saw him take out his phone and step away, looking down like he was texting. Her phone lit up with his picture, and she answered. "Hello, Snoopy to Pop Tart," he said. "This is Snoopy to Pop Tart, come in Pop Tart," he said quietly.

"Okay, settle down," she said. "I'm coming over."

It was hot, and June had confirmed her sundress was very Instagram Mom. She slid the huge tortoiseshell sunglasses on, but she had to step out of the car before she could add the enormous hat. With the tote over her left forearm and the rhinestone water bottle in her right hand, she started toward the parking lot.

"Antiques" did not mean only "antiques," it turned out. Or, at least, not what she would have considered antiques. There were not one but two entire tables of trading cards, one of which was exclusively basketball, and one guy had boxes and boxes of old magazines. As Laurie passed his table, he unloaded five years of *National Geographic* to a guy in khaki shorts, a black Metallica shirt, and a cowboy hat. She was hyper-casually eyeballing a display of vinyl records when she heard Ryan's voice in her earbuds.

"Hey, good morning," he said. "How's it going?"

It was a little bit hard to hear the guy in the background. But, as they'd hoped, it wasn't too hard. "Going great, let me know if you have any questions."

"Nope, that's not him," Laurie said softly. They had seen a couple of pictures of Rocky, but they were blurry to varying degrees, and most of the guys here had caps and sunglasses. But Laurie knew she'd recognize Rocky when she heard his voice. That, she had experience with. Ryan made a couple of minutes of conversation with Not Rocky about what sounded like a collection of belt buckles—Laurie was afraid to lift her head and look over, even though he was only a few tables away—and then he moved on.

"Hey," he said again. "Good morning, how's it going?"

"It's going good, man, thanks for coming out."

"That's him," she said toward the ground. "That's Rocky."

She knew she should stay farther back, but she turned and walked over toward the table next to Rocky's, directing her face resolutely away from him and trying to look like she didn't want anyone else to try to strike up a conversation either. Just as she got near, she heard Ryan say, "Can we talk somewhere? I have a question that's kind of sensitive." They'd figured Rocky was used to this, that people would constantly want to tell him in secret about something they had in their attic or their car that they thought might be *so* valuable that they didn't even want to speak of it in the presence of random people walking around a public event.

"Sure," Rocky said. "Angie, I'm taking a second, keep an eye out."

Even criminals have women to keep an eye out.

Out of the corner of her eye, she saw him walk with Ryan over toward a big black pickup truck with a decal on the side that said FINE GOODS BY ROCK. They leaned on the truck. Laurie started picking up and putting down a series of Precious Moments figurines.

"So what's up, how can I help?" Rocky asked.

"My name's John." Yep, that was him. John No Last Name.

"Hey, John."

"And I think we know somebody in common," Ryan said. "You know Matt Pell?"

"Yeah, he's got a store in Camden. We've done some work together."

"Well, he and I have done some work together, too." Laurie held her breath. Baby figurine. Angel figurine. Figurine with a little sheep. This pause was long. Uncomfortably long. Glacially long.

"Have we met before?" Rocky said. "Did you grow up around here?"

Didn't I know you in college? Didn't you date my sister?

"No," Ryan said.

"I could have sworn. Like, I've seen you."

"I just have one of those faces."

"You're sure we've never met?"

"Sometimes people think I look like the guy from *Suits*."

Another pause. "Oh yeah. I think that's it."

Laurie tried, but couldn't help it: She coughed with her fist over her mouth so that nobody could see her trying not to smile. But of course, this was the extremely easy part.

"So," Rocky said in his slightly muffled voice, "you know Matt."

"Right. I think he gave you a piece. A duck. Yeah? A Kittery."

"Let's say he did."

Laurie flicked her eyes over and saw Ryan turn to face Rocky as he leaned on the truck. "He's full of shit," Ryan said.

"That's often the case, yeah."

"He's specifically full of shit about this. He and I dummied up that duck. It's a fake. We found it, we thought it might be a Kittery, but it wasn't. So we did some work on it until it looked like it was. We were supposed to be going fifty-fifty."

Rocky put his hands on his hips. "What happened?"

"I got nervous. I told him I thought we needed to lower the expectations, sell it as a nice piece but not a Kittery. Too much money involved, too complicated. I didn't want to pursue it, you know? Because it was kind of fraud?"

"Ah, shit," Rocky muttered.

"He didn't want to hear it. We had a big fight about it, and he told me we could talk about it again and figure out what to do. Next thing I hear is that he's trying to sell it through you. And he's cutting me out."

"He showed me proof, though. Pretty solid."

Laurie's heart sped up. She could feel a crackle in her skin.

"What did he show you, exactly?"

"Hang on."

Laurie watched as Rocky went around the side of the truck, opened the passenger door, and leaned in. He looked like he was opening the glove box, and when he got back to Ryan, he was holding an envelope, which Ryan opened. "Wow."

He couldn't say, *Wow, look at this certificate of authenticity and photograph of Carl Kittery carving this specific duck?* He couldn't say, *Wow, look at this letter from the Bar Harbor Historical Society?* He couldn't even give her a hint? Just "wow"?

"Wow is right," Rocky said. "That's the contract to do the clean-out on the lady's house. And in the picture, that's the lady. That's according to the letter."

The lady, the picture, the letter?

"Yeah, he told me he was going to do this, but I wasn't sure he really would. I have bad news," Ryan said in a dry voice that seemed barely his. "There's no lady. I mean, there is a lady, and he cleaned out her house. But that's not where he got it. It didn't belong to her. We found it, we fixed it up, we tried to sell it. She didn't have anything to do with it."

Thank God, Laurie thought. *This is one of the things we were ready for.*

"So he just happened to clean out her house?"

"No," Ryan said. "He was looking for somebody who would be believable. Believable as somebody who might have had this thing all these years without anybody knowing. He was looking for, you know, a spinster. Found this lady, got hold of some of her pictures, the rest is history."

Spinster. Even as a line, Laurie hated it.

"And he faked the letter."

"Yes. Contract's real, lady's real, letter's fake, picture's just him watching a lot of YouTube videos about compositing in Photoshop." Ryan reached into his back pocket and pulled out a folded piece of paper. And even though she couldn't see it, Laurie knew that at the top, it said, in blue letters, WESSON & TRUITT. "Appraisers knew what this thing was right away. Didn't fool them at all, even though we'd tried to jazz it up."

> Wood duck decoy, approximately 2008. Produced in bulk in the style of Carl Kittery and distributed to museum and souvenir shops as part of a promotion commemorating the history of American folk art. Also sold at traveler locations including Logan Airport. Original sale price approximately $25.99. Current value similar. Many examples available through online auction sites and estate sales, selling for approximately $30.00. Further appraisal not necessary or recommended.

Laurie could see Rocky reading the letter and shaking his head. Getting rid of the lorem ipsum and the dummy text at the bottom had been as simple as Nick putting an index card over it when he copied it behind the reference desk.

"He set me up. He knew we might get caught, and he set me up."

"Look, I told you, he's not a genius. He just holds his breath and hopes he can sell something for a ton of money without anybody getting it appraised. He doesn't know what the hell he's doing, you know that. You have to know that. He's faking his way through it, which is what he's been trying to do from the beginning. He's just a bullshitter."

"Why are you telling me this? Why didn't you just go to him?"

"Because fuck him, that's why. He would've told me a dog ate it. And also because . . . I might have a buyer for it."

Rocky laughed. "After all this, you want to sell it."

"Not like he does. Not for a hundred grand. Just to the grandson of a nice rich lady who thinks it will remind her of her late husband. He's going to give me six thousand dollars. And instead of getting a measly bite of a bunch of money that's not coming and maybe going to jail for fraud, you'll get half of six thousand real dollars. But it has to be now, because that's when he wants it."

"How do I know this is even true? How do I know you're not just trying to get it away from me?"

"Call him yourself," Ryan as John No Last Name told him. "His name is Nick, and you'll find him answering the main number at the Whipwell County Public Library. You can look it up yourself."

One piece left.

Rocky took his phone out of his pocket. Laurie watched him poke buttons, looking for the number. Then she looked down at a row of silver rings while she listened closely. "Hi, is this Nick? Hi, Nick, this is Rocky. I'm here with your friend John, and we're making some arrangements about your purchase . . . Yes, I have it. It's in my truck right now."

Laurie's mind was an overactive toddler all of a sudden: *Holy moley, wow wow wow, it's in his truck right now, they are leaning on the truck and it's right in there.* The undoubtedly very nice man behind the table with the rings looked like he might try to talk to her, so she turned away from him and made herself look preoccupied by doing the very first thing she could think of: googling "famous ducks." She continued to listen.

"And what price did the two of you agree on? Right, right. And you understand it doesn't come with documentation, you're buying it as an art piece, as is, yes? . . . Oh, it's a great example, no question. I think she'll love it." He looked at his watch. "Oh, wait, you need it today? Oh, I see. I see. Her party is at six-thirty?" Again, looking at his watch. "Well, that's a little bit of a problem, because I'm here at this event until six."

Ryan—"John"—broke in to say in a stage whisper, "I can take it to him."

"I'd really rather handle it personally, to tell you the truth,"

Rocky said into his phone. "Maybe I could come by with it during the party, make it a surprise?" Putting away her phone, Laurie moved to a table of scarves staffed by a young woman who seemed engrossed in her book and unlikely to try to chat. She pictured Nick with the front desk phone cradled in his shoulder, emphatically repeating that he absolutely had to have the piece by 5:30, or there was no deal. "Hang on a minute," Rocky said. He muted the phone, then went back to talk to Ryan. "I don't like it, I want to be there, I want to see the money."

"He's a *librarian*," Ryan said. "He likes *books*. He tells people to stop *talking* for a living. What do you think, he's lying?" Nick would undoubtedly say that Ryan was enjoying this a little bit too much. Putting a little too much mustard on it, as Laurie's dad used to say.

Finally, Rocky went back to the phone. "Okay. John's going to bring it by your work and pick up the money . . . yes, good working with you too, I hope she gets a lot of enjoyment out of it. I'll speak to you later." He hung up and slid his phone back into his pocket. "That's that, I guess."

Laurie looked over at the truck, where Ryan was standing by the back wheel on the driver's side. Rocky walked around and opened the passenger door again, and he took out a canvas bag. He walked over to Ryan, and she could see it. Her duck. She could see her duck, as Rocky put it in Ryan's hands. "Take good care of it," he said. After a minute, he handed over the canvas bag, too, and Ryan put it inside. "Might as well take the whole thing. How are we meeting up so I can get my money?"

Ryan took out his phone. Well, not his phone—his burner phone. The one he used for anything where he didn't want somebody to have his personal number. He had considered it a delightful marker for fame when his agent had told him it was time to get one. "Gimme your cell number," he said. Rocky rattled it off, and Ryan typed it into his phone. "Here, I'll text you, and now you have my number.

Text me where you want to meet in a day or two, and I'll have the money."

Rocky nodded. "What am I going to tell Matt?"

Ryan shrugged one shoulder. "Tell him somebody broke into your truck. What's he gonna do? Call the cops?"

"He'll be pissed."

"He's not Al Capone," Ryan called out as he slung the bag over his shoulder and started to walk away. Just as he passed the tables, just as he passed probably ten feet from Laurie, a voice rang out.

"Oh my gosh! You were on *Halls of Power!*"

Ryan froze. He turned to look at a woman, probably in her twenties, who was holding a painted teapot in both hands. "What?"

"You were the guy from the congressman's office! I just rewatched that one!"

As Laurie stood, frozen, Rocky started to walk toward them. "Oh, I'm sorry," Ryan said to Teapot. "I think you're thinking of somebody else, but I'm very flattered." He turned toward Rocky. "See? One of those faces." He shrugged. Teapot frowned, watched him for a few seconds, and went back to her shopping.

Laurie spent an interminable couple of minutes browsing at a glassware table, and then she tried so very, very hard to mosey in a relaxed way across the slightly sloped lot and down to the sidewalk. Down the sidewalk to her car, which Ryan was already inside. She slid into the driver's seat.

"Did you hear that? She recognized me."

"I heard it," she said.

Without another word, Ryan held out the duck to her.

Laurie held it in her hands. Whatever Rocky had done to clean it had made it look a little better, a little smoother, a little nicer. She ran her fingers down the back, over the tail feathers, back up to the head, the green crest, the lively eyes. When she looked up at Ryan, she was surprised to find herself a little teary. "Thank you," she said.

"Hey, I'm just the actor. This was all you." He took his hat off and put his shades back on. "Let's get out of here. I don't want him to change his mind if somebody looks in the window and thinks I'm Matt Bomer."

"Mm, optimistic," she said.

"Hey, don't be mean," he said. "I just saved your duck."

"Wait, what did he show you? What picture, what lady, what letter?"

"Oh boy," Ryan said. "We have to talk."

Chapter Nineteen

D ot had a whole collection of collections, and one was a collection of sunglasses. Laurie had found ten or twelve pairs around the house in drawers and purses and peeking out from behind the coffeemaker. Round green frames the size of a tennis ball, square red frames with gold flecks, tortoiseshell cat-eye frames with sparkly gems in the corners. None looked expensive; they all looked like they could have been picked up in drugstores or at gas stations, and more were likely abandoned in cabs and left behind on café tables. In Polaroids taken by her traveling companions, she wore them at the Eiffel Tower and the Grand Canyon, and they perched on her head as she sipped a cocktail at a table sheltered by an umbrella.

So when Ryan told her that Rocky had showed him a picture of a woman he was certain was Dot in a long print dress, wearing a pair of huge mirrored lenses in bright blue frames, she wasn't the least bit surprised. In the picture, he said, Dot was next to a gray-haired man, her arm wrapped around his waist, her head resting on his shoulder. From the research Laurie had brought home from the library and showed to him, Ryan had recognized the man as the esteemed artist Carl Kittery. And Carl was holding a wood duck decoy, unmistakable with its bright green head and the crest Laurie had memorized with her fingers. He was extending it toward the camera a little with both arms, Ryan said, like Carl was presenting it as a gift.

Rocky had also shown Ryan a letter that Ryan could not quote precisely, but that he could paraphrase. It said that this duck had a few variances from Kittery's other work and he'd never carved wood ducks otherwise as far as anyone knew, but the one Rocky had in his possession was made in his style and the mark was a variation of his, likely one applied to personal gifts. It seemed by all appearances to be the same one Kittery was holding in the photo. He had most likely given it to the woman in the picture as a gift, which explained why it was found in her home. The picture itself was recovered from Kittery's house in Bar Harbor, from a box in his office, after he died. On the back, in faded ink, it said, *D, 1972*.

During his life, the letter said, Kittery had talked about being friends with a woman who lived in Calcasset. Although he hadn't shared her name, he had indicated that they were close, and that they had spent a lot of time together. It seemed reasonable to conclude that the duck had been carved by Carl Kittery somewhere around 1972, and that he had given it to Dot, and that she had kept it in her home until it was found by Matthew Pell during the collection of her possessions.

The last sentence said the letter was being written by Kittery's granddaughter, who had lived with him and his wife for a time. It was signed *Rosalie W. Kittery-Kane*.

Ryan explained all of this with the duck on his lap as the car wound its way back toward Calcasset. And when he was finished, Laurie just stared at the road, the little houses, the lighthouse in the distance, thinking about Dot taking this duck from this man and tucking it in the bottom of a chest. What Ginger had said about rumors of Dot and a married man; it had to be this.

Maybe this piece of his work was the only thing of his that Dot ever had. If their relationship was a secret, if he was cheating on his wife, then she couldn't have had his company in public, she couldn't have had him all the time. Maybe that's why she had this, this precious thing. For all its value, for all the fuss over it, for all the stealing and stealing back, maybe this was a consolation prize. That would explain why she hadn't told anyone she had it. It would explain why she hadn't told anyone what it was or how valuable it was. That was why she'd hidden it. He never left his wife (of course), so she got the parting gift.

Dot's life had been opening itself to Laurie like a book for more than a month now, unfurling folded pages she'd never known anything about, letting Van Halen tickets flutter out, writing footnotes with Polaroids and plastic sunglasses. Like any good story, it had twisted once or twice: She was a collector, she was a sucker, she was neither, and now she was maybe a woman who always wanted something she couldn't have. Maybe all this travel and all these friends, the smiles in front of landmarks and the cocktail party candids, were because she was stuck with a duck instead of her one true love. In a way she couldn't explain even to herself, Laurie felt betrayed.

But all she said to Ryan was "So, it's real."

He nodded. "I think it's real."

"After all this."

He nodded again. "Yes."

"And we got it back."

"You got it back," he said. "You got it back for Dot." He

chuckled. "Boy, she'd have gotten a kick out of it, too. You had these guys for lunch, Laur."

"What are you going to say when he calls you and he wants his money?"

"I've been thinking about that. I might not answer, but I might answer and say somebody broke into my truck and then say, 'What are you gonna do, call the cops?'"

"I like it."

She felt him turn to look at her from the passenger seat. "What are *you* going to do?"

"I think I have to go talk to her. The granddaughter. I think I have to meet her." Laurie frowned. "That might be the wrong thing to do, I don't know. But I'm definitely not ready to talk to the rest of the family, because I don't know what we'll do if it's worth money. Everybody's kind of been assuming Dot's estate wouldn't amount to much other than the house. I don't want to get a whole thing started if it's not necessary."

"There's not going to be a fight, right? They wouldn't all start rolling around in the mud, Mom and her sister and her cousins?"

"I don't think so. Dot's will is clear enough. I just don't want people spending money they don't have yet. I don't want the aunts to book any spa vacations or buy new cars. The letter and the picture are enough for me, but I don't know what the process is for something like this, if we even want to sell it. And maybe we don't want to sell it; maybe we want to keep it in the family. Maybe it's an heirloom now. Maybe it's the kind of thing you pass on to your kids. I mean, not mine, but yours." She turned up the air-conditioning. "I just think I have to start by talking to his granddaughter. If she talked to that weasel, she'll probably talk to me."

"She's not going to be happy to learn he's a weasel."

"Probably not, no."

"Well, I'm excited to hear what happens next. I should get back to my wife, because I desperately want to tell her how I impersonated a con artist to nab a potentially valuable duck." He sighed. "I can't wait to see her."

"You've been gone like three days," Laurie said.

"Laur," he said, "you know I don't care if you ever get married, and you know I don't care if you live by yourself or live with somebody else. I don't even care if you give in to whatever this thing with Nick is. But if you're surprised that I'm excited to see Lisa after four days, then I'm glad you didn't marry Chris. Because you deserve to miss the hell out of somebody after four days, and you deserve to have them miss you too."

"I have to tell you, I don't think it's in the cards."

"Eh," he said. "My softball buddy just got married, and he's older than you."

She groaned. "It's different. When men are single when they're forty, people think it's adorable. 'Oh, now that he's done whatever he wanted for the first twenty years of his adulthood, maybe he'll settle down.' I mean, do you know how many times I've seen a guy on a dating site who's forty-five, who is open to dating women who are, like, twenty to thirty-four?"

"But you're not trying to date that guy."

"I know. I'm just saying, it's a system that's rigged against women who want those same twenty years of doing whatever they want."

"I don't know if a bunch of dating-site clowns are a system."

Laurie rolled her eyes and nodded. "You know how when you turn on the tap, you expect water to come out?"

"What?"

"Answer the question."

"Yes, I expect water to come out."

"Well, that's a system, too, but you don't think about it very much, because of how flawlessly it works for you. This is the same thing. You are a good-looking young guy with a cool job who wanted to get married young. I can read countless books from past centuries and hear women in my position described as practically dead."

"I can read books from past centuries in which people thought interracial marriage was a sin against God. Fuck 'em!"

Laurie nodded enthusiastically. "Exactly. That's a terrible system, too. I'm not on the only hard path; I'm not even on the hardest one. I'm only saying this is not just a bad-luck Saturday night of app-surfing. This is something you don't notice because you don't have to."

She could feel him looking over at her. "You're very smart for someone I could always beat at Connect Four," he finally said.

"I let you win," she answered.

They crested a hill with a billboard that advertised the maritime museum ten miles north of Calcasset, which Laurie had visited on a sixth-grade field trip—just like Ryan had, and Scott and Joey and Patrick had. The only thing Laurie could remember about it was buying a lighthouse keychain for her mother at the gift shop. Much about those years was a blur of brothers and embarrassments (for a while, Joey hung her bras from the light fixture over the dinner table when he found them in the laundry room), and much of the time, all she really remembered was noise. Constant noise, from the kitchen and the family room and the driveway and the backyard, until she would go up to her bedroom and put a pillow over her head, because it was before she had headphones that could block it all out.

When she was looking for her place in Seattle, she had asked everywhere about shared walls. She made everyone be silent while she stood in the bedroom for two full minutes and listened for neighbors. This place would not be noisy, except when she wanted it to be. And just in case, she would have every machine and oscillating fan and earplug it took to make it quiet when she was sleeping. Just quiet, that was all.

"What are you thinking about?" Ryan said, snapping the thread.

"Why I live alone," she said.

The question she was trying not to ask seemed determined to get itself asked: *What was all this for?* An expensive art piece that she'd insisted on retrieving because her pride was hurt at being swindled, and now she was going to know a secret she'd never wanted to know about her beloved great-aunt and a married man for whom she might have waited around for half her life?

She drove on.

Chapter Twenty

When Ryan and Laurie got back to Dot's house, he looked at his watch. "When's your flight?" Laurie asked.

"About two hours," he said. "I should get moving."

While he packed the few things he'd brought, Laurie sent a message to the group text labeled "Quack Team." She just wrote: Success.

Almost immediately, her phone sounded and she looked down to see Nick's name and his profile photo of the front of the library. "Oh, hello," she answered.

"So it worked?" he said. "You have it?"

"In my grimy little paw, yes," she said, flopping down on the sofa with the duck in her hand. She could see now that the neck was even more graceful than she'd thought, but the paint job was a little less precise. And when she turned it over, that mark, that round mark with the CKM stamp, was so beguiling. "I'm just happy to be reunited with it. Have you talked to Rocky?"

"Not yet," he said. "I'm going to call him in a little while. I plan to be *very* angry. I'm going to tell him his guy didn't show up, which is technically true, and that I don't have the duck, which is also true. So what did you find out?"

"It was crazy," she said, grinning into the phone for the benefit of nobody but herself. "Are you at work?"

"I am, but I can take my break. Tell me the whole thing," he said.

She explained about the letter that Ryan had seen, and the photo. They had probably been right that the guy whose back they had puzzled over in the picture was Kittery, and now it seemed like he and Dot had probably been having an affair. He'd even talked about her with his granddaughter, although not by name, and it sounded like the relationship was a long one. "So," she said, "I suspect this is a case of taking what you can get when you can't get what you want."

"What do you mean?"

"It's like a poet who writes you a poem or a musician who writes you a love song. He made this for her; I bet it's why he never made another wood duck. Maybe it had some special kind of significance to them, I don't know. It's probably why it has a different mark."

"I want to see it," he said.

"You've seen it," she said.

"I want to see it again."

"Okay."

"You're sure it's the same one?"

A cold chill went up Laurie's spine. "That's not funny. Yes, it's the same one. It has the same mark in the same spot, and there's a little scratch under the tail."

"You know, I think we all wind up with a scratch under the tail at some point."

"I don't even know what that means."

"I don't either. Hey, can I come over later, maybe? I'm off at seven. Bring you some pizza and beer?"

"Sure. Ryan will be gone by then, so it would be just the two of us."

"Well, that's good, because I was only going to bring one pizza."

"Then you're on."

They said goodbye, and she composed a panicked—and, she would soon realize, rather hasty text to June: Nick is coming over for dinner later, and I can't figure out if it's the kind of dinner where I have to shave my legs.

She went into the kitchen to get something to drink, and just as she took the iced tea out of the fridge, her phone pinged with a response: You never have to do anything on my account, I'm super casual. The next several seconds were like falling down a well: First, she fell over the edge (realizing the response was from Nick and not June), then she felt herself endlessly careening (figuring out that she had sent it to the group text instead of to June), and then she hit the bottom with a thud (realizing this meant the entire thread, including her brother, had seen, or soon would see, her speculating about her sex prospects).

My phone was hacked. By very dangerous hackers, she typed back.

Of course it was, Daisy answered.

I figured as much, Nick added.

Ryan came out of the bedroom with his overnight bag. "All right, my airport taxi is going to be here in about five, so I'm going to go stand on your porch like a doofus and wait." He spread his arms wide. "This was so much fun. I'm glad I got to see you, Laur."

She put her arms around him—he was so pleasantly tall and familiar, and out of all her brothers, he gave the best and most plentiful hugs—and said, "Thank you so much for your help. I couldn't have done it without you. You're a great liar."

"It's really rare that my profession comes in handy in a practical situation, so next time you need somebody to pretend to be somebody else in order to exact revenge, I'm here for you."

She pulled back from him. "You're the best. And thank you for the talk, too."

"I meant all of it, you know. I think you're exactly the right version of yourself," he said. "And whatever it takes for you to be happy, I'm on your side. You know?"

"Yeah. I love you, buddy," she said. "And don't look at the group text."

He frowned. "Well, now I'm going to look at it the minute I get outside."

"Ugh, fine. Just don't *tell* me you looked at it."

"Deal." He squeezed her hand and headed out the kitchen door.

When Ryan was gone, she looked at Dot's wall clock. Enough time to get started.

She sat with her laptop and started with a simple search for "Rosalie Kittery-Kane." At the top of her results, it said, *Did you mean Rosalie Kittery-Lane?* "What?" she mumbled. "No, I didn't mean that, why would I mean that?" It spit out a lot of "Rosalie Kane" listings, and a smattering of Kitterys: Bruce, Donna, Daniel, Robert, Tom, Margaret. It seemed like there was only about a 75 percent chance that Ryan had remembered her name entirely accurately under such pressure, with a creep breathing down his neck and nowhere to take notes. Could he have remembered it wrong? Maybe she *did* mean Rosalie Kittery-Lane. But that turned up nothing.

Assuming that Rosalie was originally a Kittery and now she was a Kane, maybe she didn't hyphenate under circumstances in which she wasn't providing the provenance for a potentially valuable carved bird made by her grandfather. Maybe the "Kittery" was for emphasis. Maybe it hadn't even said "Kittery-Kane"; maybe it had said "Rosalie Kittery Kane." So she started digging into those Rosalie Kanes.

It seemed unlikely that Matt had traveled all that far to seek her out. And if Kittery was born in 1915, she figured Rosalie was probably born somewhere between, say, 1960 and 1995. So she wasn't the one born in 1940, or the one who lived in London, or the one who had been dead since 2006, or the one who had danced the role of Clara in *The Nutcracker* in Sydney, Australia, in 2012. Probably.

But what about the Rosalie Kane whose Facebook profile, mercifully part public, placed her down the coast in Old Orchard Beach? Her birth year wasn't there—just "November 12"—but in photos, she looked to be about fifty. Right on target. In two of the pictures, she was standing in front of a school, although all that showed of the sign were the letters ING STREET SCHOOL. A little more poking around placed Rosalie Kane as an art teacher at Nocking Street School in Old Orchard Beach. A celebrated artisan having a granddaughter who was an art teacher had a certain logic. This might have been wrong, but it was the best place she could think of to start.

It took a few tries, but Laurie managed to compose a Facebook message.

> Dear Ms. Kane: I'm writing with a curious question. Are you by chance the Rosalie Kane who's related to Carl Kittery, the decoy carver? I'm so sorry to impose, but I've recently found out that your grandfather might have known my great-aunt Dot Bennett, who died recently. I'm hoping you can help fill in some gaps in her history for me if you don't mind. I'm happy to come down from Calcasset to see you, perhaps for coffee? Delighted if you can help, and if not, that's totally all right, and enjoy the rest of your day. Best wishes.

She fretted a bit over whether it was too formal or too casual or too much to ask, but if Rosalie had made time to write a letter for a dirty dishrag of a human being like Matt Pell, she would probably be willing to make time for Laurie. She hit Send, and as she'd done so often since she'd come back to Calcasset, she felt like she was sending off a wish with a flare gun, just hoping someone would see it and want to make it real.

Chapter Twenty-One

She had showered, using the soap and the shampoo that smelled like gardenias. She had changed. She had picked up in the living room, and the bathroom, and the kitchen, and the guest bedroom where she slept. Did that count as having expectations? Didn't she *have* expectations? Didn't he already *know* she had expectations? Didn't the entire group chat know she did? Would pizza and beer give her dragon breath? If he had the same dragon breath, would that cancel it out?

Laurie flopped down on the couch on her back and put her bare feet up, throwing her forearm over her eyes. "I am going to be fooouuurrrrr-teeeeeeee," she declared firmly. "This is so dumb." She lightly slapped her cheek a few times. "Stop it, stop it." She thought about Nick sitting next to her at the library desk, lit up by the monitor, trying to solve her mystery. She'd been chasing the duck for a while by then, but in that moment, she'd been distracted by his shoulder, his neck, the corners of his mouth, the familiar timbre of his voice.

June's wedding eight years ago had been at the Presbyterian church in Thomaston on one of the hottest days of the summer. Before Chris, before Angus. Laurie was a bridesmaid, and her dress was mercifully simple: tea-length, blue, sleeveless, affordable, and at least moderately resistant to looking sweated-in. Charlie's younger brother walked her down the aisle; he was a twenty-year-old who looked at his phone for most of the day and ordered a vegan entree he didn't eat. She first spotted Nick during the ceremony, sitting with Becca about halfway back. She felt her hand tighten around her flowers, and she briefly thought she might snap the plastic handle. She had last talked to him on the night they broke up. Now he was married, and he was older, and he was *right there*.

He was in a blue jacket and a white shirt, and that Superman curl still sat above his eye. Becca was pretty and her hair was impeccable, Laurie noted with an unwelcome sense of resignation. She'd known Nick would be here—in fact, she'd told June it was perfectly fine, she wouldn't feel awkward. And she mostly didn't, because it was so far in the past, until she suddenly did, because . . . it was Nick.

It was watching him sit with his wife that made Laurie suddenly and acutely aware that she had spent the last few years chasing the feelings of comfort and trust, and the magnetic and uncomplicated drawing together, that she'd felt with him. There had been good relationships with other people, good sex with other people, good times with other people. But that feeling that she was connected like the sides of a locket to the other half of herself, that feeling had never returned. Maybe that feeling belonged to being younger, and not to him, but what if it *did* belong to him?

She was thinking all of this jumbled together in a disorganized flood of sensations when he suddenly flicked his eyes over and they saw each other for the first time as adults. It seemed to drag on forever, the wondering whether he would hate her, or worse, whether he barely remembered her and would, at the reception, clap her on the back and say something lightly heart-ripping like "Good to see ya!" It was always possible that he thought of their history the way she felt like she *should* think of it, with casual warmth that didn't get in the way of anything, warmth like she felt when she thought about going to high school football games or watching *Ever After* with June at the Seaside Twin, back in the age of the cheap theater with only two screens, before they tore it down and put in a multiplex.

Maybe she had imagined all of it, maybe it was just dating in high school and college, maybe he never thought about her, maybe he didn't recognize her, maybe he was going to pretend he didn't recognize her, or maybe he was going to ask her to dance later because he and his wife felt sorry for her because she was at the wedding alone.

And then he tipped his head almost imperceptibly to the side, and he smiled. Or rather, his formal wedding-watching face softened, and his eyes were still just so brilliantly green, and the corners of his lips ticked upward. Laurie felt her face turn hot, or hotter than it already was under the laboring ceiling fan, accompanied by the regular rhythm of sweat beads rolling down her back. Looking at him, she felt like she was eighteen and like she was forty, it was then, it was now, and it was later, and they were kids on the same fourth-grade trip to an art museum in Portland, and they were at the prom, and they were having sex in her room while her parents were playing bridge, and they were breaking up while the Old 97's played from a cheap portable speaker.

She smiled back.

Later at the reception, she was at the bar trying to figure out how to carry a little plate of mini crab cakes and a napkin while also picking up her glass of champagne when she heard him say, "Need help?"

It was like a breeze blew and a train went by and the shot of whiskey she maybe should have ordered instead went sliding down her throat. "Well, hi," she said. "I think I'm okay, I'm just trying to make it over to one of those tall tables over there." She gestured with her chin.

He held up his glass of red. "I just got this; I'll go with you."

Over at the high-top table, she set down her snack and her drink, and she took a deep breath. "I'm really lucky these shoes are comfortable—that's June for you."

"Well, you look great," he said.

"So do you." The band was pretty good, especially with pop and ballads; less so when they tried to play jazz or rather disastrously wandered into reggae. "So, how have you been?"

"Been good," he said. "I'm still in town, I still work at the library. My wife, Becca, is around here somewhere, I'll introduce you. How are you?"

"Good too," she said. "I'm out in Seattle now. I'm working at *The Outdoors*. It's a real job with health insurance and everything. My parents are thrilled. How are your folks?"

"They're good. They're just starting to think about when they might retire. I think Mom's going to get very deeply into her ceramics and Dad's going to get very into driving Mom out of her head. How about yours?"

"They're in Florida now. It seems to agree with them, for the most part. My dad has back problems, but they're good. The boys are good, Ryan's starting to get a little bit of work, Patrick's taking out appendixes—appendices, whatever—Scott's doing well, and Joey met a very nice girl who raises orchids."

"Well, that's good." He leaned over and eyed her plate. "Can I have a crab cake?"

She nodded. "I have lots."

He chewed it slowly, offering up a series of exaggerated ponderous faces until he finally swallowed and nodded. "Very good, very good, I like it."

Laurie laughed from what felt like an unfamiliar place. "It's really good to see you, Cooper," she said.

"It's really good to see you too," he said. "I've thought a million times about messaging you on Facebook or asking June for your email, I just never got around to it."

"Yeah," she said. "I've thought the same thing. Time is really . . . slippery. It's embarrassing. I just keep waking up and being older."

"You're thirty-two," he said lightly.

"I know. It's just always later than I think."

He nodded, and then he put his hand on her forearm. "Hey, can you stay here, and I'll go find Becca? I want you to meet her, I think you'd like her."

"Oh, actually, I need to go and find Junie; I'm supposed to be helping her with a bunch of things. Maybe find you later?" She was already starting to turn away from the table.

"Okay. Find you later."

But he didn't, because she managed to always be somewhere else every time he tried.

And now, his divorce and her broken engagement later, she was try-ing to kill the last hour before he would be there. As she stretched and twisted on the couch, she saw out of the corner of her eye Aunt Dot's copy of *Persuasion,* in a stack between *Shōgun* and *The Spy Who Came in from the Cold.* She plucked it from the stack, and when she opened it, a receipt Dot had been using as a bookmark— dated 2010 and showing a purchase of aspirin and cough drops— fluttered out. Dot would have already been eighty-two then, carrying a basket at the CVS, plucking what she needed. Maybe she was reading the book in line, staying busy like always, and she slipped it into the pages when she turned to go home.

Laurie had meant to put on at least a little bit of makeup, but she got to reading, and she was lucky just to get her hair dry by the time he texted and said he was five minutes away. That was just enough time to brush her teeth again, do one last check to make sure there wasn't anything like underwear or ice-cream containers in weird places like next to the bed, and get out some paper towels and plates to put on the coffee table.

She was just barely ready when he rang the bell at the front door, and she ran to get it. Nick was coming from work, so he arrived with a messenger bag over his shoulder, a pizza in one hand, a six-pack in the other, and a sunflower laying on the pizza box that he gestured at with his chin. "That's for you," he said. "I wanted it to be a rose this time, but I settled for what I could find."

"That's okay," she said, stepping aside for him to come in, "roses will just stab you anyway." She took the flower and set it on the coffee table, and he put the pizza and beer beside it. They dropped onto opposite ends of the couch. "I think thanks to you, I've gotten more flower action in the last few weeks than in the previous ten years. How was work?"

"It was good," he said. "Today, I mostly got to actually answer questions and be helpful instead of chasing people around and telling them not to do things, and the people who were supposed to be working showed up on time. That's a good day for me. Maybe not as good a day as you had, though. I want to see the big prize."

"Well." She went into the kitchen and came back with the duck, which she displayed grandly, as if she were selling it on *The Price Is Right*. "This beautiful weird thing has been returned to its rightful home." She handed it to him.

"Unbelievable," he said. "It worked exactly like it was supposed to."

"Mostly," she said. "Ryan was very confident that he wouldn't be recognized, but he's about five percent too famous to do this kind of thing safely. He got busted for being on *Halls of Power* with about thirty seconds to go."

"That show," he said, shaking his head. "But he played it off?"

"Fortunately, the kid really came through. He managed to convince everybody he just looks very generic." She took the opened beer bottle he extended. "But yes, the guy handed it over, we brought it home, and Ryan is getting a new burner phone. Hopefully, that's going to be that, and how it disappeared is going to be a problem that stays between one creep and another."

"What do you do now?"

She sighed. "Well, the really interesting part came when Rocky showed Ryan the authentication stuff that Matt had shown to him." She explained the letter, the picture, the Facebook message she had already sent. "Now I'm waiting to see if I can put a couple more pieces together."

"Have I told you recently that I think you're pretty cool?" he asked, lifting up a slice of pepperoni.

"If you have, I never mind hearing it again. And I've got to say, you have done some pretty tremendous friend work these last few weeks. I never thought research could be so beguiling. Cheers." She knocked her beer bottle against his.

"Cheers. And I'm glad you liked it. I know it's hard to believe, but I've known guys who didn't think knowing how periodicals were indexed was going to impress women."

"Ridiculous," she said. "For me, it's pretty much: cool car, big shoulders, facility with reference materials. But not in that order."

"So, what are you going to tell this lady if you find her?"

"If she really did talk to her grandfather about somebody who really was Dot, I want to know what he said, I guess. Because even though Matt is a rotten potato of a person, he might have had this right. He found Rosalie, she made the connection when he showed her a picture of Dot that he probably stole, and the duck originally went from Kittery to Dot as a gift. That seems plausible to me. I also want to tell her what happened, I guess, because I feel like she has a right to know. If she was trying to help and he was lying to her, well . . . I'd want to know, if it was me."

"And then what? Do you think you'll sell it?"

She smiled. "That's a whole other thing. If my mom and her sister and their cousins want to sell it, then we'll sell it, obviously, and it won't be up to me. But if they ask me what I think, I think that regardless of the kind of relationship it was, she wouldn't have tucked it away like she did if it didn't matter to her. I don't know, I can't think about it yet."

"What would you rather think about?"

She smiled at him sideways. "I was thinking about June's wedding. How I saw you at the reception for a minute and then not for another eight years."

"You took off like a rocket," he said. "I kept looking for you, but every time I spotted you, you'd be someplace else by the time I got there. It was like trying to grab a drink with Carmen Sandiego."

She laughed. "Well, I wasn't super excited about meeting Becca. It was an emotional day, just helping Junie and everything, and I didn't have a date. I think I felt like if I met her and I didn't like her, or if I really liked her, it would throw me for a bit of a loop."

"You definitely would have liked her," he said. "And she would have liked you. But I understand. Even though I knew you would be there, actually seeing you wasn't as uncomplicated as I'd like to say it was."

"Were you mad at me?" she said. "About how it ended? Were you still mad when we were thirty-two?"

"Not mad," he said. "After all, you turned out to be right—I live here and you don't. But I never thought about breaking up with you until the minute you broke up with me. My parents got together when they were in college, and I always really envied the fact that they connected so early."

"Can I ask you something else?"

"Sure."

"Tell me about Becca."

He started peeling the label on his bottle of beer. "We met senior year. She was interested in botany."

"Oh, a plant person," Laurie said. "My mortal enemy. All the best people are animal people."

He laughed. "Sure. But, you know, I overlooked it. We started dating, we were very happy. We both went to grad school in New York, and then we came back here, got married, because I was going to work for my mom and dad. But I think she thought it was temporary, you know? I think she thought we'd be here, and then we'd go somewhere else after a few years. And that felt okay to me, too, in theory. But then my folks were retiring, the branch closing came up, the job started to get harder, and at that exact moment, she got this amazing opportunity to go a very long way away. And I said, 'I can't leave right now,' and she said, 'Well, when can you leave?,' and I said, 'I don't honestly know,' and she said, 'Well, in that case, I will be packing my stuff.'"

"Do you ever wish you'd gone?"

"To Michigan? Not really. We almost got back together like a year after we separated. I was truly miserable and I asked if we could get together, and she was very kind about it. But when I got out there to visit, it was like the window had closed, right? She had new friends, new stuff, new things that she wanted to do. It wasn't like anybody was mad anymore by then, it was more like . . . putting on an album you haven't listened to for a long time and realizing it's not your taste anymore. You have that *well, I guess this isn't mine anymore* feeling even though you used to want to play it every single day."

"Is it terrible if I say I feel that way about being in Calcasset sometimes?"

He shook his head. "It's not terrible if that's how it is."

"I'm sorry you were miserable," Laurie said.

He nodded. "It sucked, but it ended. I told you it was kind of amicable, and that's about as amicable as it gets."

"And now you're single again."

"It seems so, yeah. Unless I want to hunt for a new dentist, I guess."

"Poor you."

"Yeah. Poor me."

Pizza and beer turned out to be exactly what Laurie wanted as a celebratory dinner on the day she had pulled off what she hoped would be the most daring caper of her life. There were two pizza joints in Calcasset, and Laurie and Nick both preferred Olive & Mario's, which had been downtown since 1980 and made a slightly spicier sauce than the newer and slicker Three Brothers, which had sixteen locations and was thus slightly less trustworthy. The only locations Olive & Mario's had were the counter, the tables, the restroom, and the kitchen—and maybe the spot out front on the sidewalk where Mario and his brother sometimes sat in lawn chairs.

They handed the roll of paper towels back and forth, cleaning their hands and smacking grease onto the necks of their beers. And when they were full and a little buzzed, they decided to watch Ryan's arc on *Halls of Power*. In only two episodes, his congressional aide had stolen a congressman's documents, sold them to an opposing political operative, attended a state dinner, attempted to seduce the first woman president (President Hall, of course), and died in a yacht explosion. Ryan was good; he had a curled lip and he looked sharp in a suit, and even Laurie wanted to throttle him after about ten minutes.

She put her hand on Nick's knee when the first title sequence hit. He put his hand over hers. When a senator was stabbed in the leg during a failed coup attempt, she hid her face in Nick's neck, and he wrapped his arm around her shoulders. By the end of the first of the two episodes, she was turned toward him with her knees pulled up and her head resting in the hollow under his jaw. By the time the state dinner rolled around, they were tangling and untangling their fingers, tracing each other's palms. She was holding his hand and looking at the inside of his wrist, how pale and soft the skin was, and she kissed it and looked up into his eyes.

They did not see the yacht explode, because by then, they were stretched out on the couch, and she was on top of him, kissing him like he was exactly what he was: just the most delicious thing. His hand slid up her back under her shirt, and she muttered "mm-hmm" without meaning to, like she was appreciating a cupcake.

"Do you feel okay about this?" she asked as he traced her ear with his tongue.

"Very okay, do you feel okay?" he asked as she pressed herself closer.

"Yeah, I feel okay. Nothing we haven't done before, right?"

He pulled back from her a couple of inches. "I'm a lot better at this than I was in high school, I promise."

She nodded. "I know. Me too." She kissed his jaw. "There's just one thing, though."

He froze. "What?"

"This couch isn't mine. It's part of the estate. It technically belongs to my mother and—"

"Oh, don't tell me that," he said, burying his forehead in her shoulder, and she laughed.

"No, no, I won't say the m-word, but . . . I'm just saying, not on my aunt's couch."

He made a wary face. "Not in your aunt's bed either, though. That's a lot of years of . . . I mean, it's a lot of years."

"No, no. I'm not sleeping in there anyway. I'm sleeping in one of the guest rooms." She pointed. "It's that way."

"So we're going that way," he said.

"We are," she answered, and climbed off him.

She took his hand and they started toward the stairs. "Should we bring the duck?" he said.

"I don't like it *that* much," she said.

Chapter Twenty-Two

don't believe in undressing other people," Laurie said into Nick's shoulder as he kissed her neck up against the inside of the bedroom door.

He stopped and pulled back. "Why not?"

"I believe in them being naked, don't misunderstand me, I just think undressing other people is inefficient," she said, digging her fingers into his hair. "I've spent twenty years trying to figure out how to smoothly take somebody else's pants off, and I always wind up feeling like it would be easier without me." She kissed his jaw. Then she stepped away and pulled her shirt over her head in one rapid motion, tossing it onto the chair in the corner of the room. "See? Easy peasy. Would that really be any better if you did it?"

"I think," he said, holding up one finger and then resting it in the hollow of her throat, "that the idea is that I would do it in some kind of very hot way; I would do it with a lot of oomph."

"Well, yes," she said, putting her arms around him and feeling the fabric of his shirt on her belly. "But I already have my shirt off, so how much more oomph do you want?" And when she kissed him now, it felt different, and she almost saw herself from the outside as a half-naked woman crawling up his body. "The trick is not to fall behind."

He crisscrossed his arms to grab the bottom of his shirt, and as he tried to pull it off, it got briefly hung up getting over his head.

"Boo," she booed, cupping her hands in front of her mouth.

He laughed through the shirt, which still clung to his neck. "Don't boo me when I'm vulnerable." The shirt came free, and he tossed it on top of hers.

When Laurie was a teenager, she didn't like having a bigger chest than her friends, and then in her twenties she got to like it, but now that she was about to turn forty, she again wasn't quite sure. Nick seemed to have no such reservations, and he put one finger under the bra strap on her shoulder and said, "Can I take this off?"

She narrowed her eyes, fluttery just from his finger on the skin of her shoulder. "I don't know," she said. "Can you?"

He kissed her as he reached behind her back and undid the hooks; she typically tried at this moment not to think about whether men would notice, positively or negatively, that they had perhaps taken off a lot of two-hookers, and she had a four-hooker. But Nick moved to the corner of her mouth when he did the second hook, the other corner when he did the third, and back to the center when he opened the last hook and pulled the bra free. He held it up, pointing at the tiny bow between the cups. "Cute," he said.

She pulled him close and he threw it over her shoulder, and where it might have landed, she wasn't quite sure. He tasted like beer, and despite what Ginger had said about beer drinkers, she sort of liked it. But that might have been because it was him, or because it was them, or because it was the beer that he brought over to celebrate their victory. This was the real thing, the big time, the whole shebang about to shebang all over the guest room, and when she stepped back from him for a minute, she put her finger on a round birthmark on his shoulder. "I forgot all about the lucky penny," she said.

Nick moved his hand down her side, from under her arm toward her hip, and it triggered a memory, rather mortifyingly, of Chris. He would press one finger deeply into the soft side of her until he created a well in her flesh, and then he would smile and say, "I *like* this," as if it were the alternative to "I *hate* this," or "I can't *believe* this." Nick didn't say anything. He just trailed his hand around to the front of her waistband, where her jeans buttoned. Into her ear, very softly, he said, "Is helping out a little bit allowed?"

She breathed that it was, and he opened the button, and everything started to melt. She reciprocated by popping open the button over his belly, and then she stepped back again. "Meet me over there," she said, practically out of breath, pointing to the bed. He nodded. She pushed her jeans and her underwear down, felt that brief moment of fresh air and nerves, balled her clothes up and put them on the chair, wishing she'd thought to match all her underthings. But he didn't seem too concerned about it, given that by the time she got into bed and pulled the sheet up loosely over her legs, he was only a couple of steps behind her, and then there was nothing between them at all.

He smiled. "I forgot you pull the sheet up."

"I am who I am," she said, propping herself up on her elbow. "Speaking of which, I'm not on the pill. I went off it after Chris. I never liked it. And I probably wouldn't get pregnant anyway at this point, but that's probably not a 'probably' we should rely on."

"I got you," he said. He sat up a little and spotted his wallet where he'd left it on the nightstand. He leaned over so far to get it that half of his bare ass came out from under the sheet. "I'm sure this is very alluring," he said as he grabbed a clutch of three condoms from his wallet.

"When did you put those in there?" she asked warily. "Tell me it wasn't, like, 1998."

"It was today, smart-ass," he told her as he turned back to her.

She laughed. "Okay, I apologize for impugning your extremely fresh condoms. And I admire your optimism."

He tore one packet off and put it on the very corner of the nightstand, with the other two pushed farther away. "I've actually been putting three fresh condoms in my wallet every day since you left, in the hopes that you would one day return to town and I would get to have sex with you again."

"That's commitment," she said. "I'm glad it worked out for you."

He pulled her close, kissed her with urgency, put the heel of his hand against her ear with his fingers dug into her hair. She could smell it, the smell of his clothes from high school, the smell of his neck, now mixed with sweat and gardenias. This was his hip now, his shoulder now, this was how he kissed now, this was where he put his hand when he wanted her to come closer now. Nostalgia is toxic, false, an impulse based in a desire to escape the present into the imagined past, she knew all that. But it was Nick, and after years of assuming she would never see him again, let alone all this, when her eyelashes brushed his temple, something inside of her went pleasantly slack, far from work and family and a canceled wedding.

It was slick skin and familiar hands, a little trial and error and a little return to form, some rushing and some lingering and some carefully aligned timing, and it was the logistics of adults who are grown and the daring of people who are passing by each other briefly and trying to hold on, secure in the knowledge that whatever is complicated will be over before it matters.

After, she shut off the lights and got back under the sheet, pulling up the light cover to her waist. She lay on her side, facing him, curling her arm under her head, and they stayed there, quiet, with their index fingers hooked, his hand pulled over close to her. "Is it okay if I fall asleep?" he said. "Are you going to wake up at two in the morning?"

It was almost completely dark, just a few bars of light coming in through the blinds. "Of course you should fall asleep," she said. "And I think you've relaxed me as much as I can possibly be relaxed. So I'm optimistic. This mattress is good for my back."

"Mine at home is too soft, I think," he said. "Half the time I wake up in the morning and I feel like a pretzel."

"Warm and salty?"

"I wish," he said quietly, from inches away. "I keep meaning to buy a new one, but then I have to get rid of the old one, and getting it up those stairs in the first place was such a pain in my ass that I think I'm just going to keep it up there until I'm ready to tear down the house."

"Oh, you should invest," Laurie said. "You'll love it. It's great for back pain, and you spend hours and hours on it, so you should at least like it." She let her eyes fall shut, and she said, "Do you need anything? Glass of water?"

"Nope. I think I'm just going to close my eyes."

She leaned toward him one more time. "Where are you?" she said.

"Here," came his voice out of the dark, and she found his mouth and kissed him with presumptuous familiarity, like she'd do it again tomorrow and every day after that.

"If you wake up before me, there's iced coffee in the fridge."

"Thank you."

"Good night, Nick."

"Night, Laur."

. . .

Laurie opened her eyes, and it took a few seconds to reorient herself: She was on the wrong side of the bed because of Nick, whose body lay heavily next to her. She could hear him breathing. Her foot was tangled in the sheet, and she gingerly tried to extract it without waking him. She moved like she was underwater, freezing when she heard him inhale and relaxing when he sighed and then was out again. She had a little stiffness in her hip, and kept thinking about how good it would feel to turn over and sleep on her other side, facing away from him, but it would be hard to do without kicking him or bumping him.

She closed her eyes and tried to fall back to sleep. She had slept with Nick. She had slept with Nick, whom she had specifically decided it would be a bad idea to sleep with a couple of weeks ago. She had slept with Nick, who seemed convinced she should come back here and live in Dot's house, or one like it. And what if she did? She could be near the Atlantic instead of the Pacific. There would still be water, boats, green places to go. The winters would be colder, but it would rain less. She'd be farther away from her friends out there, but she had friends here, too. She could watch June's kids grow up, throw summer parties for neighbors where Daisy and Melody would come over and play music on the deck.

She could fall asleep with Nick, wake up with him, have dinner with him, have coffee with him. He could be there to read her first drafts, and she could listen to his stories about patrons and bosses and the pain of public service. She could have sex with him on a better mattress, whenever she wanted. She could stand by the stove making breakfast and wait for him to come up behind her and wrap his arms around her waist, and maybe she would reach her hand up over her shoulder and touch his cheek, and maybe sometimes, they'd go right back to bed.

She could watch *Halls of Power* on the couch with her feet in his lap, and they could try to remember song lyrics and make out in the shower and just try hard to be very, very happy. Didn't she deserve that?

Laurie slowly reached her arm backward, over her shoulder, and she felt on the nightstand for her phone. She picked it up and touched the screen to wake it up.

It was 2:08 in the morning.

Chapter Twenty-Three

Laurie woke up on the living room couch. She was in the shorts and T-shirt she'd taken off a pile of clean laundry on top of the washing machine after she gave up and climbed out of bed naked at 3:00 A.M., convinced she would not go back to sleep. Moving as silently as she could, she'd come out to the living room and dropped onto the couch, pulling an afghan over her middle, leaving her bare legs out. She was asleep before she had time to think about how much longer she'd be awake.

And now she was up again. She folded the blanket and returned it to where it had been, resting across the back of the sofa. It was light out, and her phone said it was 7:50, so she padded down the hall in her bare feet until she came to the open bedroom door. She stepped inside and saw Nick, still dead asleep, his face half pushed into the pillow and one arm crooked under it. She took a step toward the bed, then another, and then she lowered herself down next to him, a few pounds of her body weight at a time, then settled herself next to him, facing him and listening to him breathe.

This wasn't bad, this knowledge within minutes of being awake that someone was going to drink coffee with you and have breakfast with you and ask you how you'd slept. She envied his ability to sleep through her leaving, through her returning, through her crawling back into bed. His cheek was stubbled, and she put her fingers up to her own face and wondered if it was pink with friction.

"Are you watching me sleep?" He didn't even open his eyes, but when he spoke, she jumped.

"Sorry," she whispered. "I didn't mean to wake you up."

"That's okay," he mumbled into the pillow. "I was going to get up anyway."

She reached over and kissed his bare shoulder. "I like seeing you so early."

He opened his eyes and rolled onto his side. "You should see me after I get to brush my teeth."

"I think there are some unopened brushes in the medicine cabinet," she said. "They were probably for guests of Dot's, come to think of it."

"Thank goodness for sex after eighty," he said, and as he crawled out of bed and pulled on his jeans, she flopped onto her back and put her hands behind her head, whistling as lasciviously as she could manage. "Okay, lustball," he said, "let me at least make myself beautiful before you get started."

"You want coffee?"

"You read my mind." He walked toward the bathroom.

Laurie went into the kitchen and took down two glasses, then she took out the pitcher of iced coffee. She poured hers over ice, and then she paused and went down the hall toward the bathroom. She asked through the door, "Do you want milk or sugar?"

"Both, please," he said.

In the kitchen, she fixed the coffee and brought both glasses over to the breakfast table.

Wearing his jeans from yesterday and his untucked shirt, Nick sort of rolled into the kitchen, barefoot and wearing glasses that looked very good on him. "Wait," she said, "do you wear contacts?"

"I do," he said. "Ever since college."

"When did you take them out?"

"After you fell asleep," he said. "And before you got up again." He sat down across from her.

So he had woken up after all. "I'm sorry about that," she said. "I hoped you'd keep sleeping."

"Oh, I did," he said. "Then at some point, I turned over and realized you weren't there. I figured you had a case of the two A.M.s and had probably wandered off somewhere to get some real rest. And then I realized I was going to wake up with my contacts stuck to my eyeballs, so I took them out before that happened. I also might have come out to the living room and seen you snoozing away with your legs out, but I decided to let you sleep instead of licking your calf."

She smiled. "I'm glad you didn't. I might have kicked you in the head."

"I'm just glad you found a place that was peaceful."

She yawned and shook her head. "It wasn't you," she said. "It truly wasn't. I really liked being there with you. It's the nicest falling-asleep I've had in a very long time."

He shook his head. "I didn't take it personally, don't worry. And thank you for the coffee."

"Do you want anything else? Breakfast? I could make . . . toast."

"No, I have to get home and change anyway, as much as I'd like to smell your shampoo on my shirt for the next twelve hours. I think I'm going to grab a bagel on the way."

"Wait, do you work today?" she asked. She looked at her phone. "It's almost nine now."

"I don't, fortunately. I've been on for six days straight. You want to do something later?"

"Honestly, I should keep working on the house," she said. "It's been a big couple of days, but I still have a million boxes to go through, and I only have a couple more weeks to work."

"Do you want help?"

Wait, why *didn't* she want help? Why did she suddenly imagine, with longing, an entire day in the middle of the living room floor, sorting boxes into smaller boxes, leafing through books, listening to something diverting, until it started to get dark? She had only so much time with Nick, so much time to kiss him and watch movies with him and sleep with him and tell him everything and gloat about the duck, so why did she know she was about to say no before she actually did? "You should go have a day," she said. "I've got this, and if you stay here, you'll distract me with your deliciousness."

"That is definitely the most flattering way I have ever been told to buzz off," he said, leaning over the table to kiss her on the cheek. "Can I call you later?"

She nodded as he stood back up. "Of course you can call me. But don't be sexy on the phone, because I'm going to be busy."

He headed for the door, picking up his messenger bag on the way. Once it was over his shoulder, he used both hands to grandly gesture down his body, from head to hips. "Just remember, play your cards right, and you could have hot librarian sex every day," he said. "You really want to give this up for constant pouring rain?"

"All right, get out of here," she said, balling up a napkin and throwing it toward him. He winked and let himself out, and she picked up his glass and poured the ice from his coffee into her own.

She texted June: Nick stayed over last night. And then she added a smiley face. Then changed it to the smiley face with the yikes teeth. Then the smiley face with the heart eyes. Then the one that was sweating. The exploding head, *The Scream,* the party hat, the praise hands? She finally settled on the little emoji of a pair of exclamation points, which seemed silly, since she could have just added two actual exclamation points.

June replied very quickly: And?

It's going to be complicated.

June again: What a surprise.

Chapter Twenty-Four

Laurie used Facebook so rarely that she had almost forgotten what this particular sound even was when she heard it that night, this slightly different tone. But when she picked up her phone after a weekend of ping-ponging between her place and Nick's, she saw the notification right away: It was a new message from Rosalie Kane. She opened it, holding her breath.

Laurie,

Hello! Yes, Carl Kittery was my grandfather. As you probably know, he died in 1995. I am 52 (eek) and was born in 1969. I lived with him for about three years, from 1988 to 1991. I believe he did know your aunt Dot. Maybe you know about this, but I recently was able to identify her in a photo we have of him from 1972 where he's holding a decoy I believe he gave to her. I think they were quite close, although he never said a lot about the particulars of their relationship. (His marriage with my grandmother was pretty complicated.)

I would love to meet! My grandpa was very special, and I am sure your aunt was, too. I might learn just as much about my family from a conversation as you would learn about yours. I am a teacher, and I am off for the summer, so any afternoon you're free, I'd be happy to welcome you down here. I think it would be a lot of fun to talk!

Best, Rosalie

Laurie wrote back quickly, asking whether Rosalie really meant any day—she wasn't going to be in town long, so was it possible that they could meet the day after tomorrow, Tuesday? It was. Rosalie gave her the address, and when Laurie looked it up, she found photos of a charming little cottage with a brightly colored metal sculpture in the front yard. The home of an art teacher, for sure.

The next two days were blurry: Monday was lunch with June and dinner with Nick and boxes and boxes of Polaroids. He stayed over again on Monday night, and she woke up at two in the morning again, and this time, she slept on the bed in Dot's room until the vibrating alarm on her phone buzzed at 7:00 and she got back into bed with Nick. This time, she stayed in bed while he hopped into his car and ran out to Frederick's, the bakery a few blocks from Dot's house, where he grabbed muffins and coffee and brought them back with the muffins still warm and dotting the paper bag with oil. Breaking the muffin in two, still lying on her back and picking the crumbs off the front of her nightshirt, Laurie laughed as he explained that it had taken a little longer than it would have if he hadn't run into his mother in line, because she wanted to know what he was doing at Frederick's when he lived over by The Cozy Cup, and because he wasn't yet prepared to explain to his mother that he was spending nights with Laurie, he had decided to tell her that Frederick's had better coffee, which turned into a disagreement he didn't care to have about a thing he didn't actually believe.

"So," he said, "if you run into my mother, make sure you don't act surprised if she tells you that I've developed some strong and unjustified opinions about coffee."

He couldn't tag along to Rosalie's, even though they both would have enjoyed the ride down together, because he had promised to help a friend of Ginger's figure out her iPad, so Laurie said she'd call him when she was home and promised him a full report.

It would take her about two hours to get down there, and she'd told Rosalie she'd try to arrive around 1:00, so after she'd had enough coffee, she gathered up some of Dot's 1972 Polaroids, just in case Rosalie recognized anyone, and some of her own family: her grandfather who'd been Dot's brother, her mom and her cousins, Laurie's brothers, and Leo, the only suspected boyfriend of whom Laurie had a good picture to show. She also took a couple of pictures of Dot's house on her phone, and at the last minute, she pushed into her bag the phony appraisal Matt had given her, because that story was probably going to come up, as much as Laurie wished she didn't have to explain it.

She took Route 1 south instead of 95, because nobody came to MidCoast Maine to drive down 95. They came there to drive down Route 1, with the views of the water and the billboards for motels, the tourist towns with their views of the water and their postcard aesthetics.

When Laurie was young, she'd taken this drive for granted, zipping up and down the coast for short vacations and summer camps, never anticipating it would become unfamiliar the way it was now.

When she pulled up in front of Rosalie's house, she saw a little red hatchback parked in the street with a bumper sticker that said YOUR TEACHERS ARE PROUD OF YOU. She put her tote bag on her shoulder and headed up the narrow sidewalk, and she tapped on the door knocker, which was in the shape of a black cat.

"Hello, you must be Laurie." Rosalie Kane had a broad smile and a gray braid, and she was wearing a sleeveless blue jersey dress with white slip-on Keds just like the ones Laurie's mom always wore to get groceries. "I'm so excited to meet you, come on in."

"Thank you for inviting me," Laurie said, stepping into the house. While it was small, it was open and airy, with plants in every corner and pottery that looked handmade lined up on a table in the front hall. When Laurie stopped to look at it, Rosalie stopped, too.

"Kids give me pots they make," she said. "My husband and I came to an agreement that when this table gets full, I have to rotate a few pieces out."

Laurie pointed to one that was made of smooth blue coils, about the size of a soda can. "Some of these are really pretty."

"You have great taste," Rosalie told her with a laugh. "My son Kevin made that when he was in fourth grade. He's an architect now. I still think it's some of his best work, but I can't get him to design a building that looks just like it." She gestured toward the back of the house. "It's such a nice day, should we sit on the porch? It's got screens to keep out the bugs."

"Of course, that would be great."

The porch was already set with a tray of glasses and a pitcher of iced tea. Laurie told Rosalie about the trip, and about the way she had wound up taking care of all of Dot's possessions when she wound up at—what had Daisy said?—the bottom of the funnel.

"And you found out that she knew my grandfather after you found the decoy, I suppose."

Laurie nodded. "Yeah, exactly. There was a very nice guy in Wybeck who told me that your grandfather might have made it, and it didn't make any sense to me, honestly. She never told any of us anything about it, she didn't leave anything about it in her will, she didn't say anything about him—I mean, I'm sure he was very important to her, but you said he was quiet about her? She was even quieter about him. Some of her friends probably knew, but not many of those friends are still living and around here, and her younger friends, the ones she made in the last ten years or so, I don't think they had any idea."

"I hadn't thought about it for a long time, honestly, until Matt Pell came to see me. I guess he knew someone who knew I had done some work with my grandfather's history, so he came by to ask me about your decoy. At first, I was confused, because the mark wasn't quite right, and he'd never made wood ducks as far as I knew. But then he had a picture of Dot, and when he showed it to me, it looked so familiar. I couldn't figure it out, but then I thought, 'Oh boy, I think that's his friend.'"

"His friend?"

Rosalie shifted a little in her chair. "When I lived with my grandparents, I had left college. I was kind of taking a break, and I came up and lived with them. They didn't have the Bar Harbor house anymore, they were in Waldoboro. My grandmother was in a nursing home full-time by then. Mostly, I spent my time with him. And one night, we were talking after dinner, and he started to tell me about this friend he had years earlier, this woman."

Laurie nodded. "What did he say about her?"

"Well, let me say that you should understand that my grandmother was sick for most of her life. She had a lot of physical problems, she seemed like she was constantly having surgery, but she also had a lot of other problems that I still don't know all the details of. I think some of it was depression, I think some of it was probably dependency on some of her pain medication and some of her anxiety medication. And she lived in various places, hospitals and things, from when I was little. I don't ever remember her living at home, really."

"Did he spend a lot of time with her?"

"He visited her every day he could, as far as I know. When I lived with him, he did. If he had to miss a day, he would make sure somebody else went. When I was little, they would just tell me she was in the hospital, so I barely knew her. But it was very hard on my mother, I know, that her mother was in this very difficult situation. And my grandpa didn't want to make it worse, but I think he needed . . . company. Companionship. Something like that. And so he told me that he had this friend. He never told me her name, but he did tell me she had lived in Calcasset."

"Do you know how they met?"

"Apparently, they had a friend in common. They wound up at the same, I think, New Year's Eve party? And they got to talking. He said they had the same favorite book."

Laurie nodded slowly, remembering the piles of books, the endless piles of books. "Did he tell you what book it was?"

"John le Carré," she said. "*The Spy Who Came in from the Cold*. He absolutely loved spy novels. Couldn't get enough."

"Dot did, too," Laurie said. "I came across her copy of that book just the other day."

Rosalie smiled. "You never know what it's going to be that brings people together, I guess. Anyway, I remembered this when Matt talked about Dot and mentioned Calcasset. And I knew I had this one picture of this friend that he had showed me, so I went and I got it, and I put it with a picture of Dot that he brought with him, and I'll be damned if they weren't the same person. And even though he'd never made a wood duck that I knew of, he was holding it in this picture, and I hadn't even registered it, really, in all this time. And when I saw the duck Matt had, even though it seemed different from some of his work in some ways, it was easy to recognize his technique, and it's not that surprising that if he gave it to her, he may not have bothered with his regular mark. The photo was pretty convincing. So I wrote the letter to authenticate it, and I gave him the photo, and that's the last I heard of it until you wrote to me."

"Well," Laurie said, "I wish that had been the end of the story." She took a breath. "Unfortunately, Matt Pell was kind of a . . . he

lls you how important it was. And what do I know? Maybe
d her friends. Maybe she told her sister. But they're all gone.
eople she knew then, the people in her Polaroids from that
they're gone, or at least I'm not going to find them."

I wonder who took the picture," Rosalie said. "The picture of
two of them together with the duck. They looked comfortable
gether. I'm sorry I don't have it to show you, but they really did.
hey looked happy. So they knew someone. Someone knew them.
They had a friend together."

Laurie nodded, and she suddenly had a thought that landed on
her like a weighted blanket: heavy, but almost comforting. "I'm
never going to know," she said. "I'm never going to know this whole
story. He's gone and she's gone, and most of the story is gone. The
story is over. He gave it to her, but I'm not going to figure it out
beyond that."

She smiled. "It wouldn't even matter if they weren't gone,
though. The default is forgetting, not remembering, isn't it? You've
forgotten more about your own life than you remember. I have, too.
I look at those pots in the front hall sometimes, those pots that
some wonderful kid I love put in my hands and wanted me to have.
And every one of them, I wrapped up and brought home and put
there myself. I am certain I thought about that kid when I put that
pot or that ashtray or that vase on my table. But now? I don't remember exactly who made what anymore."

"Why do you keep them, then?"

She shrugged. "Oh, even if I don't know which is which, they're
my only hard proof that there's any reason for me to have been over-
worked and underpaid for the last thirty years. I don't have to know
which pot came from which kid, you know? All the pots came from
all the kids."

Laurie nodded. "I'm a reporter. I have a hard time leaving things
unresolved."

"I'm an artist," Rosalie said. "I do, too."

was a . . . con man, I guess I w

"He got the authentication from

appraisal from Wesson & Truitt that

wasn't real."

Rosalie was very quiet. "Why would he

"He told me it wasn't anything important,

fifty dollars."

She sat back in her seat and put her hand to h

no! Oh no, I'm so sorry, I wish I had thought to ge

you directly. Oh, why didn't I do that? I feel awful. Ca

get it back?"

"As a matter of fact, I have it back." Laurie slowed dow

because this story was much more enjoyable to tell: Rocky

closet, her brother, the parking lot of the church, and the fact t

her duck was now safe and sound in Dot's living room.

"And you haven't heard anything else from Matt?"

"Not yet," she said. "He has a problem, right? If he comes to me

and he's mad about it, he has to admit that he scammed me—he

wouldn't be mad about something that's worth fifty bucks. He also

probably doesn't have any way of proving exactly what happened,

although I'm sure he's going to put together that I have it at some

point."

"Well," Rosalie said, "I can honestly tell you it gives me a lot of

comfort to know it's back with you. I know my grandfather cared

about Dot very much. It might seem like a small thing, I guess, giv-

ing a gift to someone you couldn't give a lot else to, but for what it's

worth, I think they had a lot of happy times, in spite of how compli-

cated it was."

"She kept it for, what, almost fifty years?" Laurie thought about

what this meant, that Dot had been keeping this safe for ten years

by the time she herself was born. "I think it's safe to say it meant a

lot to her. Maybe the fact that she never told anybody about it or

gave anybody any idea she had it or knew him, at least as far as I

Chapter Twenty-Five

When Laurie got back to Dot's, she drew a bath—you can do anything in the middle of the day when you work for yourself—and she climbed in with a big glass of white wine. She filled the tub until the suds were threatening to spill over the sides, and she lay back and let her neck rest on the cold porcelain.

It was an affair, maybe. It was a tragedy, maybe. It was lovely, maybe. There was nothing to know. He made Dot a duck, and he gave it to her, and she put it in the bottom of a wooden chest, and it was still there when she went to China, when she saw *Avenue Q*, when she traveled to Patrick's wedding, and when she lay dying in the hospital. It was still there when Laurie said she would see to the house, and it was still there when Laurie started on that bedroom and opened the chest and wondered what was under all those blankets.

She must have told her boyfriend John, the one from the "ducks, darling" letter, what had happened. She must have confided in him, and so he had made a joke about selling it if she ever got desperate. But she didn't sell it; she kept it. It would only have gotten more valuable over the years, but she kept it.

When Laurie's fingers wrinkled and her face started to sweat, she stood up in the tub and was suddenly hit with the chill of being wet and naked in an air-conditioned house. She wrapped a big bath towel around herself. "Talk about *The Spy Who Came in from the Cold*," she muttered, briefly pleased at her dumb joke and disappointed that no one was there to hear it, since she was, after all, a sort of a spy, and—

Laurie stopped drying her hair and froze. She remembered a ticket falling out of a book, money falling out of a book, a clipped newspaper article falling out of a book. She pulled on the stretchy joggers and the clean T-shirt she'd folded on the clothes hamper. Out in the living room, she ran her finger down several of Dot's towers of books until she found it: *The Spy Who Came in from the Cold*. She'd picked up *Persuasion* from right next to it only a few days ago. She'd been right next door.

It was a beat-up paperback that looked like it had probably been read a lot, maybe lent to reluctant friends and reread during terrible moments. And ultimately, it was a beat-up paperback that bonded her to someone she loved. Laurie thumbed the pages, letting them flutter past, until something floated to the floor. She put the book down.

She carried the picture to the couch and sat down. In the photo, Dot was in a long print dress. Sunglasses. Mirrored lenses. Big blue frames. She was exactly as Ryan had described her in the photo that Rocky showed him. But in this photo, Dot was alone. It had to have been taken at the same time, because in her hands, she was holding the duck. The entire time Laurie had been here, there was a photo of Dot holding this duck, right in this book. Right under her nose.

It would have told her that given Dot's age, the duck could not be a contemporary reproduction that was sold in airports. It would have told her that Dot had this duck so long ago that she cradled it in her arms while she still had dark hair.

And as she peered at the photo, she realized there was something written on the back. Something peeking through just a little. So she turned it over. On the back, in what she now knew must be Carl Kittery's handwriting, it said:

I have never been so proud. —C

Laurie frowned at it. Proud? Oh God, not another clue. She wasn't even sure she wanted another clue. She wasn't sure she wanted the clues she already had. But she had come this far, and now she had to go a little further with this ghost: He had given this to Dot to mark some kind of an accomplishment. She thought back across what she knew and came up empty. What was he so proud of her for?

And while she was squinting at it, what was that on Dot's hands? She picked up the magnifying glass on the coffee table. Dot had something on her hands. Something . . . green? It was like makeup or—

It was paint. Dot had green paint on her hands. Laurie slid the magnifying glass across the duck Dot was holding, over to its vibrant green head. She looked across the living room in which she was sitting, to the duck that was on the mantel. To *its* vibrant green head.

I have never been so proud.

She looked at the paint, at the duck, at the paint, at the duck.

And then, Laurie put down the picture and the magnifying glass and almost tripped over her own shoes running down the hall to Dot's bedroom, where she threw open the closet doors and took down boxes of paints and markers and beaded bracelets until she got to the big blue plastic bin with the permanent marker writing on the side: IN PROGRESS/UNFINISHED. She'd never even opened it. She pried off the lid.

The top layer was seven or eight rough carvings of ducks. They looked half expertly done and half not, precisely as they might look if one person started one and the other person finished it, maybe one demonstrating and one practicing. The ones near the bottom were small, crude, done on cheap wood blocks, not much more than roughed-out silhouettes. Toward the top of the bin, they got better, sharper, with less of a clear distinction between the more perfect and less perfect sections. In the bottom of the bin, there were pictures of ducks that looked like they were cut out of magazines. One was a big full-page shot of a majestic wood duck, with its green head held precisely at the angle Laurie had spent so much time admiring.

A few of the unfinished carvings were painted—several nice-looking examples. Laurie turned one of the nicer ones over and looked at the flat bottom, where a mark would belong, and in what looked like it was probably just black Sharpie, it said, DOT B. Another also said DOT B., but someone had drawn a heart around it.

"Oh my God," Laurie said, as she sat down on Dot's bed, running her hands over and over this one, this one with Dot's name inside a heart. She lay back on the bed and threw her right arm across her eyes. She was completely out of breath, and she heard herself yell "HOLY SHIT!," and then she sat up and pulled out her phone.

"Hey, Laur," he answered on the first ring.

"Nick, I know what happened. I know who made the duck."

"I thought Kittery made the duck."

"He didn't."

"Wait, after all this, it's *not* real?"

Now she was laughing. "Oh, it's completely real. It could not be more real."

"Who made it, then?"

"Dot did," Laurie said. "*Dot* made it."

There was a long pause, then he said, "I'll be there in half an hour."

They sat on the floor in the living room facing each other with their legs crossed, their knees almost touching. Laurie bent over the duck and pointed to a painted pattern on the wing, overlapping rows of markings for feathers, little black outlines of drop shapes, like tiny spaceships. "This was his thing, right here, this kind of wing," she said. "But the ones I've looked at, they're more pointed, and Dot's are a little bit more rounded. You can see he taught it to her, but she did it her own way."

Nick's hair brushed against hers as he leaned down to look. "It's amazing. That's so much work, and that doesn't even count carving the thing in the first place."

"Yeah," Laurie said. "The ones I told you about in the bedroom, some of them aren't that much better than you or I could do with a week of practice. But then they keep getting better. She must have worked on them for years. He must have started teaching her, I don't know, five years before she made this? Ten years? There are probably thirty of them in that bin. Some of them are almost as good as this."

"Do you think this is the only one she ever finished?" he asked.

Laurie shook her head. "I just don't know. She never said anything to anybody about it as far as I know. She had this whole thing she knew how to do, this beautiful thing, and she just learned it and kept it to herself. Or I guess between the two of them. She must have told the one boyfriend, John, the scientist, though. It makes sense now, what he wrote in the letter—'there are always ducks, darling,' you know? He didn't mean she could sell it. He meant she could make them. If she was ever desperate, she could make ducks. He wrote that a year after she made this. She must have told him."

Nick ran his fingers over the bird's tail. "I can't imagine knowing how to do this. I can't imagine knowing how to start with a block of wood and end up with this." Then he looked up into Laurie's eyes. "Do you think he's still alive? The boyfriend?"

"I hadn't even thought about it," she said. "I haven't chased boyfriends, friends, really anybody. I mean, I've seen a couple of pictures of him, and they look like they were pretty close in age, so he would be getting up there. I doubt he's around."

Nick looked her in the eye, and he smiled, and he said, "You have got to be so pumped that you did this. That you figured it out. I've never solved a puzzle anywhere near that cool. I literally sit under a sign that says INFORMATION, and I've never found information like this."

"I wish I felt great. I actually feel terrible," Laurie said, putting her hands behind her and leaning back. "I feel like a jerk."

"What? Why?" He had such a good heart.

"Nick, it never even occurred to me. She had done everything, she had met everybody, she had gone everywhere except Mars, she had studied every craft short of butter-churning. And I still, when I found this thing, I still never thought . . . hey, maybe it was *her*. Maybe this was *her* work. Maybe it wasn't something she bought, or something she collected, or something some man gave to her. Maybe this was her own work, her own time spent learning how to do it. I never included that on my list of possibilities until I literally saw paint on her hands."

"I don't think you can be blamed for not intuiting that Dot was an expert-level decoy carver," he said.

"I loved her like crazy. She's the only reason I survived having four brothers in a house that couldn't hold us, and I didn't know anything. I was completely clueless."

He shook his head. "You weren't clueless. You knew. Maybe not exactly, but you knew. You knew it meant something that she put it in that chest, and that she didn't show it off with all her stuff. You knew her, and you knew how she worked, and that thing in your head that makes you want to understand everything kept poking you and poking you until you figured it out. You don't have anything to feel bad about."

Laurie refused to let the tightness in her throat turn into tears. It would complicate everything. So she coughed a little. "I spend my whole life wanting to be independent and wanting people to respect what I can accomplish, and I didn't even think to assume that if there was a mysterious beautiful thing in her house, maybe she herself is the answer to where it came from."

"But why does that make you feel bad?" He put his hand on her knee. "Laurie, something is obviously wrong."

She stood up with her hands on her hips, then sat on the edge of the couch. "I wanted to be a champion for her, I guess. I wanted to stick up for her life, for the way she was and the way she lived. I wanted to give her the same respect she would have gotten if she'd made different choices. I wanted her pictures and her precious things to be counted, even if they weren't being fought over. And I can't help feeling like I failed a little. I almost missed this huge thing, this big part of her life. I could have missed it. I could have given that duck to that jerk very easily."

"But you didn't."

"I almost did. Almost."

"Laur, 'almost' will drive you out of your head. I *almost* went to Michigan to work for the university when Becca did. I *almost* stayed married. I almost got back together with her a year after we were separated because I hated living by myself. A million different things almost happen."

"I almost got married," she said.

He nodded. "But you didn't, and here you are."

"And somehow, I still feel terrible."

"Has anybody ever told you that your rich emotional life is full of pools of lava and trapdoors?"

She smiled. "I know. I know how it sounds. And the thing is, I love being here. I love Dot's house, because Dot's house is not sad. Look at her life, look at all these things she did. I was trying to be the one person who really thought I *got* all that about her too, and I never thought to give her credit for this amazing thing she kept to herself. I feel like I let her down."

He rolled his eyes grandly. "Oh, *brother*. Laurie! I mean, what does being independent mean to you when you say it like this? When you talk about how much you care about it? What do you think you have to prove? What would happen if you stayed here, if you let yourself enjoy your friends and all these people who care about you, if you crawled into bed with me and we were happy? What is so scary about that? What do you think it's going to cost you?"

Laurie thought first of her big bed at home, and the way she liked to sleep right in the middle, stretched out however she chose, various pillows arranged to facilitate the ideal splaying of her limbs. "Look, to be honest, I was going to say, before—yesterday even— that maybe I would do that. I was thinking about it. I thought about it a lot. But I can't."

He let out a breath. "*Almost* again, huh?"

She shook her head. "I'm not a person who's ever going to want to share everything with somebody else, like my parents do, or like Junie and Charlie do, or like I think you want to. When I didn't marry Chris, I started to suspect it about myself, and when I realized that I was very relieved about calling that off, I knew it."

"Knew what?"

"That I would never get married," she said. "To anybody. Ever. No matter how great they are." Did she say this to him, *for* him? Did she say it for his benefit? She wasn't even sure, until she saw that he looked just slightly stung by it, that she had disappointed him, just a tiny amount. And she knew then that, yes, she had wanted to make sure that this was something he knew as they were lying in bed together, if in fact they ever did again.

"You can't imagine a situation in which you'd ever get married?" he said. She shook her head. "No matter what." She shook her head again. All he said was: "Okay."

She took a breath. "Nick."

"No, I heard you." He got up and resettled himself in the big armchair. "I heard every word, and I understand what you're telling me."

She wanted to kiss his neck, but she also wanted to tell him to stop it. "Nick."

"Sass, I'm forty, and you're going to be forty, and I'm too old to bullshit. Your slamming the door on what we're doing here makes no sense at all to me."

"What do you have in mind?" she said. "Because Seattle to Maine is a very, very long way. What's the endgame? What, if this worked out, you would leave here? Move away?" She could see it in his face. "No, right. You think I'm going to come back here, and we'll live in Dot's house, and everything will stay the same for you as it's always been. That's how you see it turning out."

"Are you the only one who's allowed to want what you want?" he said. "And for the record, I don't want you to be open to this because it's how I see it. I want you to be open to it because I think you might be happy. Have you not been happy here?" he asked. "Have you not been happy around Junie and Daisy and Melody and going out to my grandma's crazy house? Have you not felt settled here? Because you seem settled here. You seem good. I can't tell you what to do, but I think you should at least consider possibilities that might make you happy, even if they interfere with whatever vision you have about yourself."

Laurie went over to sit on the arm of Nick's chair and pulled out her phone. She showed him a photo. "This is my house. I planted those flowers out front. I chose them over all the other flowers, in all the other colors. They go pink, purple, blue, yellow, then pink, purple, blue, yellow, because that's what I wanted. I picked them out, and then I dug in the dirt and I put them in the ground. I made this home for myself. You know how much I love my family, but I like the fact that none of them would plant exactly these flowers. Nobody I've ever dated would plant them. My friends wouldn't, June wouldn't, *you* wouldn't. I got to make it the place I wanted."

He pointed to the house numbers, which were tall and narrow, and which she had spent an entire Saturday searching for. "I like these," he said.

"Me too," she agreed. "And when I walk up to that door, I know that when I open it, it's going to be quiet, and that is the best feeling I have ever had walking into anywhere I have ever lived. Including the house I grew up in. Including this house." She flicked the screen with her thumb. "This is my neighbor Sandy's dog, whose name is also Sandy. I don't know how that happened, because I've only met her twice, but I want to learn." She flicked again. "This is Brynne. We worked together at *The Outdoors* when I was on staff. She took me to the surgery center last fall when the doctor had to poke around my insides because I was bleeding when I wasn't supposed to. I'm fine, by the way."

He nodded. "Well, good."

"This is Erin. She came over the night I called off the wedding. She got me drunk and then she drove me to her house and tucked me into bed in her guest room, and in the morning, she brought me coffee and made French toast, and now she's going to wear my dress." Flick. "This is Anne. I met her at yoga, and even though I hate yoga, I like Anne, so we go out from time to time and have coffee." Flick. "This is Jen and Toni, they're in the—"

"I understand," he said. "You have friends. I understand."

"I have a whole life, Nick," she said. "I have a whole life that I *really* like, and I'm not interested in giving it up, even though I loved Dot and I love Junie and . . . everything else. Calcasset is not home to me anymore. My sister-in-law doesn't even like to visit here, remember? And they're trying to have kids. There are reasons this is not the perfect place for everybody."

"I'm not sure the Pacific Northwest is a progressive paradise either."

"It isn't!" she said. "I'm not trying to win an argument with you about whose city is better, I'm just . . . I'm trying to be honest about it."

"I get it, Laur, but your version of being honest about it is sticking me with being the asshole who's trying to get you to give up your whole life, and I never said that. I thought you were happy—I thought *we* were kind of happy. If you're not, then nobody is stopping you from leaving." She could almost see him trying to stop talking right at that point, before the next few words came out of his mouth. "It won't be the first time, right?"

"Are you kidding me? Is that what this is about? You're upset because I left in, like, 2002?"

"No, I'm upset because you're always the one who leaves and I'm always the one whose fault it is. You can't even just say you're leaving because you want to. 'I choose something else.' You act like you're being driven off by some set of expectations that presumably I have? And I don't think I have them. I never said it was here or nothing, never. If you're not even up for a conversation about meeting halfway, that's fine, but don't put the whole thing on me."

"Halfway?" she said. "So, what, Minneapolis? Is that halfway? There's no halfway here. You go off with somebody, and they want one thing and you want a different thing and it's not halfway, you just end up trying to win and lose an equal number of times. Especially with big things, and especially when you're older like we are, what's the play? I'm not going to give up everything. I have spent too much time on my life to decide I don't need it anymore because of however I feel about you."

"However you feel," he repeated.

She set her jaw. "Nick, I knew it was going to get harder for me, I knew I was going to make a complete mess out of it, and I'm sorry if I made it harder for you too. It sounds crazy, but how I feel about you is absolutely not the point. It's not you. It's that I wake up at two in the morning when I sleep with other people, no matter who it is. I want to sleep through the night. I don't want to fight over waffle makers. I don't want to negotiate vacations every single time, I want to go where I want to go, like Dot did."

He nodded. "You want the pictures and the spoons and the books, but really you don't want anything."

Laurie stood up and walked into the bedroom. She had been sorting Polaroids for weeks now, and she had a big box that was labeled PEOPLE. It was sitting beside the box that was labeled FAMILY. Laurie stacked one on top of the other, and when she carried them back out to the living room, they were heavy, heavy with the years and years of *click-flash, click-flash.* She went over to the chair where Nick was and put both boxes on his lap with a hard thump. She pulled the lid off the PEOPLE box on top and pulled out a handful of Polaroids. She took Nick's hand with one of hers, turned it palm up, and pushed the pictures into his grip. "It's not about not wanting anything," Laurie said. "It's about what I know how to have. Do you get it?"

"Not really," he said. "But I know you mean it."

She sat beside him and put her hand on his knee. "I'm incredibly glad we did this," she said. "Incredibly glad. You will never, never know how much I appreciate the fact that we got to spend time together again."

He nodded slowly. "Yeah. Me too."

He left not long after that, kissing her at the door, but quickly. Just as she shut the door, Laurie had a text from June. Hey, Charlie's at a bachelor party and I have to feed my kids and I could really use an extra hand. Any chance you'd like to come over for dinner?

Laurie tapped back right away: I would love to.

Chapter Twenty-Six

Over at the Devons', June was part of the way through making spaghetti sauce, and Bethie had just finished a complete meltdown over Tommy breaking one of her headbands. She was now up in her room reading while Tommy watched videos in the living room. June's face had the slight puff of someone who might have recently been in tears, and she kept peering down at the pot of water on the stove. "It won't boil," she said. "I swear, it has been on there for fifteen minutes and it won't even simmer."

Laurie came up next to her and put her arm around June's shoulders. "Hey. Heat works, I promise. Boiling still works. You can see the tiny bubbles on the bottom. It's going to happen."

June smiled weakly. "Right before I texted you, I was sitting at my dining room table with my head down, and I was chanting, *I love my kids, I love my kids.*"

Laurie gave her a squeeze. "Of course you do, but they can also be pains in the butt, Junie." She picked up a wooden spoon and stirred the sauce in the skillet. "This looks good. Smells good, too."

"I hope it is good," June said. "I really thought we were going to have this nice mom-and-kids dinner while their dad is out at this stupid thing he didn't even want to go to, and then I burned my hand, and Bethie started screaming about the headband, and she told her brother she hates him, and he said he hates her too, and they're probably both going to be fine in fifteen minutes and I'll still be standing here with my head exploding."

"I'm so sorry, Junie," Laurie said, continuing to stir next to her oldest friend. "I'm glad you told me. I appreciate not thinking about my duck for five minutes."

"How are things with Nick?" June asked as she peered again at the bottom of the pot of water.

Laurie hesitated. "I don't want to get into my thing, we're dealing with your thing."

"My thing was that I needed you to come over here and stand next to me so I didn't start screaming. You are officially allowed to get into your thing. Maybe it will take my mind off this fucking pot of fucking water."

Laurie laughed and put the spoon down, and she leaned up against the counter. She told June about her visit to Rosalie, and about *The Spy Who Came in from the Cold*. She told her about the paint on Dot's hands, and the bin of unfinished ducks, and the way Nick had come over, and the way he had left. "I think," she said, "it might be over. Like, not over-over, but . . . I see how it's going to be over."

"Oh, Laur," June said. "I'm sorry to hear that."

"Well, you called it." Laurie shook her head. "It was doomed from the start, no matter how much I wish it weren't."

June stepped away from the stove and went to get a bottle of wine out of the fridge. "Well," she said as she pulled the cork, "I mean, how much *do* you wish it weren't?"

"A lot," she admitted. "But not enough to come back. You know what it's like? It's like when I asked Bethie about her Legos and she said she was making a barn. It was going to be a school, but all she had was a rectangle, so boom, it was a barn. That's how I felt about meeting other people when I was in my twenties. You meet them, all you really have so far is a rectangle, it's your life, but you're still putting it together. If you happen to meet somebody else, you can turn it into a barn pretty easily." She looked at June, who was smiling a little while pouring wine into two glasses. "What?"

June handed her a glass. "Nothing. I am very impressed with this entire metaphor. It's going to change the whole way I look at Legos."

"But now, you see, I've already built the school. I built the windows, I put in the desks, I put on the bell, I've got whiteboards, I've got erasers—"

"This is a very involved Lego school."

"Stop making me laugh, you're being too literal, June. The point is that now, I've done all this building already. And when you've done a bunch of building and you meet another person, and they already have a whole barn, well, now you're trying to figure out how to put a school together *with* a barn. And there's this romantic bullshit idea that the most you can possibly love another person is to love them so much that you tear down everything you've made so far. You love them enough to turn yourself into a little piece that fits into what they already have and makes it perfect. Like you're the missing element in a plan that already exists. That's what Nick wants, that's this fantasy that he has where this all turns out well and I come back here and I live in Dot's house, and we have brunch at Ginger's, and it's exactly the thing he already has, except with me. And I'm not saying I'm any better; I'm exactly the same. I think about telling him I want him to come live, like, down the street from me, and he'll get up and leave after sex so I can sleep. And then he's just a piece of what *I've* already built. Neither one of those things is right."

"Did you tell him this part?" June asked.

"Which part?"

"Did you tell him that there's any part of you that wants to find a solution to this, or did you just say no to the thing you thought he was suggesting?"

Laurie narrowed her eyes. "I'm not sure."

"Well, why not?"

"June, I don't care what he says, he's never going to leave here. He's the shadow mayor. They love him. He picked this place over staying married."

June looked skeptical. "I'm not sure it was only about this one job. She was just more ambitious, and he was more settled. Charlie and I always thought they made kind of a weird couple."

"You don't think it means he'd never leave?"

"Laurie, I don't know. You don't know. Neither of us knows, because you haven't asked him. You think he's making this approach to you—what if you came back here, what if you bought Dot's house—and all you're doing is saying no to that. Which is great, and right. Laurie, you are braver than anyone I know when it comes to knowing what you don't want. You've always been pretty sure you didn't want kids, you know you don't want to get married, you know you don't want to share all your space. But none of that means you don't want somebody in your life. It doesn't mean you don't want him. You aren't even telling him what you want."

Laurie bit her lip. "I don't know exactly what I want."

June sighed. "I'm just going to tell you one thing, and I hope that you understand that I'm saying this out of love. Like, decades and decades of love. Okay?" She came over and put her hand on Laurie's arm. "I find the way you approach this exhausting."

To her own surprise, Laurie laughed. "That's direct."

"Well, my kids have worn me out." She sighed. "You talk like you're choosing between having this relationship and preserving your identity, you know? Like down one road, you're in a church with a ring and you're fusing yourself with somebody else for the rest of your life, and down the other road, you're this lone wolf hiking around the world and only stopping to make satellite phone calls to your parents so they know you're alive. I keep wanting to reassure you—you know, I am still myself, even though I got married and even though I had kids and even though I let somebody else make some of the decisions about what color to paint the living room. And I really think no matter what you do, you are going to be on your own sometimes, and you are going to be dependent on other people sometimes. As I was today when I started this spaghetti sauce by myself and then texted you because I needed an assist. And you came."

"I did," Laurie agreed, looking down at her wineglass.

"Laur," June said, "you don't have to be single to be independent. And you don't have to be married to be loved. That's not the choice. And I think you owe it to yourself to at least figure out what options you have before you assume that what you really want is impossible." June took a big slug from her wineglass, and then she went back to the stove. "Oh, look. Water's boiling," she said. "You were right."

Chapter Twenty-Seven

Laurie startled awake the next morning when there was a sharp knock on the door. She dragged herself out of bed, pulled her hair back, and called out that she would be just a minute, then she pulled on soft pants and her Springsteen shirt. She opened the front door and found Matt Pell on her doorstep, shifting back and forth on his feet. "Matt," she said.

"I need to talk to you." His smile was gone, he was wearing a plain gray shirt, and suddenly, she believed that she was actually seeing who he was.

"That's great," she said. "Because I need to talk to you, too." She stepped aside, and he followed her in. She shut the door behind him and said, "I'm going to go first. I want you to look at something." She went to her bag and found the fake appraisal. She pushed it into his hand. "This is fake. It's fake, and it's not even a good fake."

She half expected that he would defend it, that he would start to tell her that this was a completely legit document, and that the auction house was lying or denying their work, or maybe that there was some big misunderstanding, and couldn't they listen to some Natalie Merchant and talk about it? So she was surprised when he frowned at the paper. "I'm sorry, tell me what this is again?"

She laughed. "This is the 'appraisal' you gave me, and I know it's fake. I talked to Wesson & Truitt. I called them on their real phone line. I know this number—this number you put here—rings that insufferable hipster phone in your store that you don't answer. They told me this isn't from them. It's not their document number, because they start their document numbers with a letter. It's also got dummy text on it, and they never looked at a duck that was supposedly a Kittery. They didn't make this." She grabbed it back from him and flapped it in the air an inch from his face.

"This what?" He took it from her and turned it over and over in his hands. "I don't know what this is."

Her ears started to ring. "This is the paper you brought me. This is the . . . the thing you gave me. This is the thing you gave me that was the entire reason I sold you the duck. This was your proof that it wasn't worth anything. This was the appraisal you promised me."

He held it in his hands. He looked at it. He looked, for whatever reason, at the *back* of the sheet, as if he barely understood what paper was to begin with. "I don't recognize this," he said.

Laurie felt something in her chest start to expand like a balloon full of lava. "You gave this to me in this living room," she said. "You gave it to me *over there*." She pointed. "We were right there, and you came in, and—"

He shook his head. "This can't be a W&T appraisal. It would start with a letter. Plus that's dummy text at the bottom. I wouldn't have given you this."

"Why are you repeating what I just said? Of course it's not a real number. But you certainly did give it to me. You brought it over, you said 'Oh, I'm going to let you read this for yourself,' you said you were sorry it wasn't the news I wanted—you even gave me a pep talk about how good I was being to my aunt."

He shook his head. "I don't think I could have done that."

She stepped back from him. "Are you a *game show host*? Is there a hidden camera? Is this *Memento*? Are you heavily sedated? What are you doing?"

He held out both hands. "I think it's some kind of a misunderstanding," he said. He dug in the messenger bag he was carrying and pulled out a sheet of paper. He handed it to her. "This is the receipt I got from you when I paid you for the piece. It says here you sold it to me for fifty dollars, you were transferring ownership of it to me—this is what I'm going by, this is what I remember," he said, speaking to her slowly and gently, as if she were a frightened toddler.

"This is fraud," she said, holding out the paper toward him. "This is literally fraud. You can't do this. What do you think is the point of sitting here and pretending you don't know what I'm talking about? Do you think I'm going to reach the conclusion that I was imagining it, or that you have an identical twin?"

"I'm at a loss here," he said. And then he focused his eyes on her a little more intently. "I don't know how you'd prove that I gave you that. You could have drawn that up as easily as I could."

She very slowly nodded. "You *are* a game show host," she said. "You're the host of *Who Wants to Steal from Little Old Ladies and Go Directly to Hell on a Pair of Sparkly-Ass Roller Skates*? You're an absolute garbage can, you know that?"

"I haven't done anything wrong," he said. "But I'm pretty sure you did."

She looked right at him. "Oh, I did? What does that mean?"

"After I bought this piece from you, completely legally, I had an associate who was going to sell it for me."

"Oh," she said. "Right. An associate. You mean your friend who might actually dislike you more than I do?"

"Someone stole the piece from him," Matt said. "Someone took it, saying they were going to help find a buyer for it, and then that person disappeared with it. It's vanished."

Laurie nodded. "That's sad for you."

"According to my associate, he was supposed to be selling it to a librarian named Nick Cooper. Does that name mean anything to you?"

"I've heard of a Mini Cooper. And Gary Cooper. There's also Alice Cooper. Are you sure your guy wasn't going to sell it to Alice Cooper?"

Matt crossed his arms. "I know he's your old boyfriend, and I know you've been doing whatever with him this summer."

She shook her head. "I think we must be having a miscommunication. Are you saying you sold the duck to Nick Cooper? Because maybe you should ask him where it is."

"He says he never got it. It seems to have gone missing while it was in the hands of a third party."

"A third party?" she said. "Who?"

Matt hesitated. He didn't like sharing this part. "I don't know who."

"Your associate gave it to somebody who lost it, and you don't even know who it was? That sounds terrible. You know, it really seems like that's the person you should be looking for. You should call the police. Tell them everything that happened. Have them call me."

"This isn't cute," he said.

"You know, I have to say, you have really changed," she said. "You have become a lot more hostile in the time since you defrauded me. I'm not sure I like this side of your personality."

He pulled his shoulders back and puffed out his chest, such as it was. "I know you have it. I know you took it, and I have a receipt that says it belongs to me. So if you're smart and you don't want trouble, why don't you give it back right now, and I'll forget this whole thing?"

She had been trying so hard not to yell, but now she was yelling. "Are you fucking serious? Are you threatening me? *You'll* forget it? You're a felon, for fuck's sake. You're a thief and you're a liar, and you steal from people who are grieving. You're a solid man-shaped pile of decay, and the world has way too many of you, and you're in no position to make threats."

"You need to return what you stole," he said.

She could have just explained it to him: The thing was not a Kittery. The thing was a Dot Bennett original. He had defrauded her for nothing. In fact, she might have saved him from trying to sell a fake to someone else. But telling him this did not, in the moment, seem at all like the thing to do.

"Do you think I'm scared of you?" she said. "You left 'lorem ipsum whoopsy dingdong' at the bottom of your forged document. Somehow, I'm guessing you are not a master criminal as much as you are a small-time creep who turned to theft because he ran out of ideas for apps people could use to buy pet rocks on the internet."

"Well, good luck selling that duck once I report it stolen," he said.

"You're not going to report it stolen," she said, "because then we would have to talk to the police about all the other stuff you've pinched while you were running your bereavement ransacking business."

"What the hell are you talking about?"

Laurie stepped toward him. She raised her eyebrows. And then she said, "I know about Betty Donnelly's tiger clock. I suspect there's more where that came from."

Laurie would remember a lot about that summer for the rest of her life, but the look of the blood draining from Matt's face was something she wished she could photograph, paint, etch, or just sculpt out of Rice Krispies Treats and eat for breakfast every day for a year.

"Who the hell have you been talking to?" he demanded, just like a man who was used to assuming that voice would work on people.

She cringed. "Ooh, that's not a very innocent response, I'm afraid. That would be something more like 'What tiger clock? I have no idea what tiger clock you could possibly be talking about.'" She walked over to the door and swung it open. "Get the fuck out. And if it's not already obvious, you're very, very fired."

"We have a contract."

"Try to enforce it and see what happens," she said.

He tried for one more menacing stare, then turned away and started to leave. When he was almost to the door, she jutted her chin toward his back. "Hey."

He turned around. "What?"

"Did you really read my piece about the Texas blue lizard?"

He smirked. "I'm not much of a reader."

"Yeah. It shows. By the way, I'm sorry I never found those darn Andrew Wyeth letters. I know you were really excited." She pushed the front door so that it closed with a loud bang, and then peeked through the window to watch as he kept on going, down the steps and to his car parked in her driveway.

Chapter Twenty-Eight

Laurie had called June on the day she got into her second-choice college, and on the day she didn't get into her first-choice college. June called her when she got engaged, and even though she and Charlie waited to tell everyone else they were pregnant both times, June called Laurie as soon as she saw the plus signs on the home tests. Laurie called June right before she broke up with Chris, and right after. June called Laurie on the day her mother was diagnosed with cancer and on the day she was declared cancer-free. Laurie called June when she closed on her house, and June called Laurie when she and Charlie had just had their first appointment with a couples counselor.

So while her parents called on her fortieth birthday, and her brothers all texted by the end of the day, and her Seattle friends Face-Timed her with party hats on, it felt right that June's was the first voice she heard, while she was still pouring herself coffee. "I knew you would be awake," June said, "because I know this is the time of day when you look at Twitter and do half of the *Times* crossword."

"You were right. Although sometimes, I do more than half."

"Well, happy birthday, anyway. Do you feel different?"

Laurie stood by the sink in Dot's kitchen and looked out into the yard, where a robin was hopping around picking something out of the grass. "You know, I don't think I do feel different. Should I feel different?"

"I don't know why you would. I'm just congratulating you on being an absolutely amazing forty-year-old, much like yesterday you were an absolutely amazing thirty-nine-year-old. And I love you, and I'm so happy that you've been here this summer."

"Thank you, Junie." Laurie walked into the living room, where the duck was sitting on the coffee table. "I love you too, and I promise, I'm not going to stay away so long next time."

"Do you have big birthday plans?"

"I don't at all. I think I'm just going to keep working over here, because I'm almost done. I think I'm within reach of tackling the last box in the last closet, can you believe it?"

"Well, the kids and Charlie are all very excited for you to come over and have a birthday dinner with us. I'm going to pick you up so you can drink wine if you want, and Charlie's going to cook out on the grill, and Bethie wants to show you something she learned in gymnastics. I'm just going to warn you, she calls it a somersault, but it's more like a stop-drop-and-roll poster."

"I'm sure it's stunning."

"How are things with Nick? Have you talked to him?"

It had been four days since she had pushed the Polaroids into his hands, and while they had exchanged some texts and she had gone over to his townhouse for dinner one night, she hadn't stayed over. "No. All I've figured out is that I want it to be a shorter distance, I guess. I want teleportation. I want it to be a short train ride, or a day trip in a car."

"Well, I don't think those things are going to happen, so keep trying. I'll see you in a little bit."

Laurie was within days of finishing the house. She had contracted with a new service—one that she'd vetted with no fewer than six references—to take care of the junk and the donations, and June would let them in after she was gone. She had boxed up some things for friends of Dot's in Calcasset, for friends elsewhere, and for people in the family who had asked to have something. She had touched just about every item from attic to basement. The duck was still in the living room, on the coffee table, and it was still her favorite thing in the house. She'd started to put her things in the laundry, then back in the bags she brought them in. She had a flight booked, and in a week, she would be back in her own bed. Thank God, Erin texted. It's been way too long without a debrief.

At about six, she took a shower and changed into her most comfortable jeans and a V-neck black tee; there was fortunately nobody at June's to impress. When June's car pulled up out front and she climbed in, she looked at the face of one of her very dearest friends and said, "Oh no."

Maybe it was June's *slightly* too dressy sundress. Maybe it was the fact that she had a little bit of makeup on, or maybe it was just that Laurie was secretly, somewhere in the deepest depths of her soul, aware of what was happening all along. "What?" June said.

"Who is at your house, June Marie?" she said.

June blinked. "What do you mean? My kids and my husband. Put your seatbelt on."

"Who *else* is at your house?"

June took a huge breath. She held it. And in a squeaky voice, in the voice of the scheming event planner, she said, "Nobody?"

Laurie's shoulders slumped, and she reached over to put on her seatbelt. "You should not go into espionage. You are the worst liar in the world."

"Look, I told you it was a birthday dinner. I never promised you

nobody else would possibly ever show up. I can't control what people do. I don't know everybody's schedule."

"Just drive," Laurie said. "Now I want to see for myself."

June turned to her. "It's not going to bother you when you see
that my entire house has been re-wallpapered with black 'Over the
Hill' napkins, is it?"

"You know, you only think that's funny because it's not your
birthday."

June cackled. "Well, you'll just have to be very brave, because
this is happening."

It was a very short trip from Dot's to June's, and Laurie spent
most of it wondering if she should have dressed up more. She had
to assume Nick was going to be there; what if this was the last time
they saw each other before she left? What if he looked incredibly
good and she looked like she was planning on eating burgers with
children? What if he smelled like the library? What if he smelled
like *Nick*?

Before she knew it, they were parked outside the house.

"You have to go inside," June said. "I promise it's not bad. It's not
a circus. You've been in my house before. You're going to be okay."

"This is going to be way too much attention for me."

June put one hand on her shoulder. "Don't make me ruin it for
my very excited children, who have never participated in an ambush
before. You trust me, right?"

"Junie," she said pleadingly.

"Out you go, birthday girl," June said. "It's time to face it."

Laurie followed June up the sidewalk and saw Bethie's inflat-
able pool and Tommy's scooter leaning up against the steps. "Can I
swim in the pool?"

"No."

"Can I ride away on the scooter?"

"Laurie, don't be a baby." June opened the door to the house,
which was dark in the evening light. Laurie followed her inside,

into the front hall where the family's shoes were neatly lined up on a rack.

"SURPRISE!"

Fortunately, there weren't very many people. Nick *was* there, and June's husband and her kids. Nick's grandma Ginger was there with newly tinted pink hair, Daisy and Melody were relaxing on the couch, and Violet and Louise, two of Dot's younger friends from church who had helped take care of the house during probate, were running things in the kitchen. Laurie had cooked for them one night to say thank you, and she'd invited June, too.

She gritted her teeth and said, "You guys, thank you so much!" Daisy walked over and offered her a glass of wine. "Oh, I'm so glad you could come," Laurie said.

"We're glad to be here," she said. "We couldn't resist when June told us you were turning a hundred and twelve."

"Thank you, Daisy," she said. "That's exactly it, I am one hundred and twelve years old."

Louise and Violet brought her flowers, and June's kids had made cards with glitter and glue. Ginger put her arms around Laurie and pulled a Calcasset Claws hat down on her head. "New merch," she said, pronouncing the word "merch" like it were a cut of steak. "We just started making these in this beautiful green." Directly into Laurie's ear, she said, "I'm so happy for you, and you're going to love being forty, darling. I hadn't had practically any fun yet when I turned forty, and look at me now."

When Ginger went off to play with June's kids—and "play with," in this case, meant that they told her very, very long stories about TV shows they had watched and she gasped and laughed and begged to hear more—Nick slowly walked over, and he was still so good and so solid. To be honest, she wasn't sleeping well alone now, either. "Hi," she said as he leaned over to kiss her on the cheek.

"Happy birthday," he said, and he touched her cheekbone with one finger.

"Thank you. Thank you for coming. I'm glad we're ending this adventure on a good note."

"We are," he said. "The last thing I want to do is make it so we don't talk for ten years." He held out a small square box wrapped in polka-dot paper with a red bow on top. "I did bring you a present, and I promise it's not jewelry or anything weird."

She took it from him. "Should I open it?"

"No," he said. "Open it when you get home and then call me."

"Wait, it's a present we have to talk about on the phone? Did you get me bad news for my birthday?"

"Not at all. I just might have to explain some things about it."

She frowned. "Are you sure I can't open it now? Because you're kind of killing me with the suspense here."

He leaned over and said into her ear, "I'm just taking one more opportunity to tease you before you go home." He did smell like Nick, like books and soap and apparently some kind of insane pheromone load, because her knees almost buckled when his hair tickled her temple. *Oof, right to the nethers,* she thought.

"Okay," she said a little weakly.

"You're blushing," he whispered.

"You're making me," she whispered back.

"By doing what?"

"Standing there being all . . . you. Go stand over there." She pointed to the table where the drinks were, and he smiled like he was choking on a laugh. He walked off, and June caught her eye and glanced down quizzically at the box. Laurie shrugged and went to drop it into her purse.

She got home around midnight, dropped off by Charlie rather than June because Bethie had woken up wanting *only* her mother, no exceptions, no fathers allowed. She got out of the car with a paper grocery bag dangling from her fingers by its handles, holding the box from Nick and a few other small gifts that were meant to comply with the request not to give her any gifts—or at least nothing that would be a pain to cart home with her on the plane.

She didn't know whom she was trying to fool, opening everything else first, like she wasn't dying to know what was in the little polka-dot box. It wasn't as if the rest didn't matter: There was a pendant that she was fairly sure Daisy and Melody must have picked out on one of their jaunts to some art fair or other. Ginger gave her a small compass in a brass case with a note that said, *So you can always find your way*. And June and her family had given Laurie a framed photo of Dot's house that had been taken in 1974 (thank you, local historical society), side by side with one taken earlier in the summer.

Laurie sat at Dot's dining room table with the box in front of her, and finally she eased the bow off the top and tore away the paper. When she opened it, there was a piece of white copy paper folded inside. She unfolded it and drew in her breath. It was a grainy photocopy of an article from a 1995 college alumni magazine, reporting on the retirement of the chemist John Edward Harlan, class of 1950, longtime resident of Bangor. It said he had spent most of his career studying the structure of proteins, although Laurie got a little lost in the specifics. He was married and he had four kids, and he hoped to spend his retirement gardening and traveling.

Pointing at the bottom of the page was an arrow written in black marker, which Laurie recognized as the universal, if nonsensical, sign for "turn me over." So she did. And on the back, it said, "John E. Harlan, Gatecrest at Ivywood, Apartment 215, Carrywick, ME." It took only a minute to look up Gatecrest at Ivywood and find that it was an assisted living community.

Nick's phone rang only once. "Hello, Sass," he said.

"He's alive?" she said. "He's still alive, just chilling in assisted living?"

"He was when I talked to him yesterday."

She started tapping her fingers on the table. "What did you talk about? What did he say?"

"Well," Nick said, "I just told him that Dot Bennett's great-niece was trying to put together some family history and thought he might be able to help."

"And?"

"He knew Dot had passed, and he told me that if there was anything he could do, he'd be happy to talk."

"Do you think he'll let me come by?"

"I can do better than that. He's expecting us. Well, you. Well, no, us. If that's okay with you."

"Of course it is. But when? I'm leaving soon."

"That's why I told him we'd come tomorrow. Sorry to spring it on you, but I asked June, and she thought you could spare the time in the afternoon. I didn't really think you'd be mad."

Laurie shook her head, even though nobody could see her. "I'm not. I'm not mad at all. I would love to go."

"That's great," he said. "It will be nice to take one more trip together before you have to go."

"It sure will," she said.

"Happy birthday, Sass."

"Thank you, Nick."

She went to bed restless, wishing he were there, thinking maybe this time she would have slept better that way.

Chapter Twenty-Nine

Gatecrest at Ivywood was at the end of a long driveway that wound between two low green hills. It was made up of a central brick building and two broad, flat wings that sprawled out on both sides. Lots of the windows had bird feeders or hanging planters, and a white-haired woman came out through the front doors walking her dog just as they pulled in to park. "This doesn't seem like a bad place to end up, all things considered," Nick said as he turned off his car. "It must be working out for John, I guess, if he's ninety-four years old."

"You know, if he moved here after he retired, he's probably been here for twenty years? Longer? He's been here on this property since . . . oh boy, Nick. He's been here since we were dating." She whistled. "Either he's been here a long time or our history is not as old as I thought."

"Little bit of both?" he said, locking the car and gesturing toward the front doors. "They know we're coming."

They did. The very kind woman at the desk had their names, and she directed them to the elevator and said John's apartment was up one level and to the left. He was one of their longest-term residents, she said. He'd arrived not long after they opened, in 1998. She gave them visitor badges to wear and reminded them there was no smoking.

Armed with all this, Nick and Laurie walked down a long hall to the elevator and stepped inside. It was large, undoubtedly to accommodate carts and wheelchairs, and when they stopped moving, the doors opened onto a blue-carpeted hall and a serene hush. They turned left and were soon at the open door labeled JOHN HAR-LAN. A painting of three boats hung on the wall outside his room, and when they stepped inside, they saw him sitting in a chair by the window, looking at the newspaper. Nick knocked on the open door. "Excuse me, Mr. Harlan?"

He looked up and over at them. "Yes?"

"We spoke on the phone yesterday. I'm Nick Cooper, and this is Dot's great-niece, Laurie."

"Oh yes, oh, come in, come in." Laurie followed Nick into the apartment, which was compact but immaculate, with a TV in one corner and a raft of family pictures in another. There were two armchairs arranged across from where he was sitting, and he gestured at them as he carefully laid the paper down on a small table. "I asked them to pull up a couple of chairs so you wouldn't have to stand." As Laurie approached, he turned to her and his face filled with warmth. "Look at you. You do remind me of Dottie."

Laurie smiled and reached out to shake his hand. "That's nice to hear. I'm Laurie Sassalyn, Mr. Harlan, thank you so much for your help."

"Oh, call me John, please, I feel like we're almost old friends."

She sat in one chair and Nick sat in the other, and she took out a photo of John and Dot that she had found in a box, labeled D & J. It wasn't one of Dot's Polaroids; it said 1962 on the back, and it predated Dot's fascination with photos she could launch right out of her camera. In it, they were sitting on a bench under a tree, his arm slung around her, her hand—rather daringly, Laurie thought—resting possessively across his knee. "I found this, and I thought you might like to have it." She handed it to him.

He held it close to his face. "Well, I'll be damned. That's us, all right. That's the bench out front of F.C. Glass, where I was working. She used to come see me. One of my buddies probably took this for me. I sure could never have enough pictures of her."

John told them that he and Dot met in the mid-1950s when they were both in their twenties. She was working at the elementary school in Calcasset, and he was doing research for a company in Bangor, and they met at a friend's wedding, drinking champagne under a canopy. They started dating, and he asked her to marry him, but as he put it: "She told me she didn't think she was a getting-married kind of woman. Which, you know, back then, you didn't hear that so much."

Nick and Laurie glanced at each other, and she remembered wanting to smash the crystal ball with her wedding date on it.

After that, John and Dot didn't see each other for a couple of years, but then they ran into each other at a party, and they were both still single. They went back to dating, but only in secret, since his family knew she had turned him down and they would not have approved. They stayed together until John was thirty-five and beginning to think that if he wanted to settle down and have children, he needed to go ahead and do it. "We talked and we talked," he said. "But there's not a lot of common ground between getting married and not getting married. Or especially between children and no children." So they broke up for good, and just six months later, John met his wife. John said he and Dot exchanged letters from time to time for another fifteen years or so. "So the one you found, I would have written after I was married," he said. "It's nice to know she kept it, that I rated so highly, even in my absence." Laurie could see the man in the pictures in his face now; his eyes were the same, and his smile.

"I know this is a strange question," Laurie said, "but I'm wondering if you know anything about her relationship with Carl Kittery."

"The duck man!" John said brightly. "Don't tell me you know the duck man."

"I very much don't," Laurie said. "He died quite a while ago. But when I was cleaning the house, I found this very nice carved duck decoy."

"The wood duck?" John said.

Laurie physically reared back a bit with surprise. "You have a good memory," she said, handing him a picture of the decoy.

"For a guy who's ninety-four, you mean," he said with a smile.

"For anybody," Laurie said. "I regularly don't remember why I came into whatever room I'm in."

"Well, she sent me some pictures of that particular piece, and I kept one on my piano at home, so I looked at it for a long time. I called him Woody. Not too creative, I know."

"She . . . she made it, right? She made it herself." Laurie didn't breathe for a moment. She wasn't ready to hear that she was wrong. She wasn't ready to start again, and she certainly wasn't ready to be disappointed when she was so close to the end of this.

"You bet she did," he said. "The duck man taught her. She was with him probably . . . ten years? I don't know, maybe ten years. And he taught her. I got a lot of pictures of what she was working on over the years, and I wish I still had them. Sometimes they worked together, but she loved that one because she did almost all of it herself. I'm surprised she never told you about it." He paused. "I suppose that would have meant talking about the duck man. Maybe not a thing you tell family. But I'm glad you know she made it. That would make her happy, I think."

"It was hard to figure out because it has part of his mark on the bottom." Laurie showed him another picture of the bottom of the duck.

"That's right," he said, pointing. "I remember that. She said he liked it so much that he put the studio mark on it, like she was an apprentice, I guess. I'm sure they didn't realize they were creating such a mystery for you, though."

"Left off the dots for his wife and daughters," Laurie said.

"Yeah," John said. "That seems right. It was a little messy, certainly. But as far as I know, they were pretty happy. You know, fifty years ago, not too many men were looking for women who were going to be just as good at whatever they were doing as they were. I think the fact that he wanted to teach her, wanted her to get really good, that was part of why she liked him."

"He was married the whole time, though, right?" Laurie said.

"He was. And she knew, he didn't lie to her. But if I remember, his wife was sick. For Dottie, I suppose it really wasn't a bad situation, because he was never going to bug her to get married like I was. She got to have somebody, but only so much as she wanted."

"Do you know how long that lasted?"

He stopped and closed his eyes. "Well, when did she carve that, early seventies?"

"In 1972," Laurie said.

"I don't think it was too long after that when they broke it off. He had children, and they were even having their own children, and it was getting a little more complicated. So probably a couple of years after that."

"Can I ask why you two fell out of touch?" Laurie said.

He shook his head. "You know, there wasn't any big fight or anything like that. I think it was just she started traveling so much, doing so much, she had so many friends. And I had my kids, and they were getting older, too. My wife and I, of course, we had rough times like everybody. It didn't seem right to be talking to Dottie about all that, telling her my problems. Not really fair to her or my wife. We just lost track of each other, kinda slow."

We just lost track of each other, kinda slow, Laurie repeated inside her own head, looking at Nick and looking down at her hands. "But we still knew some people in common, so I'd hear how she was doing now and then. At least until everybody got so old." He chuckled. "But a few years after my wife was gone, this would have been maybe five years ago, I did call her." For a minute, he just looked down at the picture. "I was lonely. Bored. I called her up, said 'Dot, how have you been?' And we were on the phone probably two hours. Talked about you, talked about your brothers. Your mom. My kids."

"That must have been really something," Nick said.

"It really was." He reached over and put the photo on his windowsill, propped up in front of a small flowerpot. "I sure loved her."

"I did, too," Laurie said.

"She was proud of you, you know," he said. "When we talked, she was 'oh, my niece the writer' this and 'oh, she's in a magazine' that. Don't tell anybody else, but I think you were her favorite."

"She was my favorite, too."

They stayed with John for a couple of hours. They ate lunch with him in the dining room, where they sat at a big round table with a couple and two single women in their seventies. Everyone who walked by would put a hand on John's shoulder, ask him how he was doing, drop a piece of gossip or ask him how the food was. The food was forgettable, honestly, institutional and resolutely acceptable, but the place hummed with overlapping casual and less casual bonds, like a college dining hall.

When it was time to go, John walked them out to the lobby. Laurie admired his straight back, his confident walk. Dot would have added him to her list of people in their nineties who aged well.

In fact, she probably had. He took both of Laurie's hands and said, "I am so glad that you came by."

"It was my pleasure," she said. And she leaned over and kissed his cheek. She picked up a Gatecrest brochure, plucked a pen off the desk, and wrote her phone number on the back. "Call me anytime you want to chat. Really."

"Nick," John said, and they shook hands. "Thank you for putting this together for us."

Nick nodded. "If you don't mind my saying so, sir, you might enjoy meeting my grandmother. Maybe I'll bring her by sometime."

"What a good idea," Laurie said, thinking about his need to connect things to other things, people to other people, a person to a book, a woman to her family.

"I'd love that," John said. "You stay in touch." Laurie could tell John didn't really think this would happen, and she couldn't blame him. He would logically think this was the hollow *let's get together soon* that you say at the end of a class reunion, but that was only because he didn't know Nick. Laurie, on the other hand, would have bet a hundred dollars Nick would be back here with Ginger within a month.

They drove home the longest way possible, taking apart and turning over every detail of what he had told them. That Dot had made something beautiful, something she and someone she loved were very proud of, but something she didn't think she could talk about. It had been enough for her to have it, to keep it, and maybe to know that someday, someone would find it when she was gone. You don't keep a thing for fifty years by accident, Nick said; not even a secret. He figured that Dot might even have known that Laurie would be the one to find it, the one to figure out what it was. Maybe this was a stretch, but it was as good a version of the story as any, and Laurie gravitated eagerly toward it. This faith in Laurie's capacity to discover might not have been true of Dot, but it felt true to Dot.

By the time they pulled up in front of Dot's house, it was gray and the air was heavy, and it had started to drizzle. "Do you want to come inside?" Laurie said. "I can make tea or something."

He looked over at her. "I know that you're leaving in a few days."

"Yes."

"I just wanted to say that before I come in, because I don't want you to think I'm not listening."

She nodded. "Let's go in."

There was not tea. They stumbled through the kitchen wrapped around each other, up the stairs with her tugging his hand, into the bedroom with their shirts already halfway off. In the big bed they sweated and laughed and she tried to memorize exactly how it felt to be under his weight, or hovering over him with her hair falling onto his cheek, or lying with her face buried in the side of his neck with her eyes closed while their hands worked under the covers. She couldn't keep it, this feeling. It was a thing she had started, knowing that it would end. And while she would not be the first woman to ever feel a love story slipping away, she wished she could stitch it or carve it or quilt it and then save it, tucked into the bottom of a cedar chest and never entirely gone.

Chapter Thirty

They fell asleep with the damp gray afternoon darkening the windows, and by the time they woke up, it was raining. "I should get home," Nick said. "I know you have a lot to do." He rolled out of bed and started pulling on his clothes.

"Are you okay?" she asked.

"Yes." He turned around to smile at her. "I'm okay. I mean . . . I'm going to miss you, Laur. But I'm okay." He put on his watch, which he had set on the nightstand, and he looked back at her, still stretched out in the bed in only the T-shirt she'd pulled on before she fell asleep. He raised an eyebrow at her. "I'm going to remember you exactly like this. Forever. In my dreams. When I'm John Harlan hanging out with my ninety-year-old friends griping about the food in the dining room, I'm going to remember you mostly naked while it pours down rain outside, and I'm going to be the happiest guy there."

She scowled. "I guess I'm honored, and I'm glad you still expect to be that horny, congratulations on that."

"Why wouldn't I be?" he asked.

She got out of bed and put on a pair of sweats, and she walked him downstairs. They stood in the kitchen, and he put his arms around her, and she grabbed on to his waist and rested her cheek on his shoulder. "Do you need an umbrella?" she asked into his neck.

"I'll be fine. I'm just headed home."

"I'll call you tomorrow?" she asked, even though it wasn't technically a question.

"Sure," he said. "I want to see you before you go."

They pulled apart. He slid his hand down her hip as he went out the kitchen door. When he closed it behind him, Laurie stood still, listening to it rain, listening to Dot's kitchen clock ticking. She closed her eyes and put her hand on the edge of the countertop and gripped it, resisting the gravity that wanted to pull her right through the door, to his car, where she would push him against the door and keep him from opening it and getting inside.

But she didn't; she heard the car start, heard it drive off, let the silence settle again. She went into the living room and lay on Dot's couch. The feeling was so familiar: *I don't want this.* She'd had it trying to register for wedding gifts, and when Angus talked about how great a mom she'd be, and she'd had it when Nick started talking about her living in Dot's house. It was a surfeit of negative space, just like June said. *Don't want, don't want, don't want.*

This was different, though, maybe: a negative of a negative. *Don't want him to leave. Don't want to give up. Don't want to say goodbye. Don't want to miss him. Don't want to make a mistake and tell him no, tell myself no.*

"Oh, hell," she muttered. She slipped her shoes on and grabbed the car keys from the post by the front door.

• • •

She wasn't far behind him, only a few minutes. When she pulled up in front of his house, he was on the porch, pulling mail out of the box. He looked up only when she shut her car door. He looked confused. "Hey," she said.

He smiled. Oh, it was such a good smile. It was a good smile when he was ten, and when he was fifteen, and it was a good smile now. "You know, somebody once told me not to start conversations that way," he said. "People suspect it's an indiscriminate 'hey.'"

She walked up the driveway. She liked his house; in fact, she was pretty sure she'd left a toothbrush in the bathroom. "I had a very bad feeling after you left," she said. "And I wanted to talk to you." He didn't say anything. She couldn't really blame him. "This is not what I want," she said. "I don't want this, where I leave and we just . . ." She made a motion with her hands like the puffing of fluff off a dandelion.

"Okay," he said. "What do you want?"

Well, there it was. And now, with it upon her as she continued to get rained on, she was surprised how it tumbled right out. "I want to be with you. I mean, ideally," she said. She didn't say "*be* with you," like a song; she said "be with *you*," like a decision.

Nick stood still. "You do." Not "you do" like a declaration, "you do" like a discovery. He looked around them and pushed the damp Superman curl off his forehead. "You want to come up on the porch and get dry?"

She nodded. She walked up until she was next to him, outside the door, feet from the rain. It was so quiet other than the water drumming lightly on the roof. Laurie took a breath. "What if I said I didn't want to get married, and I didn't want to live with anybody, and I didn't want the kind of relationship that my parents have or your parents have or Junie has, but I didn't want to let you go either? That I . . . want to keep this. Us."

His forehead wrinkled. "You want to date? Seattle to Maine? Do you think that's realistic?"

"I don't think it's realistic at all," she said. "And I'm not talking about just dating forever, I promise. That's not where I want to end up. And I really don't want to write polite letters when you're married to someone else."

"You're there," he said, "and I'm here, and I don't know what you have in mind."

She took a big breath. "Could you really never leave?"

"You mean move to Seattle? I've never even been there."

"I don't mean move there now. I don't even want you to promise to move there. I guess I mean . . . I mean, what if you visited me and I visited you, just so we could see, just so we can know each other more? And we just didn't let go yet? Is that even possible?"

"You can't come back, but you want me to leave." He could have said this angrily; he didn't.

"I realize that geographically speaking, I may be asking you to meet me more than halfway. Because like I said, halfway is Minnesota, and I don't want to live in Minnesota, it's just too cold."

"Agreed."

"Everything I have been able to think of is very hard," she said, "because we are too old to make everything from scratch. This is . . . advanced relationship stuff, I realize. I don't know how to make it any less so. I don't know how to be any more honest than that I am probably in love with you but I'm not going to break everything just so it all fits together, and I don't think you should either."

"So what do we do?" He ignored what she had said, the part about being in love with him. In that moment, it was a kindness.

"I don't exactly know," she said. "Because of course, of *course*, maybe you want to stay just as much as I can't stay. And that's fair, and if that's how you feel, then yes, we are John and Dot, going different ways, and there's nothing to be done. We should say goodbye, and I will miss you and I will be a total mess—and maybe you will be one too, I don't know. And I swear to you, if that happens I will understand and I will always love you and I will always be glad we did this.

But I am just saying that even though I don't want to get married, and even though I will always need space of my own, and even though this isn't my home anymore, I wish, I *wish* I could have you. I wish I could negotiate something, figure out something—"

"I thought you preferred to be on your own," he said.

"I don't prefer it," she said. "I'm just not afraid of it." She looked out into the rain and saw a bird cross the sky in her rippled field of vision. "I want to be . . . a bird who can fly by itself some of the time and know that the rest of the birds aren't too far away, you know? Maybe it would look strange to everybody else and not to us. Maybe we would live in a duplex, or upstairs and downstairs. Maybe I'd figure out how to fall asleep with you because I love that feeling so much and then how to get good sleep, too. Maybe I'm always going to want to rattle around at two in the morning and I'll keep doing that, or maybe it's melatonin or the sound of the ocean or something I haven't thought of. Nick, I don't know what it would look like. And maybe it's not my house. Maybe it's not my city. But it's not going to look like living in my aunt's house in my hometown, even though I know that would be simplest. And I just thought maybe you would, you know, want to be Citizen of the Year somewhere else someday."

The corner of his lip raised. "You're making a very romantic appeal to me in the rain, you know. I mean, we're on the porch, but I think it still counts."

"I didn't have time to wait for a sunset. I was feeling impatient."

He turned to face out toward his front yard, ignoring the water that was now pouring off the gutter in thick streams. "I don't know," he said. "I don't know if I could be anywhere else, Laur. I am so crazy about you, I want to tell you yes, but I would be lying to make you happy if I said this sounds easy."

She stepped closer. "I don't want you to feel like I expect you to bend your whole life around me just because I can't bend my whole life around you. And maybe it won't work, I don't know."

He looked back at her and squinted a little. "So, you don't want to get married," he said, "but it's more than dating. What you're talking about."

"Yes. Not married, and not living together, like *together*, in the way a lot of people do. I have to have my own kitchen cabinets, I think."

"But it's not casual."

"No."

"It's committed."

"Nick, yes," she said, grabbing his hand. "I'm not a split-the-closets person, but I'm . . . I don't know, I'm a partnership person. And for the last few weeks, you've been an outstanding partner to me and I have really, really liked it. When I say I want to make it work, I mean I want it to work as you and me, just you and me. For good. I want to be able to go chase turtle traffickers and then I want you to be there when I get back. And then I want to be there when you get back from whatever you can dream up."

"That's your vision," he said with a small smile, and for a minute, she thought he might be making fun of her. But then he looked over at her. "I get it." He ran his hands over his damp hair. "It's hard, Laur," he said. "I don't know how to decide anything based on a few weeks, no matter how good they were." He smiled. "At the same time, the older I get, the more I feel like . . . when I'm happy, I want to get on with it already, you know?"

"I really do." She squeezed his hand, and now they were both looking out at the rain. "It bothers me a little to want this so much. It feels like it's not real yet. I mean, it *isn't* real yet. Or . . . you know. It's real, but it's not . . ."

"Tested," he finished. "It's not tested yet."

She nodded. "Yeah." Waiting for him to speak made the rain so loud and everything else so outrageously quiet.

"I guess we should test it," he said.

She turned to face him, and he was looking at her, and it was

1998 and it was a month ago, and it was 1985, and she was at Dot's knee and in her parents' house and in Ginger's living room, and she was at home alone and in bed with Nick, and all of it seemed right at once. "It might not work," she said to him. "I know it might not."

"I think it will," he said.

"I hope it will." She smiled.

"I think it will," he said again.

She pulled him toward her. "I think it will, too."

Epilogue

Who doesn't hate the airport? It's loud and crowded and you can't go anywhere, and people keep bumping into you with roller suitcases and speeding past you because they left the house later than they intended to and now they're literally running late. Everything is overpriced, everything is cramped, everyone is stressed, and on this particular day, Laurie felt like she was happier to be there than she'd ever been to be anywhere. Last time she'd picked him up at baggage claim, she had practically tackled him, knocking him back a foot and making him drop his bag and laugh so loudly that it echoed in the tiled hallway. She was thinking about doing it again.

The sliding doors kept opening, with different flights filing in, passengers who had poured out of planes and up ramps and down elevators, people who just wanted to grab their stuff and get out, because who doesn't hate the airport. Laurie bounced on her toes, jingling her keys in her hand. He had texted that he had landed, then that he was off the plane, then that he was on his way. And then the doors opened, and he stepped through: Nick, her Nick, with a carry-on in one hand. He grinned when he saw her, came over and kissed her, made her feel like she was being melted from the inside out. "Hello," he said, pulling back enough to look her in the eyes.

"Oh, hello," she said back. "How was your flight?"

"Long," he said. "How was your wait?"

She laughed. "Not as long as the flight."

They stood by the carousel until his dark green suitcase slid around a corner, and he plucked it off the belt. She picked up his carry-on. "Oh, thank you," he said. "You don't have to do that."

"Hey," she said, "you get the pickup service, it includes all the extras. We're that way." She gestured toward the long walk to the parking garage.

On the ride home, he told her about Ginger's shoulder surgery, which had gone well, and about June's kids both coming down with the same bug, which had been a mess. The library was undergoing a major renovation, and the Claws had finished at the top of their league for the season, which had made everyone very, very happy. "What's going on with the duck piece?" he said.

Laurie had successfully pitched the story of Dot and the wood duck to one of the outlets for which she often wrote. They were allowing her several thousand words to explain about the decoy, the scam, and especially what it meant to learn that her great-aunt had a talent that went unrecognized throughout her life. Nick was convinced it would be a book; she told him she had to take it one page at a time.

"Are you sure you can take having me in the house for a week?" he said as they sped along the highway. "Not too much togetherness?" he said. "Because I can still stay somewhere."

"Are you kidding? It's eight days. I'm going to absorb you through my pores," she said. "I'm going to breathe you in like you're an inhaler. It's going to be positively creepy how I attach myself. It has to last me an entire month, so consider it a down payment."

"But you'll wake up in the middle of the night," he said.

"I have a guest room."

"What will you do when I crowd you?" he said.

"I'll go for a walk. I'm sure you can entertain yourself."

"You probably won't be surprised to hear I brought books."

She laughed. "By the way, Erin's been telling the rest of my friends all about you since you were here last time. She just calls you The Librarian. They're irate they haven't been introduced yet."

"I'm flattered," he said.

"I think they're going to ask you about the Dewey decimal system," she warned.

"Now, see, you're kidding, but I could fill about an hour talking about Dewey versus BISAC."

"I don't know what that means."

"That's why I need an hour."

She had an hour. She had a week, and she had work, and she had a beautiful wooden duck on her mantel at home that everyone had agreed she should keep. She had a bed someone else could sleep in or not, a kitchen someone else could make coffee in or not, a front door she was excited for him to walk through again, and a linen closet door she needed to call somebody about because it didn't quite close. She had friends in two corners of the country and family in even more. She had a WE'RE #1 foam finger marking the accomplishments of her first hometown's baseball team, and she had a paperback book in the glove compartment where she was gradually checking off the best places to see wildlife in her second hometown. There might yet be a third.

Maybe she would bring him with her in a day or two to look for black bears and bald eagles, or maybe she would leave him with something to read and speak to no one for hours, peering through her binoculars and taking pictures with the hotshot rig she used for work. Or maybe she would take her new instant camera, so that when she got back, she could hand him a picture of the best thing she saw, and he could hold it in his hand, turn it over, take it with him, take it out when he missed her. Maybe he would put it in a drawer and save it, and one day they would find it again, among their things, among *his* things, in whatever space they made.

Acknowledgments

My agent, Sarah Burnes, advocates for me fearlessly and understands my writing implicitly. My editor, Sara Weiss, helped me navigate the complicated and very unnerving second-book blues without blinking. They are my partners in getting this story out of my head and onto the page.

My dear friend Jesse Thorn loves old things and *Antiques Roadshow*, so I explained to him that I was writing a story about an old thing, but I hadn't decided what old thing it should be. I told him what kind of a thing I wanted, and he was the one who said the critical words: "Duck decoys." It's fair to say there is no book without that conversation—or at the very least, there is not this book. (He suggested carved eagles as well, and that also sounds like a good book.)

My friend Erik Adams developed the full plot of *Halls of Power* with me onstage at an event for *Evvie Drake Starts Over* in 2019.

My sister Susan is my role model in general, but is also a

beautiful soul who, like me, has had a life with multiple chapters. I'm so glad we have each other.

One of the best things about publishing a second book is getting to thank the people you didn't get to thank, or didn't know to thank, when you wrote the first book. So I'm delighted that I can now have a moment to thank the spectacular Emily Isayeff, who is everything a publicist and facilitator and booster and friend should be. It's because of Emily that I understand why people thank publicists in acceptance speeches.

I have been so fortunate to work with so many good people at Ballantine: Kara Welsh, Jennifer Hershey, Kim Hovey, Debbie Aroff, Sophie Vershbow, and everyone who copyedits and produces and sells books. I could not have asked for better, I really couldn't. And to those who have published or will publish anything I have written in countries around the world, and *particularly* those who translate and often go unacknowledged: I am in your debt.

I would not have made it through the worst of the pandemic and the writing of this story without some of the friends I got to know better during that time, including Molly Backes (and Alfie) and Kat Kinsman. And for everything I read and watched and listened to and loved, especially in the early going: *Get Your Pets! Staying in with Emily and Kumail! The Big Lasagna!*

To everybody at NPR who helped keep me talking, especially my podcast team: thank you.

In a lot of ways, this is a book about all the ways that people lift you up and take care of you. To my dear pals—Alan, Glen, Alex, Mike, Marc, Margaret, Gene, Barrie, Audie, Julia, on and on—you just can't know how much I appreciate everything. And to Stephen and Katie, for my home away from home even when I couldn't physically be in it: love to you both.

And I am so thankful for my parents, my grandparents, my aunts and uncles, my cousins, my nephews . . . I am happy to know we will appear in each other's pictures always.

About the Author

LINDA HOLMES is a novelist, a pop culture correspondent for NPR, and one of the hosts of the popular podcast *Pop Culture Happy Hour,* which has held sold-out live shows in New York, Los Angeles, Washington, D.C., and elsewhere. She appears regularly on NPR's radio shows including *Morning Edition, All Things Considered,* and *Weekend Edition.* Before NPR, she wrote for *New York* magazine online and for *TV Guide,* as well as for the groundbreaking website *Television Without Pity.* Her first novel, *Evvie Drake Starts Over,* was a *New York Times* bestseller. In her free time, she watches far too many romantic comedies, bakes bread, plays with her wonderful dog, and tries to keep various plants thriving.

Twitter: @lindaholmes
Instagram: @lindaholmes97

About the Type

This book was set in Fairfield, the first typeface from the hand of the distinguished American artist and engraver Rudolph Ruzicka (1883–1978). Ruzicka was born in Bohemia (in the present-day Czech Republic) and came to America in 1894. He set up his own shop, devoted to wood engraving and printing, in New York in 1913 after a varied career working as a wood engraver, in photoengraving and banknote printing plants, and as an art director and freelance artist. He designed and illustrated many books, and was the creator of a considerable list of individual prints—wood engravings, line engravings on copper, and aquatints.